# MEANJIN

Volume 67 Number 2, 2008

Meanjin was founded in Queensland by Clem Christesen in 1940. The name, pronounced mee-an-jin, is derived from an Aboriginal word for the finger of land on which Brisbane sits. The magazine moved to Melbourne in 1945 at the invitation of the University of Melbourne. The University has continued to be the principal sponsor of Meanjin in financial and non-financial ways. In 2008 Meanjin became an imprint of Melbourne University Publishing Ltd.

MELBOURNE
UNIVERSITY
PUBLISHING

# MEANJIN

### Editor
Sophie Cunningham

### Fiction Editor
Carmel Bird

### Poetry Editor
Judith Beveridge

### Cover Design
Chase & Galley

### Text Design
Chong

### Production
Norm Robinson

### Editorial Consultants
Natalie Book
Richard McGregor

### Office Manager
Mary Kennedy

### Website Manager
Anthony Hunt

### Volunteers and assistants
Jess Au, Laura Kerton
and Chun-Chieh Wang

### Advisory Board
Louise Adler, Kate Darian-Smith,
Mark Davis, Ken Gelder,
Bruce Sims, Deb Verhoeven,
Chris Wallace-Crabbe,
Michael Webster,
Angela Woods

### Founding Editor
Clem Christesen
(1911–2003; editor 1940–74)

# SUBSCRIPTIONS

**SUBSCRIPTIONS**

Contact the *Meanjin* office, or subscribe online at our website.

**ENQUIRIES**

**Postal address:** *Meanjin*, 187 Grattan Street, Carlton, Victoria 3053 Australia

**Website:** http://www.meanjin.unimelb.edu.au

**Fax** (+61 3) 9342 0399

**Telephone** (+61 3) 9342 0300

**E-mail:** meanjin@unimelb.edu.au

Unsolicited manuscripts are welcome but to be considered they must be accompanied by a stamped, self-addressed envelope or international reply coupon. A style guide will be found at our website.

Minimum payment to contributors is $50 for poems, $100 for prose. Fees are generally determined by word-length and will include a 5% supplement to provide in advance for copyright entitlements that contributions may attract through the Copyright Agency Ltd (CAL).

Copyright of each piece belongs to the author; copyright of the collection belongs to *Meanjin*. Republication is permitted on request to author and editor. *Meanjin* licenses selected online publication through CAL.

Published contributions by academics are refereed. See our website for details.

The views expressed by authors are not necessarily those of the editor or publishers.

Printed and bound by BPA Print Group

Distributed by Pan Macmillan

Print Post Approved PP341403 0002

AU ISSN 0025-6293

# CONTENTS

# THE CUPBOARD

A FEW weeks after I took up the editorship of *Meanjin*, based in our new home at Melbourne University Publishing, I went back to the *Meanjin* office at 131 Barry Street, Carlton. The journal was based there from 1999 until February this year. It was a melancholy visit in some ways—without my predecessor Ian Britain inhabiting the space; with files left in piles to be sorted through; and letterheads of *Meanjin*'s past piled up around the place waiting for the recycling. I was poking around the offices, not sure what to do next, when I opened a cupboard under the stairs. That is when I saw them: sixty-eight years of *Meanjin*s lined up in rows—almost every issue that has been published since Clem Christesen began the journal in 1940. It is hard to describe how exciting it is to find a cupboard full of such extraordinary history and to know you are, for a while at least, responsible for the future of the cupboard and everything inside it. I felt I was opening a door on the history of Australian book design and of Australian literature. It is this heritage I want to protect at the same time as taking *Meanjin* into the future.

We are in a phase of Australia's cultural life where commercial pressures are intensifying, the online space is dynamic, and both are modifying organisations as various as television stations, universities, newspapers, theatres and publishing houses—which is why I believe that it is precisely now that something as determinedly refined as a literary journal has even more potential. In upcoming *Meanjin*s expect more of an interaction between words and text. Expect to laugh. Expect writers you haven't heard of before and to read established writers writing about unexpected things. And expect some things to stay the same. In the most literal sense this means I plan to reprint some articles from the early issues of the journal. I also share previous editors' interest in history and memoir. *Meanjin* will continue to connect its readers to the myriad stories and experiences that, when read alongside each other, describe what it is to be Australian—and that description is, as it should be, in a constant state of flux.

Some particulars: *Meanjin* will no longer be formally themed. There will be an essay by a book designer in each issue in which they tell us the story behind a particular book cover—or discuss the design process more generally. In this issue we publish Ampersand Duck, whose piece began life as a blog post on both www.ampersandduck.blogspot.com and www.sarsaparillablog.net. I will interview an author for each issue. For this issue I spoke to Luke Davies about his new novel, *God of Speed*, and on switching between genres. You'll find the first extract, of six, of Kate Fielding's extraordinary graphic history, *Their hooks find hold deep in our flesh*, a history that has been illustrated by Mandy Ord, Clint Curé, Ben Fox and Elizabeth McDowell. I'm also keen to serialise a novel, and readers should note that Caroline Lee's wonderful piece, 'The End', is, in fact, the prologue of her novel, *Stripped*. In September we will publish the opening chapter of that novel. Whether I will get away with publishing a novel entire is yet to be established—for the author's sake I hope it gets whipped away after only an extract or two, leaving readers to wait for the published novel. We'll see.

You'll notice that the June cover has moved towards a more illustrative look. This is a first step in a complete redesign using Premier's Award-winning designers Chase & Galley (www.chaseandgalley.com). It was their bold approach to bringing together visual and textual elements that attracted me to their work and we hope to include more illustrations in the journal from September on. In September I will also introduce an 'In Brief' section to present current(ish) affairs and shorter pieces of writing. In December we will begin a series of essays on Australian cultural institutions. There are other plans afoot, including developing more of an online presence, and digitising our archives. I'll keep you posted.

I am *Meanjin*'s eighth editor. Those before me include Jim Davidson, Judith Brett, Jenny Lee, Christina Thompson, Stephanie Holt and Ian Britain, and I am indebted to them all. But while following in their footsteps is daunting, the footsteps that will take *Meanjin* forward are those laid down by Clem Christesen so many decades ago. He once said he wanted *Meanjin* to 'make clear the connection between literature and politics'. So do I. Let's see where those footsteps take us next.

SOPHIE CUNNINGHAM

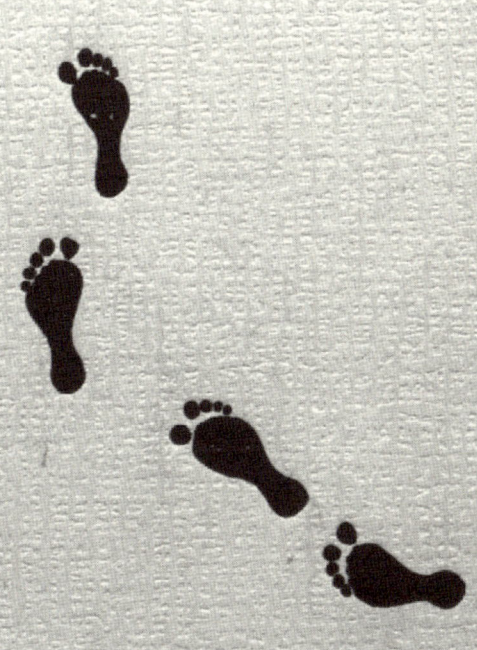

[*MEANJIN* COVER, 1943]

# EXORCISM
# IN THE
# DRIVEWAY

**PAUL MITCHELL** REFLECTS ON AN ENCOUNTER WITH MEN'S VIOLENCE
THAT'S TOO CLOSE TO HOME

IF you accept the idea that conduct on sporting fields is a mirror of society, then Australia has never been a more peaceful place. Through a combination of video surveillance and harsher tribunal sentences in the past ten years, on-field violence in both the Australian Football League (AFL) and the National Rugby League (NRL) has reduced substantially. In addition, order-off rules in minor leagues have meant that club footballers have sheathed their fists in favour of relying on their skills to do the damage to the opposition.

But it appears Australians, in a move converse to the Roman trend, have created sanitised Colosseums and made their streets and homes gladiatorial. In the period in which the AFL and NRL have become almost biff-free zones, reported violent assaults in Australia have increased 60 per cent, from approximately 9000 in 1995 to about 15,000 in 2005—a year in which 57 per cent of assaults were inflicted on men, most in the fifteen to forty-four age range. It seems that while our football fields are safer, our streets, clubs and even our homes have become places where men need to keep their guard up.

MY 35-year-old brother clambers down his porch steps and starts throwing punches at me. I grab his beefy arms and he slams me hard against his ute. His face is red and drunken, his eyes white, his mouth seething curses. Over his shoulder, I notice my parents at the bottom of the steps, shouting at us. My girl-friend Jo is moving towards me, a shocked expression on her face; further down the driveway, my kids—seven and ten—are in the back seat of my station wagon watching their father being attacked by his younger brother.

Until it happens in your own family, domestic violence is what goes on in housing commission flats or in poorer suburbs and towns. But my brother's house is a double-storey number with two living areas, four bedrooms and a wide-screen TV. His violence is not born out of poverty: although I am the one feeling the effects of the assault, he is actually wrestling with the past.

MOST heterosexual Australian men are never more physically intimate than when they are involved in a fist fight. Boxers have talked about the shared intimacy of a bout, and I remember one saying that the hug at the end of a fight is as much about acknowledging their relationship as it is an act of good sportsmanship.

Soldiers, too, have spoken about this intimacy. They say that during hand-to-hand combat there occurs an emotional physicality not far removed from sexuality. That's perhaps not surprising: in acts of violence and sexuality we seek to transgress another's physical and emotional boundaries.

Think of the scene in the film *Saving Private Ryan* (1998; Steven Spielberg): a soldier lies on a combatant and grinds a knife into his chest, watching the life extinguish in the other's eyes. There's an expression of effort and satisfaction, one that could just as easily have resulted from plunging his manhood into his enemy. Likewise, upon the entry of the knife, his opponent exhibits a grimace of shock and pain that mirrors an orgasmic sexual response. In a film renowned for its realism, that scene is—along with those depicting the Normandy landings—the one most often mentioned as difficult to watch. It could be because we find the violence gratuitous. It might also be that we're reminded of our capacity to hurt or heal in our intimate relationships.

It is easy to write about one's abhorrence of physical violence. In fact, abhor-rence seems the most obvious reaction. But there are those, unfortunately, who love violence—or at least see it as an understandable response in certain circum-

[5]

stances. And some even find domestic violence to be a bit of a laugh. An acquaintance cackled when I told him I'd been attacked by my brother, and he kept laughing when I told him my kids had been watching.

With attitudes like that in our community, it seems abhorrence of violence remains an important topic. In my fiction and poetry, I've regularly dealt with the subject—particularly the violence perpetrated by my late maternal grandfather, Bill.

He looked like Errol Flynn and had similar charisma; a popular, tough and fiercely loyal man, Bill was a likable rogue with a roaring sense of humour. But he was also a violent alcoholic who abused his wife, kids and grandkids. While Bill's influence on the men in my family has been profound, my father—who admitted to being scared of him—thinks I should stop concerning myself with Bill and the 'violence' he committed against me when I was eight years old. I put the word in quotation marks here because I wasn't physically assaulted. Instead, Bill—who I knew was his division's boxing champion in the Second World War—took me out of his fibro flat in Ocean Grove and told me to 'put my dukes up'. I had said something 'smart' to Mum.

If he'd done all that in the flat, with my parents, grandmother and brothers watching, the incident might not have stuck in my memory. But he took me outside. I was about half his size and he loomed over me in a boxing stance. No-one came out to defend me. I have never felt so alone.

I wrote a short story about that incident and it appeared in *Overland* and also in my collection *Dodging the Bull* (2007). Before the book hit the shelves, I sent a copy of the story to my father and told him we should have a chat about it. After reading it he apologised to me for his part in the incident, but he added that he couldn't remember it. He also said it was time now to stop worrying about whether my grandfather's spirit continues to haunt my brothers and me.

But I don't believe spirits leave any place where they're comfortable unless they're exorcised.

I HOLD my brother's wrists but he still manages to dig his fingernails into my chest. He swears and accuses me of ruining the family. He yells that I'm not looking after my kids properly. He says—I presume because I have a new girlfriend—that I don't make my kids the number-one priority in my life.

Despite the outpouring in my direction, the source of my brother's anger is obvious to me: his love-hate relationship with our overprotective mother and his sense of being robbed of a strong relationship with his father. And here I am, not for the first time, on the receiving end of his resentment.

My maternal grandmother was passive in the face of my grandfather's physical and emotional abuse. It is probably presumptuous to say that 'as a result' of her childhood experiences my own mother felt it necessary to exercise as much control as she could over the men in her life. But I don't think a child can watch her mother being abused without doing as much as possible to avoid it happening in her adult life.

My father was the son of a woman who stated outright that she didn't want him, and of a man submissive to a domineering wife. While my father tried to hold his own in a power struggle with my mother, he gave up when I was in my teens. It may not have been his waterloo, but after one of his fights with her, he decided to leave. The next morning he was discovered in the garage, sleeping in the wagon section of the Toyota.

My brother is a successful tradesman and a caring father but, like me in my younger years, he has struggled with depression and violent outbursts. My psychiatrist has told me that my depression and anger are the result of having my balls taken away by my mother—and my father allowing it to happen, while at the same time allowing her to snatch his. My brother has been offered no such revelation, and he constantly tries to please his mother while simultaneously resenting her dominant role in his life. He tries to get closer to his father, but despises him for his weakness. My brother refers to himself, in the words of the rock band Rage Against the Machine, as the 'son of a broken man'.

But for all his disenchantment with family, my brother still sees the arrangement as a strictly nuclear one. He appears to view with scepticism anyone outside that fundamental arrangement. We have a younger brother, who, like me, is divorced. It's perhaps no coincidence that on the night my middle brother decided to launch his assault, I'd had dinner with my younger brother.

From the street, our altercation might have looked like two hoons going at it in a suburban driveway. But underneath this 'white trash' scene were years of resentment and a string of failed relationships—failed attempts at love and at being a family.

WHILE Australia's major football leagues, under scrutiny of the video camera, conduct their competitions aggressively but fairly, another set of cameras on closed-circuit television regularly captures footage of men out of control: fighting on streets and train platforms; inside and outside nightclubs and hotels; in road-rage incidents. Despite the apparent 'good example' set by sports stars, men are—in increasing numbers—solving their problems and disputes with violence.

Assaults make the news when they involve celebrities (Russell Crowe), sportsmen (Wayne Carey), nightclubs (recent fights in Melbourne's King Street), race issues (Sudanese boy Ajang Gor in Melbourne in 2007) or death. Calls are then made in the national media to deal with the apparent causes: alcohol abuse, lax liquor laws, security guard training, racial unrest, pop-culture violence, poor parenting, social disadvantage and anger management. Properly addressing all of these issues will certainly have an effect on our rising assault statistics, but there's one issue it seems we're unwilling to name as a likely cause of increased violent assaults: competition itself.

In the eleven years John Howard and the Coalition reigned over Australia, we became more prosperous and, if we believe the former government's spin on the figures, more of us were employed. The neoliberal agenda of allowing society to be ruled by competition and the market produced the promised economic results. The period of the Howard government, however, also saw the 60 per cent increase in violent assault.

If, in our workplaces, we believe the only way to get ahead is to crush the competition, what can we expect in our homes, on our streets, in our public places or on our roads? Why should we expect the businessman who is late for a meeting to accept kindly the man who cuts in front of him in traffic? Why should we be surprised that our male sports stars, who quell the violent part of their competitive instinct on the field, use their fists off it? And why should we be surprised when the tradesman, who is used to cut-throat business competition, acts out violently in a pub? Or in his family driveway?

TIME after time, my brother slams me into his ute. He shouts out his hatred of me, the brother he perceives to be an educated, Melbourne-dwelling, golden-haired boy. Off to the right of him, my mother is crying. My father has her in his arms while he's shouting at me and my brother to stop being idiots, to stop what we're doing to our mother.

'I'm not doing anything,' I say to him.

Jo's up close now, trying to reason with my brother, trying to pacify him, but his arms are taut and ready to throw punches if I let go. His curses continue and I know they're not meant for me. He wants to shout them at our parents. At thirty-five, it seems he's still waiting for his father to discipline him, to establish him as a man.

This is the third time in my adult life I have been in this situation with my brother, and I have never before thought about throwing a punch. Now I am weighing it up carefully. Not because I'm angry, but because I think, in a strange way, it's what he wants me to do. I've developed some boxing skills at the gym. I ask myself what it might mean to discipline him, to do the job my father should have done, minus the violence I'm entertaining.

If I'm going to punch him, I'll have to be quick. He's an experienced fighter and he knows that the difference between being unconscious and standing over your opponent comes in the flicker of an eye.

I keep my eyes open, and blank.


RESEARCH suggests that boys who wrestle regularly with their fathers learn better how to control their aggression. No doubt love and affection play a huge role in that learning, but as a father of an eight-year-old boy, I know that in our wrestles his pent-up energy is worked off and his need for physical intimacy is satisfied. I set the boundaries; I show him my strength and test his own. After a wrestle, relations are generally more harmonious between us.

My father didn't set boundaries by wrestling with my brothers and me. We did it ourselves. When Mum was at work after school, we'd engage in some 'couch cushion boxing', so named because we wore couch cushions as boxing gloves. I was the tallest so I knelt for my bouts, my younger brothers could fight on their feet. We set boundaries: no kicking, no punching after one of us had said he'd had enough, and no using an exposed fist by bending the cushion in your hand as you threw a punch. It might only make a limited kind of sense but, as a result of our boundaries, there weren't many disagreements. In effect, we weren't acting violently; violence is transgression of boundaries. We were, through controlled aggression, doing our best to develop, not to transgress, our limits—until Mum caught us at it and told us to stop.

Thankfully, fighting is banned and strictly punished at my son's state primary school. But so is wrestling between boys, even in fun. While there has been a shift in the past few years towards men being more involved with their children, men with kids aged five to fourteen (a peak time when it comes to sons' need for their dad) spend less than ten hours per week with their children in tasks that include taking them to and from school or sport, and other activities such as showering, dressing and eating with them. My guess is that doesn't leave much time for a wrestle, not much time for a boy to learn how to control his aggression.

As a sixteen-year-old, I had the misfortune of playing senior football in a minor Geelong league. I was clobbered behind the play and in all-in brawls. I saw team-mates and opposition players receive injuries akin to those that might be received in car accidents. To my mind, the AFL and NRL have got it right in their crackdown on violence. Their arenas have become theatres for controlled aggression. As a society, it's time Australia considered what it might mean to follow our football codes' lead and find more ways—especially for those who don't play sport—to ensure that male aggression is harnessed and not simply punished. Whereas footballers practise self-control as a result of video scrutiny, we have to teach men—young and older—that they have a camera inside themselves that can induce the same outcome.

MY brother is no longer trying hard to free himself from my grip. This is the moment: I am relaxed and ready to express, in language I know he understands, that he's crossed a boundary; he needs to know that I'm not going to tolerate his behaviour. But I decide that I will not punch my brother. I know it will exacerbate the situation if I do. Instead, I hold on to his arms as my father yells at him to leave me alone.

'Listen to your father,' I say, meaning that I want him to listen to our father now, in the past and the future. I want him to accept my father's discipline, as late as it is.

I can feel your strength, brother. Can you feel mine?

I don't know if it's an act of strength, self-control or plain tiredness, but he lets me go. As I get into my car, I can see my mother bent over and crying, with my father holding on to her. I'm shaking and sore. Jo breathes out deeply and asks whether I'm okay to drive. I tell her I am and I try to back down the driveway without slamming my foot on the accelerator. As I turn to look where I'm going, I see the frozen expressions on my kids' faces. I tell them it's okay, everything's going to be all right.

'Why is Nanna crying?' my daughter asks.

'Because she was upset by the fighting,' I say.

My son asks why my brother was slamming me into the ute.

'Because he was angry,' I say, and leave it at that for now. I don't know it yet, but it's going to take another two days to debrief the kids. When I speak to them the next day, I tell them we won't be going to see their uncle any time soon. My son lets out a sigh. 'Thank God,' he says.

'Estranged.' I've always found the word eerie and somewhat impenetrable, probably due to the fact that 'strange' is trapped in it. Whenever I heard the term on the news as a kid—'her estranged husband'—I didn't know it meant that two people were no longer in contact. I thought it meant that the husband was somehow weird or different, not entirely trustworthy. I suppose I wasn't far wrong: both parties to an estrangement are likely to feel the other is weird and unable to be trusted.

A few days after the altercation with my brother, after I had considered what it might mean to charge him with assault, his wife rang and left a message on my answering machine. She said she was sorry that things turned out the way they did. She said to give her a ring if I wanted to.

I rang her mobile and got her answering service. 'Thanks for the call,' I said, and I apologised for any way in which my behaviour had caused offence that weekend. I said that I forgave my brother, but that there were a number of other things I wanted to say to him. These were things, however, I would only communicate in professional mediation and she should pass on that message.

It's been five months and I haven't heard from my brother. It's as if I've knocked him out in the driveway. I hope to hear from him when he comes to. I also hope the ghost of my grandfather is sleeping peacefully beside him.

# THE END

Caroline Lee

IN the end when she went it was so quick. She just got up and went through the doorway. Just like that. Direct. Strong. Courageous. She just went through, and then she was gone. I was waiting there by the doorway. She knew I was there. But she just left.

We were all prepared. We had been prepared for days. People on seats waiting. Waiting for a dramatic event. But we didn't expect that. A quick exit. Like that.

There is an intense silence in the room. Mama is here. The nurse is here. The priest is here. Louise and Jack are here. Daniel is here. Martin is not here. The trip all the way out to Rowville appears to have been too much for him. This is not a surprise, just a dull truth.

And I am here.

Lillian is in bed. It appears that she is lying restfully in this bed that we hired from the hospital. We are all in the living room. It is still ugly in the living room, as ugly as the rest of the house, but at least there is more space for the bed and for the medical equipment and for us. And there is light. There are sliding doors, which open out into their barren backyard. There is a flatness of green and brown, then the fence, then roofs of other houses and then the sky.

We have all been here for a couple of days. Except Jack and Louise. They arrived late last night. It is 2.37 on this warm afternoon and a silence has descended. We are waiting. The sun is coming through the windows, bathing our legs. We are all looking out the window, even Lillian.

It is as if we are on a cruise ship, slowly moving towards our destination. As if we are in deckchairs watching the landscape roll by. Going up a river. Hills in the distance, but getting closer. We'll be there soon. And so we wait.

Then Mama says, 'What I don't understand is why it started in her mouth. Lillian was always such a careful girl, not like Sophie. Careful, and particular. She never put anything in her mouth that she shouldn't have. And as for me, I've got a good mouth too. I've always had a good mouth. People have always commented on it. What was it about her mouth that let this happen to her?

'She must have said something she shouldn't have. And it was probably the law. The law that did that. I mean she did a lot of good with that mouth of hers, a lot of good, I'm sure, not that she ever made the sort of money she should have. I mean I thought law was supposed to make you rich. So, maybe it was because once or twice she went too far and said the wrong thing, to the wrong person. Yes, went that little bit too far, further than she should have. What's that expression? on TV? Oh yes, shoot your mouth off. That must have been it. She must have shot her … mouth off—well no, actually that's not a very nice expression is it? No, not at all …

'She always did speak her mind. Not immediately, not impetuously, as Sophie does, but nevertheless, always spoke her mind. They got that from their grandfather, the girls. He was a strong man, their grandfather. Yes, Jack, that's right, *my* father. Yes, strong. Strong. That's where it came from.

'But still, why? Why the mouth? I mean she had a rosebud mouth, that's what people used to say, lips like a rosebud. Oh look, look at her lips. Look at my beautiful baby's lips …'

I look at Lillian. Her lips open. Softly, gently, a wind begins to blow. Through her lips, out of her mouth. Her mouth opens wider. Little pieces of rubbish start to come out. A leaf, a piece of cotton, a little shred of pink ribbon. And then, as the wind picks up, more and more things come out, piles of things coming up out of Lillian's mouth and hurled around the room in the strong wind: gumboots, books, glasses, gloves, papers, tears, hair, blood, an eye, a birthday cake, flowers, tubes, perfume, underwear, veins, more and more coming out of her and flying around the room.

The wind has picked up outside too. It is dark, as if a storm is coming. Dust is flying around the garden, grass clippings, bits of newspaper. A few specks of rain hit the glass. Everything is whirling, inside and out, and we all just sit there watching, awe-struck. Even Mama.

Then suddenly Lillian moves. Stirs. Sits up. 'Stop,' she says. Quietly. Clearly. Calmly.

The room calms. She gets up from the bed. She is light. She slowly gets up, unclips all the tubes, and gently eases herself out of the bed.

The wind is continuing to blow outside. But inside it is calm. Lillian gets up out of her bed, walks across the room, past Daniel, past Jack and Louise, past the glass door and then right past me to the wall, next to where I am sitting. There is nothing on the wall. It is painted a horrible shade of light blue. She stands there. Mama is looking. But everyone else is still looking at Lillian's body on the bed. Then a door opens and light comes in through the wall. Through. Sunlight. Birds chirping.

And then she just walks through.

No fanfare, no fuss. She just walks through the door. And away. She has gone, and, for the moment, I am glad. Mama and I glance at each other. Her hands are clasped together and she is smiling. Smiling and crying at the same time.

# FALKLAND ISLANDS WOLF
## Dusicyon australis

How we got here nobody knows; Holocene men
Shipped us over for company on the long voyage?
When they died out, we just dug burrows & bred.
Then the uprights returned with other fur-kind,
Our palette picked up; canine instincts kicked in.
Next Darwin's specialised hand stroked our coat;
He said our lack of fear would be the death of us.
US fur hunters took up his radical belief, offered
Fresh meat; blame racial memory, so cut-throat.
The old-world tags were the hardest to hide from,
European fears projected onto us, shape-changing
Vampire. Scottish settlers finished it; superstitions
Fuelled burning & poison; expediency torpedoed us:
A *General Belgrano* of bad luck our political death.

BRETT DIONYSIUS

# JANE AUSTEN'S ABANDONED ROMANCES

**LAURA CARROLL** ASKS WHY THE AUSTEN INDUSTRY FAILS TO ACCEPT THAT
THE AUTHOR MAY HAVE BEEN SUCCESSFUL, SINGLE *AND* SATISFIED
WITH HER LIFE

THE current crop of Jane Austen-themed entertainments has a new and annoying character. First, it is gloomy: the perversity of making Jane Austen, of all authors, into a figure associated with sadness and unfulfilment is considerable. Second, it is obsessed with Austen's spinsterhood, with her shameful virginity: with her old-maidishness and deliberate barrenness. It appears that we are not at present allowed to be even a little bit happy that Austen managed to stay unmarried and thus wrote novels.

Earlier generations of Janeite enthusiasts accepted and liked that Jane Austen was a single woman. They called her, with varying shades of irony, 'Miss Austen' and 'dear Aunt Jane', and they read her novels in the comfortable and leisurely spirit of a good gossip session, less interested in racing forwards to the climactic weddings than in relishing the accumulation of trivial and eccentric details encountered on the way. But the latest round of popular books and movies addressing Austen's life and works are troubled by her apparent lack of personal interest in the heterosexual marriage plot she did so much to disseminate, and represent her unmarried state as a problem in urgent need of explanation. I suppose this is a symptom of anti-feminist backlash. It might also signal a conviction that comedy has little in common with the monstrous figure of the single woman. The last truly comic heroine the Austen industry produced was Bridget Jones, and even she thought of herself as a besieged 'Singleton' among the 'Smug Marrieds': 'I feel like I have turned into Miss Havisham … maybe they really do want to patronize us and turn us into failed human beings.'[1] The new Austen-related productions do not quite depict Austen as a grotesque bride forever arrested in the moment of her jilting, but it's a near thing.

The focusing of our narrative appetites on self-improvement and biography is important in determining the change too: we now have Austen biopics and Austen self-help texts, all bent on elucidating instructive links between Austen's fictions and how a single woman can miraculously salvage her life. The conceit of Patrice Hannon's weird part-biog, part-advice manual *Dear Jane Austen: A Heroine's Guide to Life and Love* (2007), for instance, has the Austen of 1816 filling in time while she sits around the cottage waiting to die by receiving and replying to letters from twenty-first century misses in need of relationship guidance and life counselling. Contrary to the spirit of the real Austen's fiction, Hannon's Austen dispenses advice to the effect that the happy-ever-after ending is achieved by 'the conquering of romantic illusions and expectations', 'accept[ing] the necessity of compromise'. In the chapter titled 'Beauty Tips for Heroines', a supplicant asks how she can compete in a marriage market flooded with surgically enhanced beauties. Austen writes back with consoling words about doing your best with what you have and, for the rest, 'cultivating your inner beauty using the knowledge gained from these letters'. Even the relatively pleasant *The Jane Austen Book Club* (2004 novel by Karen Joy Fowler, 2007 film directed by Robin Swicord), while free of creepy ventriloquism and healthily acknowledging the boundaries between life and fiction, presents reading Austen as therapy, as good medicine for whatever ails: in its cosy view, bourgeois American life presents no dilemmas that can't be solved by asking yourself 'What would Jane do?'

Cleverly, the movie and television people mainly responsible for feeding the Austen media behemoth have realised they can't simply recycle the same six similar novels for ever—although it's not for lack of trying, as four new adaptations were recently made for British television—and they have now decided to move on to producing films, of as similar a kind as possible, about Jane Austen herself. *Becoming Jane*, seen here in cinemas in 2007, and *Miss Austen Regrets*, a

BBC film shown in Britain in 2008, obviously slot right into the quality costume drama genre originally mapped out and still dominated by classic-novel adaptations. J.G. Ballard accurately remarked to the *Observer* that 'there are too many hats [and] everyone is overdressed' on British television—but underneath the elegantly decorated surfaces their differences from Jane Austen's concerns are many and their distance from her essential comic mode is vast. These are films in love with their own pale and interesting mournfulness, a species of histrionics Austen consistently showed up as ridiculous. Both films ask the same narrow set of questions about Austen: how did she write as she did about love without being a lover herself? Why didn't she get married? What was wrong with her? Was she unlovable? Was she sad? (Did she smell?) Was she lonely? Was she ashamed of being single? The films demonstrate an inability to believe that Austen lived the way she did as a matter of free choice—if she did choose to stay unmarried, it must have been an unhappy choice made under difficult circumstances. The great and animating puzzle about Jane Austen is seen not as how she came to write so well, but, rather, what underwrites and authenticates her stories of the dignified triumph of rational affection and the value of companionate marriage if her own life did not follow the pattern of the fictions.

It appears that the fashion for finding or assuming a biographical core to all storytelling has made it hard for us to accept that novels, especially novels by a lady, can contain and express truths not necessarily drawn from direct experience. The way Austen's novels orchestrate an apparently spontaneous alignment of mutual passion and esteem between heroine and hero with enough money for them to live happily in material comfort for ever after does not reflect a social reality any more than it mirrors her own life. But it is a not a daydream or fantasy; nor is it simply the writer finally capitulating to the demands of the narrative formula she is working with. It is a philosophical ambition. It is the inevitable corollary of her conviction, and related technical demonstration through the medium of free indirect speech, that women are independent and fully human beings, with complete inner lives, who can and therefore must think for themselves. Pressed to marry a rich man she neither likes nor respects, *Mansfield Park's* timid and dutiful Fanny Price voices an idea new in literature: 'I think it ought not be set down as certain, that a man must be acceptable to every woman he may happen to like himself … How was I to have an attachment at his service, as soon as it was asked for?' Marriage for love is an ethical goal in Jane Austen's writing and to register its full idealism and ambitiousness does not have to mean that she sought it for herself. It is enough to read her novels.

Virginia Woolf says we know Austen as we know Shakespeare: we know nothing about her, and everything, and we know her through her work, her mind:

> When people compare Shakespeare and Jane Austen, they may mean that the minds of both had consumed all impediments; and for that reason we do not know Jane Austen and we do not know Shakespeare, and for that reason Jane Austen pervades every word she wrote, and so does Shakespeare.[2]

As James Ley recently observed, what the truism that we don't know enough about Shakespeare the person really means is that we are unsatisfied with those facts we do have: we lack 'any direct testimony from the man himself … his opinions are lost to us'.[3] This is not quite the case with Austen: from the 160 of her letters that survive, we have detailed knowledge of her opinions about food, parties, fashion, the weather, games, neighbours, health, places, travel, and a sprinkling of the books and plays of the day. If we feel we lack direct testimony from her it is testimony about affairs of love, the journallings of a mythical Emo-Austen, minutely recording heavy sighs and pressed hands and exchanges of lugubrious looks, the heavy pangs of doomed love on tear-blotted pages. No such *cri de coeur* exists so it has had to be invented.

To give it its due, *Becoming Jane* (horribly blurbed by the Qantas in-flight magazine as 'a true story of true love') is trying to be the story of an artist, a Künstlerroman; it wants to reveal or suggest something about the source of Austen's inspiration. But it's looking in such very wrong places. The press pack for *Becoming Jane* said:

> *Becoming Jane* focuses on a life-changing romance during one summer in the life of the young Jane Austen.
>
> Austen was 20 years old when she met the brilliant and roguish Tom Lefroy, who she found instantly attractive.
>
> Her romantic adventures with the dashing Mr Lefroy, at a turning point in her literary career, [are] said to have inspired her to write novels and helped create her male romantic heroes such as Mr Darcy.

Some imagination is required to construct a serious romance between Austen and Lefroy, the visiting Irish nephew of a family friend, from the historical record. They met at some dances over the winter of 1795–96 and apparently enjoyed one another's company. Certainly, she liked him. Of their flirtation Jane wrote to her sister Cassandra: 'Imagine to yourself everything most profligate and shocking in the way of dancing and sitting down together.' A few days later she uses the same joking language to tell Cassandra about a ball she is looking forward to: 'I rather expect to receive an offer from my friend in the course of the evening. I shall refuse him however, unless he promises to give away his white coat.' This is the hyperbolic, ironic voice the youthful Austen uses in her satirical sketches:

> They said he was Sensible, well-informed, and Agreable; we did not pretend to judge of such trifles, but as we were convinced he had no soul, that he had never read the Sorrows of Werter, and that his Hair bore not the least resemblance to auburn, we were certain that Janetta could feel no affection for him, or at least that she ought to feel none.[4]

We can't think she would write so flippantly if she genuinely hoped to receive a proposal, and in the event she didn't. Whatever happened between them, Lefroy returned to Ireland and Austen was cracking jokes about him shortly afterwards.

In *Becoming Jane* all the dancing and flirting between Jane and Tom leads directly to a romantic disaster of *Titanic*ally clichéd proportions. The pair get recklessly into a carriage to go off and marry, even though Tom's rich old uncle will disinherit him when the truth is known. Never mind; they have each other. But on the road Jane realises that without the uncle's money, Tom's numerous brothers and sisters back in the old country will be penniless too. To keep Tom's Irish siblings from starving to death, therefore, plucky Jane renounces him and returns home to the parsonage before nightfall on the day of her elopement, conveniently preserving both her chastity and the appearance of it. She returns to the writing she'd been ineptly pursuing before she met Tom; but with the memory of his criticism and encouragements to draw upon as well as the mysterious power of love, her style is miraculously improved, and now she has something to write about as well. So out she pops *Pride and Prejudice*, featuring Tom as Mr Darcy.

There may be something of Tom Lefroy in the genesis of Darcy. Like any writer, Jane Austen did not receive 'the fruitful idea which will give rise to a fiction', as Somerset Maugham put it, 'like a falling star, out of the blue':

> For the most part, it comes to him from an experience, generally emotional, of his own, or, if it is told him by another, emotionally appealing; and then his imagination in travail, character and incidents little by little grow out of it, until at length the finished work comes into being.[5]

But there are no grounds at all for attributing the fullness of Austen's literary gifts and achievements to the effects of having had a 'life-changing romance'. To imply this is to indulge two widespread misapprehensions about Austen the novelist and the nature of her art. The more forgivable, because somehow natural, mistake is to assume that those novels, so accurate and perceptive about social systems, so psychologically powerful, and so full of personal brilliance and magnetism, contain clues about the inner life of the person who wrote them. The other misapprehension is not so blameless. It involves suppressing and ignoring all the plentiful evidence about the hard-earned professionalism, the intent, of Austen's writing career, in favour of seeing it as a spontaneously erupting outlet for unsatisfied sexual passion.

This is a pernicious view of how a person learns to be an artist, let alone a controlled and deliberate artist. Jane Austen was an accomplished writer well before she was out of her teens; she had read extensively and had a sophisticated understanding of the conventions of the courtship novel genre; and she was determined to be a professional writer, for financial as well as artistic reasons. To pretend all this doesn't matter, or that it matters less than Austen's private erotic life, is a devaluation of what this woman writer's career means. The 'life-changing romance' hypothesis implies that before it happened she was not a writer, but after it, she was: without it she might never have picked up a pen.

If true romance as novelistic inspiration were what was wanted, the film-makers would have done better to choose another author. *Shakespeare in Love* showed that the Künstlerroman built around an abandoned romance doesn't have to represent the lives of artists as tragic and sacrificial. On being asked by a campus news service for comment on *Becoming Jane*, Victorian literature scholar Rohan Maitzen mused:

> I found myself thinking that really, if movie makers (and movie audiences) want a biopic about a woman writer's interesting, sexy life, they should really be working on *Becoming George*. Isn't the transformation of country girl (and preachy evangelical) Marianne Evans into leading intellectual, free-thinker, strong-minded woman, and renowned novelist George Eliot really as good as (really, better than) anything someone could make up about a 19th-century woman's life, and true, to boot?[6]

Or, if a film-maker genuinely wanted to dramatise the development of Jane Austen's use of the courtship novel as a vehicle for her discoveries about female agency, a ready-made and largely unexploited subject awaits in the form of Austen's 17,000-word unfinished novel known as 'The Watsons'. Austen sold her first manuscript, the novel that would eventually become *Northanger Abbey*, in 1803 and began 'The Watsons' the following year. It was laid aside in 1805, and

Austen never returned to it either to revise it or to throw it away. She appears to have written nothing further until 1809, when the Austen women moved to their first settled and secure home since the death of Austen's father in 1805. Its story is both like and unlike the Austen novels we are familiar with. It concerns a young woman, Emma Watson, innocent, unaffected, good, kind and attractive, who has been brought up by rich relations and at the opening of the story has just been sent back to live with her own family because her aunt has remarried and Emma has lost her expectations of an inheritance from the aunt. Mrs Watson is long dead, Mr Watson is a very sickly invalid, and the family is severely impoverished. Besides Emma there are three sisters, all older than her and all unmarried with no suitors. The peculiar tension of the story arises from the contrast between the idealistic Emma's dawning awareness of the desperate situation and her sisters' correspondingly drastic efforts to adapt to or escape from it. A revealing early conversation between Emma and Elizabeth, the eldest and most sympathetically drawn sister, on the topic of the absent Penelope's husband-hunting strategies establishes the scene:

> 'I am sorry for her anxieties,' said Emma, —but I do not like her plans or her opinions. I shall be afraid of her. —She must have too masculine and bold a temper. —To be so bent on Marriage—to pursue a Man merely for the sake of situation— is a sort of thing that shocks me; I cannot understand it. Poverty is a great Evil, but to a woman of Education and feeling it ought not, it cannot be the greatest. —I would rather be a Teacher at a school (and I can think of nothing worse) than marry a Man I did not like.' —'I would rather do any thing than be a Teacher at a school' —said her sister. '*I* have been at school, Emma, and know what a Life they lead; you never *have*. —I should not like marrying a disagreeable Man any more than yourself, —but I do not think there *are* many very disagreeable Men; I think I could like any good humoured man with a comfortable Income. —I suppose my Aunt brought you up to be rather refined.'[7]

The fourth sister, Margaret, is a manipulative, spiteful girl, adept at and delighting in creating psychological discomfort in others. Her entrance confirms that the dominant mode of 'The Watsons' is a singular and unflinching realism (this is also evident in the story's unusual attention to details about cooking, housework, clothing and transport), which will not be softened by comedy. Mrs Bennet's oft-repeated fear, in *Pride and Prejudice,* that Mr Bennet will die and the women will all be turned out of their home, is basically shrugged off in that novel as an aspect of her perceived taste for self-dramatisation rather than a real possibility—which, of course, is exactly what it is. The Watson sisters are clearly facing the same possibility as the Bennet girls, but unlike in *Pride and Prejudice* we cannot enjoy their predicament secure in the belief that everything will magically come right in the end. When the text abruptly ceases, Emma Watson is literally trapped in her father's sitting room, unable to think calmly of the future or to tolerate the atmosphere of strife permeating the household.

Into this dire narrative situation Austen attempted to place an escape route in the shape of Lord Osborne, a recognisable Darcy avatar who is in the process of being transformed from a rich, selfish and proud individual into an appropriately gentlemanly suitor for Emma, under the influence of her lovely face and principled sense of her own worth. But Emma is displaying signs of loving instead the modest clergyman Mr Blake. It seems inevitable that in the course of the story Osborne would make Emma an offer that her heart would urge her to refuse. But in the realist mode of 'The Watsons,' such a refusal would be unthinkable: if Emma could comfortably choose the luxury of her own private fulfilment over ensuring the physical survival of her sisters then she is not the decent, clear-sighted and honourable person we believed her to be. The choice apparently facing her is no choice at all; if the lord asks her she must in conscience accept him. The situation does have dramatic potential but it offers no scope for exploring the ethical aspects of a woman's reconciliation between the social good of marriage and the personal necessity of freedom to choose. There could be no question of Emma Watson's father telling her, as Mr Bennet tells Elizabeth, 'Let me not have the grief of seeing *you* unable to respect your partner in life.' Austen did what a real writer must do in these circumstances: she abandoned her untenable romance, broke the novel off.

I think the moment she put it away is the moment she became a great novelist. She confirmed that her real literary vocation was neither the documentary recording of the difficult lives of lower-middle-class women, nor the invention of simple wish-fulfilment solutions to their problems: it was the establishment of a novelistic language that would make it possible to represent marriage between men and women as genuinely reciprocal. In *Persuasion*, Anne Elliot observes that books have told men's stories—'the pen has been in their hands'. When Jane Austen discovered this, she blazed a trail for books that tell women's stories as well.

The narrative voice we hear and treasure in Austen's completed novels belongs to a successfully single, self-possessed mature woman artist, a confirmed spinster but not a beaten-down or ridiculous old maid: just the kind of person who, as D.A. Miller has recently argued, does not and cannot exist in the social world her books depict; but the delivery of that voice into literature enlarged its expressive horizons and, it is not an exaggeration to say, contributed to the expansion of the range of experiences and ways of being the nineteenth-century novel made available to female readers. It troubles me that the person who invented that voice should be represented as having done it on the rebound. This is an insult to Austen's deliberate decision to remain independent and pursue her art, one that is also present in the 2008 BBC film *Miss Austen Regrets*, albeit with a somewhat clearer grasp than *Becoming Jane* of the actual relations between an author's life and her fiction, as well as a more nuanced picture of Austen's difficult position within her family.

*Miss Austen Regrets* is an example of what philosopher Stanley Cavell calls a 'melodrama of the unknown woman'. Films in this genre deal with the question of how a woman achieves full personhood—also explored in romantic comedies, including those written by Austen—but the melodramas operate within a narrative 'structure of unhappiness'.[8] The heroine of an unknown-woman melodrama forgoes the form of education acquired through what *Mansfield Park* calls 'unchecked, equal, fearless intercourse'—open conversation and exchange with an equal partner (Beatrice and Benedict, Elizabeth and Darcy). Her transfiguration or metamorphosis is achieved alone, at the cost of isolation from everyone around her. *Miss Austen Regrets* opens with the depiction of a documented crossroads in Jane Austen's spinster career, presented as a scene of devastation and brokenness and a radical rejection of the idealist endings of the novels. It is 1802 and Harris Bigg, proprietor of Manydown Park, is making Jane a proposal of marriage that, if she consents, will forever guarantee the future of her impoverished mother and sister, as well as of her penniless self. She has no affection for him, but accepts out of prudence. The following morning she has taken back her promise and as the carriage drives her away Jane's stricken face stares out through a rain-streaked window and she thinks: Dear God, let me never regret this day. What Carol Shields in her biography of Austen describes as 'bodily fastidiousness',[9] that is, sexual choosiness, may have contributed to the historical Austen's rejection of Harris Bigg, who was a good deal younger than her and apparently something of a galoot, but she cannot have regretted escaping the dangerous and exhausting life of pregnancy and childbearing that marriage inevitably brought upon women. (Bigg eventually married Anne Frith and fathered ten children.)

Unfortunately for the Jane of the movie, regret is the film's leitmotif and it contrives six or seven occasions on which she remembers or someone in her circle reminds her of everything she threw away each time she refused a proposal.

Advising her young niece, Fanny Knight, about whether to marry the dishy Mr Plumptre, Jane tells her to wait until she's quite certain: 'the right man will come along'. Fanny looks sullenly at her and says, 'He never did for you.' Jane's brother Edward reproaches her for 'scribbling' and for failing to marry and lighten his financial burdens. The entrance of a handsome and clever London physician who after all is more interested in Fanny than in Miss Austen gives Jane occasion to say, 'I should never have wanted to become a doctor's wife', a line surely aimed at flattering the film audience's snobberies and prejudices.

As they sit side by side on a low stone wall, the middle-aged Brook Bridges, a neighbour who proposed to Jane in their distant youth, begs her to tell him she sometimes regrets turning him down; she can't or won't oblige him but they both look devastated, Brook presumably because he's never gotten over her and Jane because she is momentarily regretting the comfortable domestic life she would have led. (Brook Bridges is a composite figure invented for the film; there is no evidence of Austen having received such a proposal from any of the men on which he's loosely based.) In the film's most dramatic scene, a wild-eyed Mrs Austen steps forward from the depths of the kitchen's black shadows to assert that yes, she really had wanted Jane to 'sell herself for money' to Harris Bigg all those years ago. 'You sacrificed all our security on a principle, Jane—and has it made you happy? Has it? My poor lonely girl.' We see Jane sink to her knees in the forest and bawl out her grief and misery.

The film's melodrama-patterned conception of Austen extends to its representation of her most significant personal relationship as structured by sacrifice and renunciation. Through all the decisions and crises of Jane's life, Cassandra moves silently in the background, keeping Jane gently but firmly tethered to the family. When Jane is dying, it is Cassandra who nurses her and who keeps Fanny out of the sickroom. Their final conversation hints at the love and sympathy the sisters have shared all their lives but it is love that is resigned and muted by sadness: in narrative terms it is too little and comes forward much too late. 'This life I have', says Jane, 'is what I needed—it is what God intended for me.'

*Miss Austen Regrets* suggests that even though Austen lived among her family and friends her essential self always remained untouched and isolated. We understand that she paid a heavy price but the movie neglects to balance the scales by giving us a clear idea of what she got in exchange. The closest it comes is an awkward and slightly absurd scene enacting the 1815 visit Jane Austen made to Carlton House, where the Prince Regent's librarian informed her she had the privilege of being allowed to dedicate her next publication to his Royal Highness.

The author of *Emma* obviously had richer sources of satisfaction than the dubious distinction of royal approval but you would not know this from the film.

'The chief miracle' about Jane Austen's work, according to Virginia Woolf, is its freedom from the ill effects of the narrow circumstances in which she lived and worked. 'Here was a woman about the year 1800 writing without hate, without bitterness, without protest, without preaching.'[10] This is a recognisable description of the psychological qualities that have long made her fiction indispensable to us, but its 'miraculous' quality also hints at the incredulous, suspicious mode in which we now probe her biography for the traces of hidden sorrows and abandoned romances that we are so unjustifiably confident must lie buried there.

## NOTES

1. Helen Fielding, *Bridget Jones's Diary*, Picador, London, 1996, p. 40.

2. Virginia Woolf, *A Room of One's Own*, Penguin, Melbourne, 2004 (1929), p. 79.

3. James Ley, 'Germaine Greer on "a wife-shaped void" ', *Australian Book Review*, October 2007, accessed online at <http://home.vicnet.net.au/%7Eabr/Current/oct07leyreview.htm>.

4. 'Love and Freindship' (1790), in *Love & Freindship and Other Writings*, ed. Janet Todd, Phoenix, London, 1998, p. 82.

5. W. Somerset Maugham, 'Emily Brontë and *Wuthering Heights*', in his *Ten Novels and Their Authors*, Vintage, London, 2000, p. 256.

6. Rohan Maitzen, 'Becoming George', Novel Readings, <http://maitzenreads.blogspot.com/2007/08/becoming-george.html>, 18 August 2007.

7. Jane Austen, 'The Watsons', in *Northanger Abbey and Other Works*, Oxford University Press, Oxford, 2003, pp. 255–6.

8. Stanley Cavell, 'Ugly Duckling, Funny Butterfly: Bette Davis and *Now, Voyager*', *Critical Inquiry* 16.2, 1990, p. 217.

9. Carol Shields, *Jane Austen*, Viking Penguin, Melbourne, 2001, p. 176.

10. Woolf, *A Room of One's Own*, p. 78.

## AFTER LIVING TOGETHER
## FOR A YEAR

I teach him to knit. He knits,
tight, exact, the yarn's
stretch and give are gone,
this is wool as metalwork.
No stitch is given slack.
I take up the small oblong,
feel in it the tensile density
of his abdomen—
it's venous, rushing up my arm,
& the blue magnet of his eyes
runs the line between us
as taut as the next noose
off the needle.

CAROL JENKINS

# COVERING
# THE STORY

**AMPERSAND DUCK** TELLS US THE STORY BEHIND THE COVER OF
*THE LOST DOG*

I'M not a mainstream designer. I don't usually do big flash commissions, as I'm not formally trained and I get nervous when faced with professional-looking briefs on company letterhead. I never went to graphic design school, I didn't learn how many blacks you can overlay without pissing off the printer or how to avoid a moire pattern when setting up screens. I did go to art school, later in my working life, after I'd decided what I did and didn't like about print culture, and had gained a desire to explore the—now old-school—medium of letterpress and hand-set type.

I initially picked up computer layout work by hating everything I saw in the 1990s. I was studying for an MA in literature and working part-time in various offices and cruddy jobs. That was when Macs and cheap design software democratised book and newsletter layout. Suddenly people stopped using designers and started getting their staff to lay out their newsletters, annual reports and journals. The results were disastrous, and anyone over thirty-five will know exactly what I'm talking about.

I managed, with the help of a bit of nepotism (the only way to get jobs in Canberra, really), to talk my way into a position as a publications officer for an academic lobby group. I produced terrible layouts for a few years, but luckily they were fairly dry things such as conference brochures and symposia papers, and each one got progressively better as I worked out how to use the software. Being a voracious reader and a lover of books as objects, I had an idea of what good publishing should look like, or, more importantly, what *bad* publishing looks like. The former is what I've always wanted to achieve.

As a rule, I don't go out and find clients. Most of the people I've worked for have found me by word of mouth, and once they've found me they tend to use me repeatedly, which means I have enough work to keep me going. The majority of them are from the local universities, including the ANU School of Art, as they are the places where I've worked and got to know people. Over the last few years I've done mostly art catalogues, journals and all of the volumes of UNSW@ADFA's Academy Editions of Australian Literature series (following a design by Alec Bolton, someone who taught me a lot about creating an elegant page).

Since I want to do fifty million things besides sit at a computer, and I love doing more hands-on print production, I only take on enough layout work to pay the bills and maybe buy a pair of shoes a year (I wear cheap clothes and expensive shoes, but I try not to have more than four pairs going at a time). That leaves me with time to talk, cook and play with my family, and make a bit of art. Enough money is great, not enough is awful, and too much seems to be a responsibility (and something I've not yet encountered). So I work to make enough.

THIS IS THE GERM OF THE IDEA, DONE WITH SOME SIMPLY SCANNED THINGS, INCLUDING WARATAH LAHY'S IMAGE (WITH HER BLESSING!).

ON a visit to Melbourne in early 2007, I was sitting in an internet café checking my e-mails, and I found one from Allen & Unwin asking if I was interested in designing a book cover for a fab Australian author of theirs who liked my blog. It was a very seductive offer, and they pressed a few of my buttons: I've *always* wanted to design a mainstream book; I love Australian literature; and she liked my blog! Sigh. How could I resist?

I rang Michelle de Kretser from my friend's flat in Melbourne, and we had a lovely natter. What Michelle really craved was a designer who reads, and she could tell from my blog that I like a book or two. For me, the most alluring element of the job was that part of my brief was to read the book properly. Hooray!

While working at the ANU School of Art I've often fantasised about opportunities to use the work of the emerging artists around me as book or album covers. Thus, my first idea for *The Lost Dog* was to use an image by Waratah Lahy, who paints onto various surfaces such as beer glasses, blankets and flattened beer-cans. She did a dog beer-can cut-out that I thought would be perfect.

Then I played some more, using just the dog shape (see below). I've always liked really simple, elegant book covers. But while Michelle loved the actual doggie object, she said it wasn't the right sort of dog. This is when I realised that she had a specific dog in mind, and it was her dog, Gus (who has since died). Also, the dog in question needed to look *stressed*, to be more *lost* in its body language.

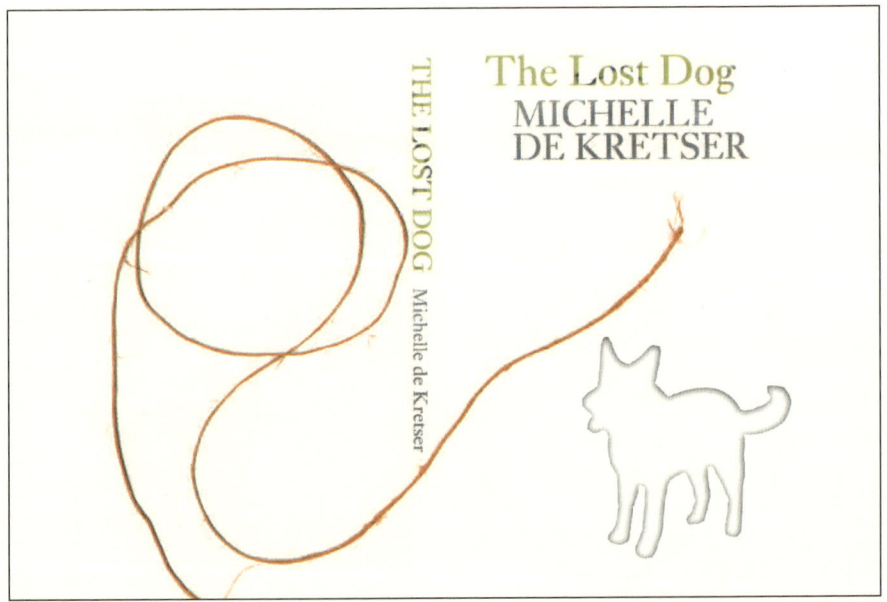

Well, of course, that changed everything. I think with those earlier drafts I had been concentrating less on the type of dog and more on the feel of the narrative. I wanted to convey a lot of feeling with very little information. I wanted it to feel contemporary, arty, airy, and very Australian. I wanted to break away from that 'Commonwealth writer' tag that keeps Michelle in a certain Auslit corner. Her last book cover was redolent with spices and palm trees. Of course, it was set in Sri Lanka. This book is set in Melbourne. It needed a 'Melbourne' feel.

Photograph by Michelle de Kretser

Gus

HMM. Back to the drawing board. Michelle and the team at A&U liked the textures I was playing with, so I jigged up some more ideas involving an empty letterpress typecase and some grungy old paper I'd photographed years ago. The paper had been lining an ancient case of wood type that had been dumped, like an abandoned baby, on the doorstep of the museum in Bega.

This is the penultimate version of the front cover.

[31]

After a lot of e-mailing we headed in a direction that made everyone happy, using the typecase (completely altered in its compartment configuration) and the paper and lots of elements that drew upon the detail Michelle lovingly renders in her writing.

IF you read the novel (and you should), it will all make some sense. We were interested in capturing small moments evoked in the pages, so nothing included on the cover is specific, except for the Skipping Vinegar Girl, an essentially Melbourne element that Michelle and I had discussed in our very first phone call. We wanted to extend the novel outside the text block, so the cover and the endpapers play their own roles in expanding the story slightly. I'm pleased that I did get to use some original Australian art: the Deborah Williams etching of the dog, cringing at the bottom of the cover. I still hope to use elements of Waratah Lahy's work for something in the future, because I think her narratives would work beautifully with someone else's.

For me the best bits of working on this book (besides reading it) was designing its internal elements, its less obvious little touches. The text design was fun—and I derived great satisfaction in designing a page I actually wanted to read—but I most loved doing the endpapers, because they're very 'me'. Michelle

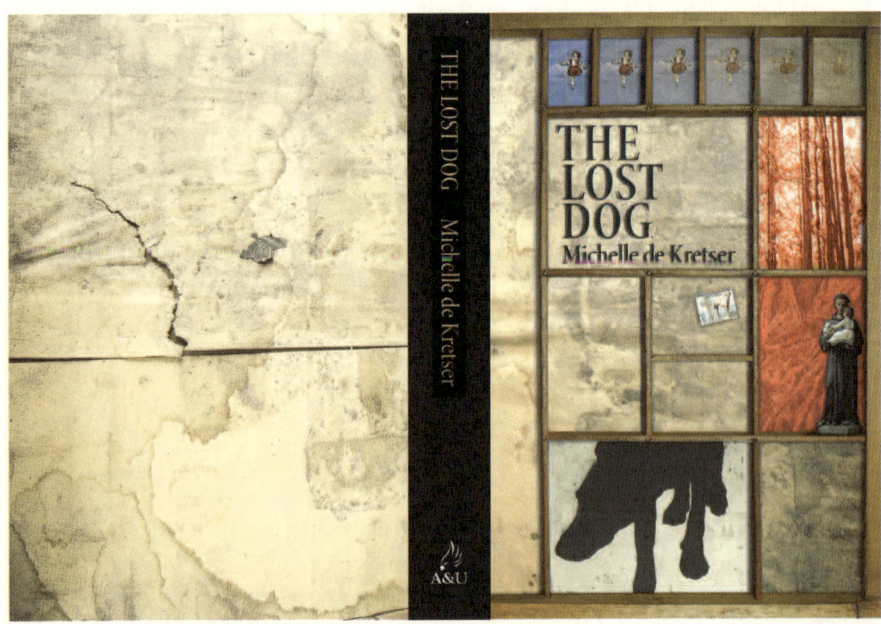

THIS IS THE FINAL VERSION, WITHOUT THE
BACK-COVER TEXT.

and A&U were inspired by the British cover of John Baxter's *A Pound of Paper*, with its samples of old book spines and covers. I thought about what we were doing, making the *inside* of a book cover, and I scanned some of the paper covers from my collection of old Angus & Robertson poetry volumes. I scanned the insides of them, with their faded and torn bits, and collaged them together to make booky underclothes. I think it worked quite well.

My practice hasn't changed much since I first started working in layout and design. In my head I still know what I want, and I'm still working out the ways to get there. I think formal design training would have locked me in a box that would have been hard to get out of, so while part of my brain suspects that I'm woefully amateur, another part treasures the fact that I'm a bit of a wildflower instead of a hothouse flower.

All of this, of course, feeds into my letterpress work, and my letterpress work feeds into my design. And my rule of thumb is: start with traditional rules and

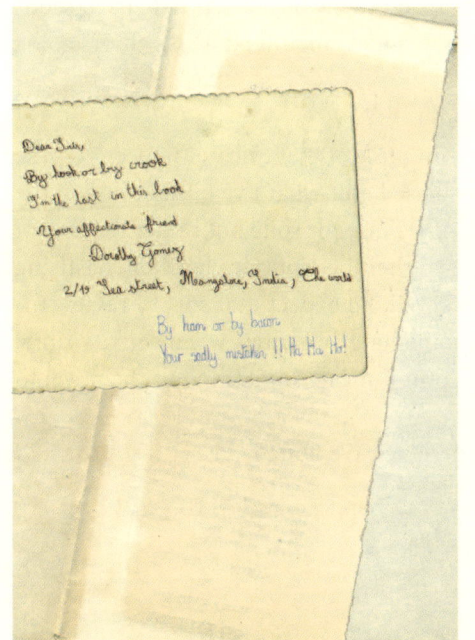
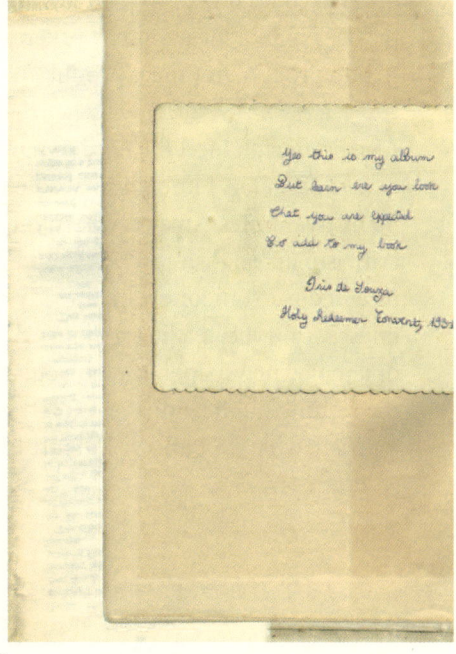

ABOVE LEFT IS THE BACK ENDPAPER. RIGHT IS THE FRONT ENDPAPER. MICHELLE WANTED AN OLD-FASHIONED AUTOGRAPH PAGE AT EACH END OF THE BOOK, WITH VERY SPECIFIC TEXT (PART OF THE NARRATIVE, REALLY), SO THEY HAD TO BE MANUFACTURED FROM SCRATCH AS WELL. I'M PROUD OF THE WAY THEY LOOK SO AUTHENTIC. THE LOVELY DATED HANDWRITING WAS DONE ESPECIALLY FOR US BY TWO FRENCH-SCHOOLED CHILDREN WHO ARE FRIENDS OF MICHELLE'S.

keep it simple. Though there are plenty of designers out there who do layered and decorative really well, and I admire much of their work, I just can't do it myself. Luckily space-and-simplicity is the equivalent of black in fashion; it never really goes out of style.

For what it's worth, my personal favourite design idea for *The Lost Dog* is the penultimate version, the one with the telephone. I think the book's title is more resolved, more appealing, in the earlier version. It calls from a distance, something I don't think the final version does. However, the final version, once you've found it on a shelf, makes you want to find out more about the story that spawned it, and that's what Michelle and A&U wanted. And in that respect it succeeds for me.

To be honest, I'm never completely happy with anything I finish, but that is hopefully a sign that I'll do better next time if I pay attention. The kinds of things that niggle at me about my work are things that others don't usually notice, and my loved ones think I'm too fussy. That's okay, it's my bugbear, not theirs. It sends me back to looking at other work, reading manuals and thinking. It's always going to be a process, not mere production.

As a postscript, I feel the need to remark on some of the reviews I've been reading of *The Lost Dog*. I know I'm absolutely biased, but what I've been seeing in the mainstream press smacks not so much of jealousy or spite but rather the sort of criticism an English teacher would give to their best pupil, a level of chastising reserved for someone who already does well. I'd expect that sort of review in-house, or maybe in a literary journal or something, but surely when you're writing in a major newspaper, the object is to communicate something of the novel to the reading public, no?

Meh, what do I know? I'm just the designer. We don't read.

# TWO EXITS & HOW TO

1
You've been here forever, but it's as though you'd moved in
just yesterday. In the end, time has had enough.
The familiar slips its moorings and goes for a wander;
walking together, you hear a blurred rushing
that slowly resolves into the articulated tumble of water.
For you, the days here are eloquent and swift; they glint
and sing. Each day, the other grows sharper and closer
while you slip imperceptibly into your own blind spot,
an image fogging the retina, becoming a ghostly presence
to yourself. Where was I? each thinks, casting around,
and not quite sure whether oneself or the other will be first
to step through the kitchen door, out into the cool black
of night, that still night, and not quite make it back.


2
But it was hardly a quandary for you, poet, who always
resisted the pompous because omnipotent drive
for conclusion, the stickyfingeredness of it all, and cheerfully
gloomily played fast and footloose with the dark, toking its energies,
taking a hit-and-miss of the worn & spanking it to newness,
a world you could count on to stay exactly where you didn't put it:
till your broken-field running stumbled, toppling you abruptly
without even a look of surprise or a bon mot
into that same river once.

ANDREW McDONALD

# DRUGS, DRANSFIELD, WOMEN AND SONGS

**DAVID NICHOLS** GIVES THE BACKGROUND, THEN **PIP PROUD** REMINISCES

My name is Phillip John Proud and this was naturally shortened to Pip Proud a few years ago. I was born 11.9.47 in Adelaide. My parents are middle class and so on, and so on. I decided to write when I saw an answer to two questions at once. What is value, and what would be entertaining for a young man. The whole thing is such a farce in that sense that I feel quite smart about it all.

SO wrote Pip Proud, brother of painter Geoffrey and friend to poet Michael Dransfield, in Thomas Shapcott's *Australian Poetry Now!* published in 1970. Dransfield (1948–1973) was a prodigious, eloquent and deservedly fashionable rising talent in Australian poetry; he published his first collection, *Streets of the Long Voyage*, that year and remains one of the best-known and -loved poets of his generation. Dransfield, a fan of Proud's before the friendship, had insisted Proud be included in the Shapcott volume.

Proud was already renowned in underground circles as the composer and performer of some of the most uncompromising and extraordinary pop music of the 1960s, exemplified in the albums *Adreneline and Richard* (1968) and *A Bird in the Engine* (1969). The popular press acclaimed him as 'a pop primitive', but the combination of his fragile, intimate vocals, naive guitar playing and raw performing style created scornful opposition alongside his hard core of devotees.

By the time *Australian Poetry Now!* was in the shops, Proud had decamped to London, where he continued to struggle. The Beatles' Apple label almost signed him and John Peel's Dandelion label *did* say yes but nothing came of it. Proud, and his loyal girlfriend Ali, were meanwhile starving, committed to his art. He was writing a novel called 'The White Forest', which Dransfield planned to (but didn't) publish.

Proud returned to Australia in 1971 in mourning, following the suicide of his adopted sister. Phonogram, his Australian record label, did not want to release his new songs (or perhaps he didn't ask them to). After some time in Sydney, where he wrote plays for the station then known as 2JJ, he disappeared to Tasmania, then to Tenterfield in country New South Wales for twenty-five years, returning to the music scene with a 1995 Half a Cow reissue of his sixties Phonogram material, entitled *Eagle-wise*. Interest in Proud was further inspired by a laudatory song from New Zealand's Alastair Galbraith titled simply 'Pip Proud' (Galbraith had inherited his mother's copy of *Adreneline and Richard*), and the 1997 success of one of Proud's old songs, 'We Crossed the Atlantic', covered by Melbourne group Hydroplane.

Proud has since recorded four new albums issued on the Emperor Jones label of Austin, Texas; the critical and consumer response has ranged from dazzled to confused. He is planning a fifth, and Emperor Jones is working on a double retrospective including a live recording from an extraordinary performance given in Melbourne in 2006. The following short memoir of a music career was recently penned by Proud, who is still actively writing.

HAVE you any idea how brave I was to do that music? It's a bit like in a video game, you lose a life every time you fail. I suppose there's a difference between strength and bravery. The less strong you are, the braver you are.

After all these years I say it now with very little feeling, but I always knew I was the bravest. Apart from those guys in Vietnam. It was almost like a whole theocracy that had to be overthrown. I wasn't alone. Maybe I was the most outrageous.

Listening to those soft words of mine, can you imagine they could outrage people? But yeah, they did.

I never understood why people laughed at my music. I still don't understand why I wrote such stuff and thought I could get away with it. Arrogance or naivety, maybe a bit of both. The trouble is I can't understand why I should have been arrogant. And with my upbringing, I certainly wasn't naive. Maybe it's a form of retardation or displacement. I think the whole hippy thing was kind of like that. We just had to escape this horrible world, so *Adreneline and Richard* carried sticks in the forest, and yeah, we're only worth our weight in meat.

I was spaso from birth. Something to do with RH-negative blood. I was knocking my knees together for a few years and then I was bow-legged. I couldn't talk properly for a long time and I certainly couldn't write. It was damning and I felt ashamed. I suppose that's why I tried to do music. It was a 'fuck you' sort of gesture. I guess that's why my lyrics are kind of dreamlike. I lived in my own world. But Christ, I was sick of being laughed at. I developed an artificial arrogance. Maybe that's bravery. Maybe it's showmanship.

All this lugging my guitar around trying to figure an E chord from an A chord. My brother trying to paint pictures. Once we rented a laundry to live in. It had a sloping cement floor with a big old cement laundry tub and a Bunsen burner for a stove, but somehow we didn't mind. We had our dreams of fame and wealth one day, but the pleasure was from the sheer iconoclasm of it all. It was bloody hard and cold, but each day seemed new. I liked pissing out the window or in the laundry tub. It was cool to see how many days we could stay awake without sleep. We used to compete like that. I think five was our record though I'm not sure who won. My brother painting and me trying to figure out how a damn guitar works.

We got some money at one stage and were determined we wouldn't starve for a while so we bought a carton of spaghetti. Like about ten kilos. But we forgot the sauce. I've had a thing about spaghetti ever since. My brother used to paint all night and all day. I used to stretch the canvases for him. It was a constant job.

Such a desperate time it was, man, ask Janis and Jimi. Every night on TV bombs dropping defoliants (in Vietnam) and the government telling us to like it. We had full employment back then and what a smug fat-arse pack of bastards we were. We were so full of shit and self-confidence we allowed the Aborigines to vote. We let them become real people! Weren't we cool!

I remember the Stones, Mick Jagger playing the harmonica like he was raping it (I thought: how incredibly spunky), and Buddy Holly on black-and-white TV. I'd go to symphony orchestras—my parents thought I was round the bend—and dances in Adelaide where I'd see the Masters Apprentices and others. I started playing guitar when I was about fifteen. I tried to learn a few Buddy Holly covers. I liked John Keats and Shakespeare and I suddenly understood how beautiful words could be. I don't remember what my first song was—some hippy thing, like 'I Love You Best when You're a Leaf'. I was living in Sydney and a stockbroker friend, Michael Hobbs, was supporting me there for a while. He bought me a tape recorder and I made fifty copies of an album called *De Da De Dum*. I took the album to quite a few record labels, and Bob Cooley from Phonogram called me up and said he thought it was okay, and I re-recorded it as *Adreneline and Richard*. I knew Garry Shead through Frank Watters and he made a film about me called *De Da De Dum*.

Really, I just freaked everyone out, they simply couldn't cope with someone outside their parameters. The bastards on TV used to try and set me up like they were going to have a joke at a performing fat woman or a dwarf. I never let them get away with it. I always gained the audience's sympathy in the end. But it was pretty hard sometimes. The blue-rinse ladies pulled me through, the young girls, and all those whimsical young poets who used to talk to me. I wonder where all those young poets are today. And those girls I signed autographs for, probably grandmothers now.

Buster Fides [an alcoholic comedian] talked to me once. He was beautiful. He said I shouldn't drink so much vodka before going on TV. We sat backstage and I drank vodka. He was a hell of a nice man.

Those dumb-arses who made these TV shows used to say 'Stand on the little red dot' on the floor and they always used to make you mime a song. I never would do that so they used to get a mike. Christ, they were fools. They could never talk me into anything, but shit, they tried. There was a kind of smugness about them. They had fake English accents. It was a huge pleasure to walk off the little red dot. It was great to make them move the cameras so far the end of the set showed. It was great to be a smart-arse, but much more importantly, it was great to run the show, to break the ice, to break the dam. Such tight-arses, man, it was great to humiliate them. I was young then, but I did it.

They used to try and set me up before an interview. They gave me stock answers to questions I'd be asked. I'd say, 'Oh yeah, yeah,' then when we were on live I could talk honestly and it used to freak these guys out, talking about peace and innocence and all these guys fighting in Vietnam at the same time.

The record company would fly me to Melbourne to do TV appearances. I hated the Hilton and used to find a groupie and go to her place instead. Got to know some strange places and some beautiful women. I had a permanent bed at this house that a Russian woman owned. She used to have pet pigs back in the old country. She shared the place with a microbiologist. The Hells Angels used to visit for three-day beer-drinking contests, and a lot of professors from Monash Uni. Strange mix of people. Anyway, this woman screwed all of us. You'd wake up in bed at night with this naked woman doing sexy things to you. The whole Russian ballet and the best minds at Monash, and me, all got a dose of some STD. All nice people. She was considered a hero. Funny, I can't even remember her name. She once tried to seduce me at a bus stop, in broad daylight, with people around. Nearly got me too, but I was scared someone would steal my guitar if I put it down.

My girlfriend Ali and I had an 'open' relationship. In retrospect that stinks. I don't think they can possibly work. But yeah, I used to like the groupies and a lot of them were good friends for a while (till they found something more stable) and I still love them. There was no AIDS back then, you might get some STD but no-one cared. I say this with a kind of bewilderment, but there was a time there when I was screwing eight women. I made house calls, half the day and all night. I was pretty spunky and I had this feeling towards all these fellow musicians who were being smart-arse and doing C13 chords and putting me down: to hell with you, I'll show you what music is all about. It's about basic chords, simplicity, a little ornamentation and the lyrics kind of falling down like the dew on the grass. But mostly, it's about sex.

Music is sex, *I* think so, it feels that way to me. At least, it's passion. Does passion have to lead to sex? I don't think so. I have a passionate love for so many people and there's no sex or desire. I really don't understand, but when I make a new song it's unrehearsed, like I've found a new lover. They're done in one take and that's the only one there will be. From my end it's absolutely exhausting. Sometimes I think I'm a real slob, but then no, a ten-minute song takes a week's energy, maybe not in calorific terms, but somehow it bleeds you dry.

We all lived at Alison's mum's flat: me, Hilary [Dransfield's girlfriend] and eventually Dransfield. Michael and Hilary used to sniff ether. He had this two-litre bottle. Christ, the place used to stink. It's a wonder we didn't all get blown up. I used to work with these two guitarists (John Black—he had two wives—and some other guy I can't remember). They never could catch my rhythms. Crazy times. I don't know how Ali's mum put up with us. Dransfield bought a deal of dope that turned out to be oregano. Ali and I smoked it on the off-chance. Meanwhile the neighbours complained about the smell and the music and Ali's mum kept bringing back hospital food from where she worked and put up with all this shit. She's a hero too.

Dransfield was always making me sign contracts for my books. I think in a way he was just trying to 'disappear' them. He just turned up at the door one day and said he was a publisher. He kind of ingratiated himself pretty thoroughly. He was so straight, worked at the tax office. I have loved and hated him, several times over. I think in me he saw something he wanted to become but didn't want to imitate. His early work was total fantasy. He had to find a niche market. His drug poems were it. Like a punk does things with body piercing and safety pins. He did escape from his parents, but what a way to go! I got really mad at him when he started offering Hilary heroin. That's when I hated him. I also got really mad at him when I realised he'd 'disappeared' my novels. They were probably crap anyway. But he was extraordinarily ambitious. I think I always knew who I was and there was really no trying, simply expressing. He didn't know who he was, he just tried different personas until one fitted.

I was kind of dismayed when I watched Dransfield killing himself. I was totally dismayed when that made him famous. He knew it would work like that. I think he thought his father would approve of him if he was famous. What a price.

I only took LSD once but that was more than enough. It lasted for three days. Your vision fractalises like on a video game, except everything for me had six sides. The ceiling turned into a Persian carpet. Music was so astoundingly clear and right inside my brain. Sex was fantastically sensitive, almost transparent, always this feeling of stark honesty, like you were cheating. My hold was so fragile. We walked to the park and the concrete footpath turned to sand and I fell through the pavement and Ali pulled me out again. I don't know, Ali saved me a lot of times in all sorts of ways.

In the late sixties I always got around with no shoes. I wasn't trying to be feral: it just felt good and I liked running. I used to run everywhere. I had this romantic notion of flying everywhere I went. It wasn't a statement or anything. I had absolutely no idea how peculiar I must have appeared. Also, so poor I couldn't afford shoes anyway. I found a pair of shoes in a throw-out once but they were a size too small so I thought I could stretch them. I boiled them in a cooking pot for a few hours thinking the leather would stretch, but the damn things shrunk and sort of set like concrete, all curled up. I didn't know anything about anything, but I thought I knew everything.

It was easy to get a job back then. You could get one any day you were short of cash. You could wake up in the morning and think, Christ, I'm hungry, better get a job today, and go and get one. They usually lasted about three days. I couldn't handle regimentation, still can't. I had this job at this car wash in Edgecliff. Three minutes. I got the internal windows section. I think they gave that job to the new guys because it was the hardest. This amazing car came in. It had a huge back window sloping at about 20 degrees and it certainly took more than three minutes. I don't know if the guy was deaf or something, but he drove off with me in the back still cleaning his window. He got a hell of a shock when I climbed into the front next to him. He let me off in Double Bay. By the time I walked back to the car wash I'd been sacked. That's typical of my work experience.

I don't feel nostalgia for those days. Wouldn't do it again but yeah, we thought we were doing just fine.

I guess back in the sixties there were as many homeless people as there are these days, but we didn't think of ourselves like that. It was pure desperado and who gives a shit. I could pack a change of clothes in my guitar case along with the guitar. Come to think of it, most of my life I played electric without an amp. Woke up one morning about three where I was sleeping in the Homebush abattoirs, under a couple of bushes. This cop on a motorcycle had his lights on me, but he pretended he couldn't see me and drove away. But I never felt homeless.

One night this cop got me for hitchhiking. Kept me in the lockup until about ten in the night, too late to get a ride. Slept in this bare field and that was a hell of a cold night. I had frost all over me in the morning. I was covered in ice. But yeah, still carried that damn guitar.

I stopped music for a long time … I mean you can only be scoffed at so much. I played guitar at a wedding party one night in about 1990 and it had this remarkable effect of stopping everyone dead in their tracks. Fuck, that was embarrassing.

In the mid 1990s I was living in Tenterfield and I started recording again. I had to learn the guitar again. I recorded to a cassette player that was hooked up to the car to power it, then a petrol generator, then solar cells. I've released four or five albums on the Emperor Jones label and I'm looking forward to doing another, a call-and-response rap album. Like the Beastie Boys, except it'll be the Pip Proud version. And I want to do it about the Third World War. It's going to have the lines 'holy shit, holy hell, holy war' stuck in there a few times. I'll probably embarrass George Bush—since he's not game to say it's a holy war. Oh my goodness, what the hell.

# THINNING THE POEM

You take the affect out of the poem
because all feeling
is underwritten
by the knowledge that at any given moment,
courage may be required—
and the question need never arise
if the poem does not ask it.

You take the self from the poem because—
dreamed or concocted or brewed—
the self is the site where one acts.

And you don't want to have to do that.

You take the sensual
out of the poem
because the sensual is the field
in which the other
steals into imaginings.

The other invites us to care:
it is where all our dangers begin.

You take quests for the common life
out of the poem:
because shared worlds
can undermine
claims to distinctive positions—
your project is pointless without them.

You take dancing, you take singing
out of the poem
because the body
is the register of the cost of language.

And you'd rather your budget were hidden.

And even though, yes,
every vein must be checked,
each experiment tried,

what is left
but an animal dying, unable to move—
though alert to each breath?

# THE FINCHES

Nobody hears them, the finches—tussocks
and mallee, copses and carpets of twig.
The sun doesn't notice—with so much
to shine on. The moon wouldn't hear them,
intent as it is on its moods. And humans—
well, why would they bother,
with so many things to fix up?
From pale, hollow grass-stalks, from claypans,
a querulous wind-drift of cheeping:
double-barred finches—as small
as a little girl's finger—are staking their claim.

They are out there right now—sotto voce,
but stubborn, unfazed. Nobody hears them.
Odd farmers. Perhaps ornithologists track them—
and make notes, and tick. And no-one
pays any attention to what they sing for.
As if their intent, compact lives were distilled
out of absence, they want to press sheer
to the absolute face of the Other, to know
themselves known.

They whirr between station and station;
they flitter through growths: piping all day,
with that miniature, sky-thinned insistence.

As loud as they can.

For an Other they cannot conceive.

MARTIN LANGFORD

# THE LAST JEWS IN HAREHILLS

**MARK DAPIN** EXPLORES THE SOMETIMES CONTRADICTORY DETAILS IN THE
LIVES OF HIS RELATIVES

MY uncle rang early in the morning to tell me about my dad. It was the first time
I had spoken to him in a decade, but I am the elder son, so he called me first. It
was a courtesy I did not deserve.

The phone in my house took only incoming calls. I had to go into the street
to ring my grandparents from a telephone box. My grandmother answered, but
she had already drifted past the point where she could distinguish her ghosts from
her dreams, so I asked for my grandfather.

He came to the phone excited, because I did not often call. His voice was
tobacco-rolled, peat-rich, loving cockney despite all the years he had lived in York-
shire. I told him my dad, once his son-in-law, had climbed out of his bath and
collapsed. Gerry Dapin had died on his bed, a towel around his waist, as my step-
mother combed his hair.

'When she told me Mark was on the phone,' said my grandfather, 'I thought
you were coming up to see us. I thought we'd go for a drink.'

I lived in the Midlands, my brother in the south of England. We met on a train travelling back to Leeds, the city where we were born. I had borrowed a dark suit. My brother was in the shirt and tie he wore to the shop where he worked. I had not had a cigarette for twelve months, but I started smoking again in a second-class carriage with my brother, who had loved my dad more than I had. It was 30 December, and the only thing I had achieved throughout the previous horrible, pointless year was to give up smoking. By the new year, I was back on a pack a day.

We stayed at my grandparents' house, a two-bedroom terrace in Harehills where my mother and her three sisters had grown up. By this time, my grandparents were the only white family on the street, perhaps the last Jews in Harehills. Their small house bore a mezuzah on the doorpost. There was a menorah on the sideboard with eight branches for Chanukah. It used to stand among a forest of wedding photographs of swarthy men in dinner suits and their brown-eyed brides, but my mother had since divorced my dad, and her twin sisters had left their husbands, and the last photograph showed my aunt Gloria and uncle Bill, wearing gumboots on their farm in Seymour, Victoria, Australia, where none of us had ever been. ('Cows and sheep,' muttered my grandma, with wonder. 'Gloria's got cows and sheep!')

There was a vast, guilty emptiness in my heart. At the funeral, my brother and I would have to say Kaddish, the Hebrew prayer for the dead. My brother could not read Hebrew, so I spent an hour phoneticising the verses for him, searching for distraction in the rhythm of the exercise.

My dad was buried in the Jewish cemetery, several kilometres out of town. I did not know most of the people at the service, a long procession of footballers he had trained and managed, each of whom wished me long life, according to the custom. The rabbi noted the large turnout, said everybody had loved my dad. I imagined the other mourners were all looking at me, thinking: everybody but him, and I was swallowed by horror.

After the service, we went back to my stepmother's small house. My brother, my uncle and I sat on low chairs, brought out for the occasion. My grandfather was the one member of my mother's family in the room. He suffered the shame of his daughter having run off with 'that Yok', but he said he wanted to 'be with my boys'. At the wake, kindly people offered my brother and me cigarettes, and made sure we—like our grandfather—always had a whisky in our hands, while they themselves drank strong tea with saccharine.

My dad's brother, my only blood uncle, kept us talking, with stories he must have told many times before, but never to me. He was a professional gambler who had once owned or managed a snake of betting shops. He had seen out his National Service in the Royal Air Force. He said he was a self-defence instructor, 'the only self-defence instructor who couldn't fight'. When he left, he worked as a bouncer, 'the only bouncer who couldn't fight'. He asked my cousin to tell the story of the time my uncle and a group of friends had been in a brawl a few years before. He told me he had employed a minder who collected debts for him, a man who looked like he could kill you but only used threats. It was the only long conversation I had ever had with my uncle, and he seemed to want me to know that, despite all evidence to the contrary, he could actually fight.

He gave me his adult life—in pieces, with punchlines—but left out the one episode I knew about: the two years he had spent in prison for fraud. My uncle was a tall man, big-bellied and beaked like an emperor penguin, a caricature of an Ashkenazi Jew. His nose might as well have been the point of a yellow star, his hair a skullcap. They would have bloodied that big nose in a British jail in the early 1960s, they would have burst open those full lips. It would have cost my uncle more than money to be who he was.

When the mourners had left, my grandfather took my brother and me for a beer. My grandfather had never had a son ('Four girls,' he used to say, 'and even the dog's a bitch') but for fourteen years he had my dad, a son-in-law, and he loved him. It hurt him that, after the divorce, my dad dropped us off at his house, and never came inside. Perhaps he thought there would be a photograph of my mother's second husband on the sideboard. It seemed to me my grandad and my dad had nothing in common but us. My dad often used to say 'I don't drink, I don't smoke, I don't back horses', in justification of some minor sin he allowed himself, such as a once-a-week poker night or watching too much football on television. My grandfather drank every lunchtime and evening. He studied the racing form and had a bet every day, and he had smoked cigarettes until he was sixty.

At my dad's funeral, my uncle said, 'I don't drink, I don't smoke, I don't chase women.'

My dad took his enjoyment from football—from watching professional games, refereeing amateur matches, and coaching and managing youth teams. My grandfather, alone among the men I knew, followed rugby league.

Yet there were similarities between the two men not apparent in the way they lived. They both had an easy manner. They made friends quickly and widely. Neither was educated. My dad left school at fourteen, my grandfather at twelve. They each loved their sport, and male company. They had both lived in the world of the people who my dad, born in Liverpool, referred to as 'the English', although my dad withdrew from it in his last years. They both came from the working class. My grandfather was a cabinet-maker, the son of a dockworker. My dad's dad was a cabinet-maker, too. I don't think of him as my grandfather, he died before I was born. I think he was born in England but not literate in English, that he spoke Yiddish in the home, but I don't know for sure. I never knew my dad's mother either. She was often sick, and my dad spent much of his childhood living with his aunt, who worked in a shop. The aunt was at the funeral, still as sharp as the nose that had frightened me as a child. She told me my dad's parents were not as poor as I had thought, that his mother had worked in a store attached to his dad's workshop. My dad was an orphan at eighteen, and only semi-literate, when he was drafted into the army. He never spoke much about his childhood, except to say he kicked footballs made of rolled-up newspaper around bomb craters during the Blitz.

I barely know my uncle, but he has a good story so I will steal it and keep it as my own. I will make it a part of me, as if his experiences somehow informed mine, although they did not. I like the picture I have painted of my family after my dad's funeral: a crowded room with whisky and rogues, like an Irish wake. It is a true picture, but barely true.

TWO years later, my grandfather was disappearing in a hospice, tended to by nuns. He said there were Yiddisher boxers in nearby beds. He said we would have to go out for a drink when he recovered, but my brother and I brought him a can of beer and he refused it, so we knew he was fading away.

I flew out to China, on a trip to Asia from which I never returned, and he was buried, three weeks before I picked up the letter telling me he was dead. My mum, Betty Benjamin, had written on the back of the envelope 'Contains the expected news'. I toasted his soul with San Miguel beer in a bar in Hong Kong. I did not cry, and I assumed I was emotionally autistic, that I cared for no-one but myself.

Another year passed, and I was sitting with some friends in Bondi Junction Leagues Club, Sydney, when suddenly I began to weep for him. My grandfather would have loved Bondi Junction Leagues Club: the cheap beer and the old men, the restaurant and the poolroom.

I was not there for my brother when my grandfather died, so I wrote him a kind of obituary. I hoped it would help him remember our grandfather, but I was also showing off my new-found skills as a phototypesetter. The piece is untitled, set flush left in Garamond, over a measure that may have been dictated by the width of bromide paper. There are two points of leading between each line, and a line space between paragraphs. I wrote:

When our grandad shaved, he used a shaving stick, a brush, a razor and blades. The hairs of the brush were soft and thick, like a cat's tail. The soap twisted out of the stick like lipstick. The head of his razor lifted to fit a new blade, then screwed down tight. The blades were wrapped in greaseproof envelopes and placed in a white plastic box. He ran the brush under the sink tap. The hot water in his bathroom was always scalding. He dabbed the wet brush onto the stick and worked up a lather. He painted his bristles in small, regular patches. He took the blade to each patch from top to bottom, scraping away his beard in short, determined strokes.

Our grandad shaved with a full kit of tools but, whenever you kissed him, his bristles rubbed your cheeks like wire wool.

Shaving is the first long memory I have of him. Before that, there are only impressions. Nana and Grandpa are poor. They live where the black people live. He drinks beer and whisky. He bets on horses. He does not like football but he fills in a pools coupon.

Nana makes mincemeat and buys wurst. She licks her fingertips and presses them into the food. She takes the bus to the market to do her shopping. He walks to the newsagent to buy the *Yorkshire Evening Post*.

They take their tea without enough milk. They use Izal medicated toilet paper. They turn off the lights to save on electricity. They are saving for their funerals in a Co-op passbook. They are saving in a tin for the Jewish National Fund. They always give us one shilling, maybe two. He cannot read Hebrew. She does not like the Russians. She pulls hairs out of her chin with tweezers. He borrows books from Sheepscar Library. A lot of things he does, nobody else has any use for anymore. One day, the man from the JNF just stopped coming around to empty the can. Our grandad went to the Shul where the working Jews worshipped. When the others died or moved away, the Shul was sold to the Sikhs.

He has his trousers let out by a tailor. With every drink he buys at the club, he offers one to the barmaid. Most times, she drops ten pence into her glass by the till.

Our grandad would buy anybody a drink. He bought beer for a Geordie scrounger who collected the glasses and helped him with his overcoat and stick. He bought beer for us, when we were thirteen years old. He once bought our dad a whisky, the only one I ever saw him drink.

Our grandad did a lot of drinking. At first, I remember him always going to the Chained Bull, then the Mansion in Roundhay Park, then the Griffin on Roundhay

Road. One year, he sometimes took Nana to the Keyhole Bar of the Arista Ballroom, which was another place nobody else went anymore, except for tattooed white boys and tough young Asians.

Before he died, he went only to the Jewish Club and the Sheepscar Workingmen's.

He had been a member of the Sheepscar Club since the war. He built the chairs in the lounge. When the lounge was being refurbished in 1987, he would often say, 'I'll have to go up there and get my chairs back.' What he would have done with a couple of dozen bar seats is anybody's guess.

At lunchtime, he would drink in the saloon bar. In the evening, he took his place in the lounge. His lunchtime mates were a bunch of old Irish labourers, big-built, glass-eyed, red-faced and loud. His evening pals dropped off over the years. They would announce the death of club members over the tannoy, and it seemed like every night somebody he knew was buried.

He had belonged to the Jewish Club since it was in the old Jubilee Hall, which faced the Sheepscar Club across an empty patch of Chapeltown. Now the Jubilee is the Trades Club, which he always maintained was Communist. Inside, Jamaicans in overalls slam down heavy dominoes on tables identical to those at the working men's club.

The new club is in the grounds of the New Vilna Shul. It is quiet and polite, like respectable lives. It holds coffee and bagel mornings, and hundreds of people play pinochle there. Only four men ever drank at the bar, and only one drank beer. The four were our grandad; Meyer Landy; a man who owned a tailoring factory; and the son of our grandad's old friend Morrie. The others wore dry-cleaned trousers and pure wool jumpers. Our grandad came wrapped in his suit, which looked as if it had come out of a charity shop.

Our grandad had some good clothes. I took his braces to go with my boots, Googie took his long, dark coat to look like a student. His taste in ties was so appalling that they would probably be fashionable today.

At the Jewish Club, they talked about family, Israel and the old days. In the old days, they used to go down to London on Remembrance Sunday and get drunk on the coach on the way to the Association of Jewish Ex-Servicemen's parade. On one of these runs, a strange woman wanked off Meyer Landy and she is still talked about today. One December, Grandad and the tailor were so drunk that their wives made them eat their Christmas dinners in the street.

Our grandad's Jewish friends had a dry, chiding humour. Their favourite jokes were about how mean the others were, although this was never really appropriate for Grandad.

Morrie's son usually drove him to and from the Jewish Club, but one day our grandad looked at the carpet and said, 'They don't come around so often since Morrie died.'

In eighty years, he had already got most of what he wanted to say off his chest. He would talk about the old East End, but only if you asked him. When Nana started to turn senile, he would talk about how hard it was to live with her. When he was very ill, he would come downstairs, gasping and wheezing, sit in the front room and wait for exhaustion. One morning he said to us, 'It don't matter what's wrong with you, some bugger always tells you he's worse.'

That lunchtime, we were in the Sheepscar Workingmen's Club. A skeletal Scot called Jock sat near us, coughed and asked Grandad how he was. He listened, nodding, as Grandad described the slow way he was dying.

'Ah yeah, Jimmy,' said Jock. 'I've got the same thing myself, only twice as bad.'

I am not proud of this as a piece of writing, and I am suspicious of my motives. If I wrote it to help my brother to remember my grandfather, why did I include details such as the West Indians playing dominoes in the building that once housed the Jewish Club? If I were generous with myself, I could say I wanted to convey the sense that he was an unchanged man in a changed and changing world, but it reads more like I had an eye to posterity, that I thought this document might one day be found among my brother's papers (whatever *they* might be) and be used to reconstruct a part of the life of the famous typesetter who bore his surname.

The piece has all the faults of my writing style. It is heavy with sharp sentences, thrown fast and short, like darts at a board, but half of them bounce off the rim and hit me in the foot. I had read only a little Hemingway, but enough to give me the idea that real writing was expressionless prose soaked in sentimental machismo.

I move between tenses as if the past and present were interchangeable. Many people do this when they are talking about somebody they love who has died; it can take a lifetime to adjust grammar to absence—but I suspect I was simply being careless.

I jump around topics with no thought for narrative organisation. I have a feeling I was trying to re-create the chaotically connected impressions of a child, to record the little things—the shaving brush, the JNF tin, the overcoat—that made my grandfather seem special to us, and different from my dad, who had a referee's whistle and stopwatch, and a trilby hat.

At times I sound like a pompous schoolboy ('… although this was never really appropriate for Grandad'). I use shamelessly formulaic expressions such as 'off his chest', doubly inappropriate since he was destroyed by lung cancer disguised for the family as bronchitis.

I remember when my grandfather said, 'They don't come around so often since Morrie died.' I was sitting on the sofa in his living room, drowsy with lager and wishing I had a notebook to help me remember the sadness of his words. Perhaps I always expected to write an obituary for him, or perhaps I wanted to steal his soul. Perhaps I saw him as a character I could turn into fiction, even then.

My coldest reservation, however, is that this piece seems to be an attempt to claim my grandfather for myself, to say I knew him best. In the last years of his life, I did a little drinking with my grandad. At first I was not speaking to my dad; then I did not feel welcome in his house; then he was dead; so whenever I returned reluctantly to Leeds, I stayed in Harehills with my grandparents. Most of my mum's family, like my dad's, enjoyed telling each other how they did not drink, but they were pleased that my grandfather had somebody to sit with him. It was probably his dream, too, to be at a table in the public bar with his grandsons, our sour cigarettes burning away in the ashtray.

I was drinking for me, not him. I found it frightening to struggle through the day without a beer, and boring to sit in my grandparents' house while my grandfather dozed in front of the black-and-white television. In the club, I would drink four pints of lager, while he chased his halves of bitter with a glass of whisky that he refilled under the table from a quarter bottle he kept in his pocket. My brother was often with us, but I sometimes went with him alone. I asked him a bit about his family, my great-grandparents. He told me his father was a Victorian, and all his family spoke like Victorians. He said he was never a boxer, but there was always a pair of boxing gloves in the East End. He told me to look after my family, because they were the most important thing in my life. I said I was looking for a job as a warehouseman. He thought that, since I had been to university, I would want to become a lawyer. I said I needed to see something of life to write about it but, in fact, I had despaired of life at twenty-three. I do not think I wanted to write the Great Warehouseman's Novel. One of my mates had found a job in a warehouse, so that seemed like something a person could do. I was economically and emotionally paralysed in the Midlands, and too broke, disaffected and stupid to move down south and get a decent job. My grandfather talked most about how he was maddened by my grandmother's madness, but he was always kind and patient with her at home. He wanted to move into accommodation run by a Jewish charity near the grounds of the synagogue, two minutes walk from the Jewish Club, but my grandmother insisted she would stay where she was, where she had lived since before the Second World War. In 1948 he had thought about emigrating to New Zealand, but she had been against that, too. He said he wished he had gone.

MY aunt Gloria moved to Australia when I was eleven years old. Before she took up what was more or less hobby farming in Seymour (she kept cows but not, as my grandma had imagined, sheep) she had worked as a teacher in schools around Victoria. Gloria was thought to be brilliant. She had a degree from Oxford University, although my grandfather—her father—had done everything he could to stop her from staying on at school. When she was younger, she had wanted to be a writer. She had composed poetry that my mum could recite by heart, and novels that remained unpublished because a complicated deal fell through, as they always do.

Gloria was the first person my girlfriend and I stayed with when we flew from Bali to Australia. I knew her from her letters, and from visits she had made when I was a child, but she had lived in Israel or Australia for most of my life. She was the relative who was most like me. She was a former member of the Communist Party who never did as she was told. My grandparents had warned her that a girl with an education—they imagined it as almost as a physical curse, like a hare-lip—would never find a husband, and she married too late for children, as they had predicted and feared.

I asked Gloria if she regretted not having written. 'No!' she said. 'No!'—her regret implicit in the fire of her denial.

We spoke about my grandfather, and she met my opinions with joyous anger. I was not describing the man she knew. I had stolen something that belonged to her, pulled it apart to see how it worked, then put it back together all wrong.

She began work on an autobiography that would tell the real story of my grandfather, but I needed the grandfather that I had written. I wanted him to be a working-class hero. I craved genealogy, a blood link with the great twentieth-century struggle of good against evil, socialism against fascism, workers against bosses, schoolboys against PE teachers.

My ideal grandfather would have been a prize-fighter and Communist Party organiser, who retired undefeated from the ring in 1936 to join the International Brigades in Spain. Upon Franco's victory, he would have smuggled himself over the Pyrenees to France, ideally disguised as a priest, and returned to England to join the Parachute Regiment, whereupon he would have liberated France, invaded Germany, and somehow become attached to the US units that rolled into the concentration camps in 1945. If he had any spare time, he could perhaps have written a slim volume of war poetry.

My actual grandfather was the son of an itinerant East End dock worker. His father's family had perhaps been in England since Oliver Cromwell readmitted Jews in the seventeenth century. His mother's family were Sephardim, descendants of the community that was expelled from Spain in 1492. His father's family may originally have been displaced Sephardim, too, but he once told me they had come from Germany. Either way, I grew up with the feeling that the Spanish Inquisition was a fairly recent event, and a profound personal insult.

My grandfather called himself Jimmy Benjamin. In the last years of his life, he asked me to address him as 'Jimmy', like the mate he wanted me to be, but I could not do this. His real name was Isaac, but it was only ever seen on official letters, such as his regular communications from Vernon's football pools. He had two brothers and two sisters. Brother Zachariah styled himself 'Alec'; Moses took the name 'Mick'.

Two of his uncles were supposed to be prize-fighters. I cannot find a record of an East End boxer called Benjamin, but Jewish fighters often hid their identities behind Catholic names.

My grandfather, Alec and Mick slept in the same bed. They grew up in the East End. He was only a boy when he was apprenticed as a cabinet-maker, and moved to Leeds because that was where the work was. My grandma had worked in a tailoring factory since she was thirteen. He met her at Lyons Corner House, made her pregnant in Potternewton Park, and married her two months later. Most of this I know from Gloria's book, which she eventually co-published with a small English arts press.

The year after he married, my grandfather became foreman at Madeloffs, a Jewish-owned cabinet-making factory. There was a strike, and he came out with the men, but the men went back without him, and he briefly lost his job. I used to think my grandfather led the strike, but now I don't know. He never spoke to me about it until a couple of years before he died, when he mentioned he had known my other grandparents. They met first when my father's father was bussed in from Liverpool as a scab to break the strike. My grandfather said he liked him, though, and described my other grandmother as 'a fine-looking woman', a description not borne out by her few surviving photographs.

When I wrote my own book, *Sex & Money*, ostensibly about men's magazines but actually about me, I used the anecdote about the striker grandfather and the scab grandfather to set up a probably false dichotomy between the two sides of my family. It was true, however, that my dad voted Conservative, while I don't think anybody in my mum's family ever had or would. My grandad mistrusted Communists and politicians in general. He did not fight in the battle of Cable Street, the siege of Madrid or the Normandy landings. When the Second World War broke out, he joined the air raid Rescue Squad and eventually went back to the East End, pulling his neighbours' broken bodies from the rubble of their homes. He saw all of the carnage of the war but did none of the killing.

When I was born, he had a workshop, a partner and an apprentice. He still lived in the same two-up, two-down terrace house. My brother and I played with his saw, his plane and his T square, as well as the box of dominoes he kept in the cupboard under the black-and-white TV. On the mantelpiece over the fireplace, opposite the wedding photographs that collapsed like his dominoes, was an eclectic collection of trinkets: a laughing Buddha, an unpainted plaster figure entitled 'World's Greatest Grandad' (part of a range my father once sold along with his greeting cards), a couple of mounted medals cast to commemorate Israel's victory in the Six Day War (which I always believed had been awarded to Gloria for bravery under Arab fire), the menorah and something—possibly an embroidered piece of cloth—with the words 'Ours is a nice house, ours is'. There was also a carriage clock that ticked like water dripping from a tap, and chimed every fifteen minutes in the twilight of my grandparents' lives. It always seemed like sunset in their house; they did not like to turn on the lights because they saw it as a waste of electricity.

Next to the mantelpiece, above the telephone, was a drinks cabinet with whisky, Palwin 11 Kosher wine, cherry brandy and the sherry my grandmother would take with lemonade at certain special times.

My grandfather, who only had daughters, loved us as his sons. The only time my grandma was pregnant with a boy, she aborted him with coathangers and knitting needles, because they could not afford another child.

My grandfather retired when I was too young to know the difference, but he quietly took a job with ghosts. When I was sixteen years old, I joined him for a week in a factory, where he stooped over a lathe with all the other retired cabinet-makers, cutting struts for bedheads. Affecting the thug look, I kept rolling my jeans to the top of my Dr. Martens boots and he kept telling me to roll them down again. We drank beer at lunchtime. I had mild, he had bitter.

My grandparents' part of Leeds was crumbling, socially and physically. The Jews had moved out in the late 1950s and 1960s. I remember the last shop selling skullcaps, prayer books and prayer shawls, and the last Jewish grocer, but they had all gone by the late 1970s. The white working-class had moved on, too. The homes they left were taken by West Indian bus drivers, nurses and mechanics, sunny people who sometimes painted their bricks pink, blue and green, like the homes they had left behind in the Caribbean. Other houses were left to fall apart, perhaps by landlords who found they could still rent to junkies or whores when the windows were boarded over and the garden walls fell down. The streets between my grandfather's house in Harehills and the Sheepscar Working Men's Club became an ugly beat for grey-skinned prostitutes, who between 1975 and 1977 were habitually raped, eviscerated and disembowelled by Peter Sutcliffe, a psychopathic lumpen gravedigger who styled himself 'the Yorkshire Ripper'. Streets in the area were closed off and bollards set in the road to frustrate kerb crawlers.

My grandfather liked the girls, and said they would help him home when he was drunk, but when I walked past and timidly ignored their 'Business, love?' they told me to fuck off.

In 1981 the sons and daughters of the bus workers and nurses rioted in Chapeltown, and they fought the police with petrol bombs and bricks in the streets my grandfather walked with his stick. His friends urged him to move, but he refused.

My grandfather was gently rough with us. He chased the cat with shears, pretending he would cut off its tail. He did not like it when my mum shouted at us. He thought it was cruel.

My grandmother went shopping and forgot what she had bought. She hid cabbages in the wardrobe. She told the same stories over and again, occasionally substituting different characters. She told my cousins and me that my brother had always been her favourite grandchild, admonished us all for ruining her furniture by sitting on it, and accused my cousin of maliciously trying to straighten out her coiled telephone cord. She often declared that she 'must be psychic' when things happened that she had failed to predict, and she said everybody else was mad.

My grandfather, tormented by her foolishness, found refuge in his clubs.

WHEN I was ten years old, in 1973, my mother left my father. My grandfather said she was dead, and would not speak to her or of her. My parents divorced and each quickly remarried. I never hoped they would get back together. I did not think of it as a possibility. I enjoyed the new arrangement. In the housing association, I had my own room on my own floor (which was shared with the garage).

I even had my own toilet. It was sad, at first, when we went to see my dad, then it was awkward when he married the woman I called my stepmother, but I hardly noticed that my family had collapsed. My poor little brother sat outside on the back step at weekends, waiting for my dad to come and pick us up. I lay in my room reading American comics.

Gloria, then living briefly in England, had to tell my grandparents about my mum. She says my mum threatened to kill herself if Gloria did not give them the news. 'After that,' she told me years later, 'there were months and months where they pretended she was dead, and wept and wailed and carried on like lunatics. It really broke something in me, as well. It wasn't because of what Betty had done, all I kept thinking was: They would have been exactly the same with me. They don't care. I kept saying, "We're all alive and we're all healthy. What are you making such a tragedy of it for?" But to them it was a tragedy, and a humiliation beyond words."'

After about eighteen months, Grandma organised a reconciliation. My mum came through the gates at the top end of Potternewton Park, where Gloria was conceived. My grandad approached through the gates at the bottom. (I think there were actual gates, but they served no purpose, since all the railings around the park had been torn out and melted down to make artillery in the war.)

My brother and I watched as they walked slowly towards each other, and suddenly both broke into a trot, then a sprint, until they met at a middle point and fell into each other's arms.

GLORIA says when I first talked to her about my grandfather, I 'sort of maddened' her: 'You were hugely devoted to Dad, but when it came to Mum, I don't think you even liked her. I thought it wasn't fair. Nobody ever saw her pleading for another bob for a vest for the twins. He was so nice, and he was full of bonhomie to all his men friends, but the cost was there was never enough money at home, and it was Mum who bore the brunt of that. We girls were totally torn. We loved it when he got drunk, and was willing to give everybody every penny he had because he was in such a good mood, but it was then that she'd get pregnant and have these bloody abortions.'

She wrote her book, *A Daughter of Leeds*, about a man who was wholly unfamiliar to me: Jimmy Benjamin before he became a benign and gentle grandfather, when he was an angry and violent parent. He beat Gloria and her two youngest sisters—helpless little girls—until his sticks broke on their backs. When the book was launched in Leeds in 1998, the *Jewish Telegraph* gave it a page of coverage. The headline read 'Troubled daughter brings family to book'. The story concentrates on Gloria's Jewishness, another excuse for my grandfather's brutality: 'At home I'd pick up the scissors on Friday night, intending to cut out some picture, an action perfectly acceptable on any other night. Suddenly a clout would slam me against the wall. What for? Why?'

In her book, Gloria writes about being sent on errands at the age of seven to a Jewish grocer who tried to get his hand inside her pants. She did not tell my grandma why she did not want to go to the grocer's, so my grandma would become enraged at her disobedience, and my grandad would come home from work and hear about it 'so he'd hit me, just to shut her up, but he couldn't hit anyone in cold blood: he had to work himself up to a rage to do it, then he hit too hard. One clout from his cabinet-maker's hands would send me reeling halfway across the living room. He didn't know when to stop … One clout was followed by more; a little girl was an easy target. He'd aim for my head. Within two minutes Mum would be terrified. "Not her head, Jimmy—not her head!" She was scared I'd get brain damage … He started to beat me with the dowel sticks he kept in my bedroom cupboard. He hit me so hard that often the stick broke and he had to get another from the cupboard … About forty years later I asked him, "What did I do that was so terrible you had to hit a little girl of seven with dowel sticks?" He was amazed. He answered stiffly, "All my friends had kids and hit them and they turned out all right. I don't know what went wrong with you lot!" '

She writes of my grandfather with a great love, always looking for excuses for him, explanations, alibis. He deserved peace and quiet. It is no wonder he ran to the pub.

My mum and her sisters launched the book. My mum, guileless as ever, said, 'I enjoyed that book but wondered if it would be of interest to anyone else.' An aunt shared Gloria's memories: 'It takes us back to my childhood,' she said, 'and to a sister who protected her younger sisters. Our father … could be quite savage when he lost his temper.'

The *Jewish Telegraph* journalist describes my aunt as 'born and brought up in the slums of Leeds during the 1930s and 1940s … She suffered beatings from her drunken father and stole money until she was seventeen from her mother, who later aborted her own foetus.'

My mum wrote to the paper, protesting that the quotes had been taken out of context. Her unusual argument was that my grandad could not be called a drunken bully because he was only a bully when he was sober. He was playful and happy when he was drunk. The 1940s were different times, when children were beaten at school. And besides, his daughters provoked him.

Gloria robbed me of a hero. I wanted him to have violence in his heart—to have dispatched fascists with fists and guns—but not that kind of violence, not violence against children. I was not angry with her, or angry with my grandfather. In a way, for a while, I was actually angry with my dad. Why didn't he beat me with sticks? At least then I would have had an excuse.

So much of Gloria's book could be mine, so many incidents recurred in my life a generation later, some of them identically. It is not big and it is not clever to be clever the way my aunt and I are clever. It is no use being brighter than a teacher or a parent. It is like being older than an ancestor. It makes it difficult to respect them, and hard to learn from them, even when they have something worthwhile to teach you.

Gloria mailed her manuscript to me as she finished each chapter. I must have objected to something she said, because two-thirds of the way through the book she stops and addresses her audience. 'Now everyone,' she writes, 'nieces and nephews and sisters, friends and husbands of friends—I beg your pardon, I know you mean well but please stop trying to adjust this document. I live my life according to my memories, not yours. I made my mistakes and rejoiced and grieved because that's the way it was for me. If I got Sean Watson mixed up with his brother Roy, and forgot the second-hand sewing machine in the kitchen, or claimed the twins were three when they were actually two and a half, what of it?'

That did make me angry, because I was trying to be a journalist, and trying to get the facts right, and because I was in a relationship with a woman who insisted all truths were relative. My aunt seemed to be siding with my girlfriend, against truth. I reject postmodernism, I don't believe all narratives are of equal value, and I don't believe the truth is unknowable. Gloria performed a service for me when she told me about my grandfather as a father. I know him better now, and I don't love him less. If she made it up, got my grandfather mixed up with his brother Alec, forgot there were no dowel sticks in the house, or claimed the twins were beaten when they weren't, her book was worthless.

It is important to get the facts right. In the end, that is all there is.

Here are the facts about me and my dad: I was born in a terrace house in Leeds in a lower middle-class street near an Art Deco synagogue that used to be a cinema. It was a cul-de-sac, a word that fascinated me with its gravity and finality. We moved, at about the time my brother was born, to a semi-detached house in a crescent. An apple tree, a pear tree and a plum tree grew in the back, along with a raspberry bush, and a blackberry bush was woven into the neighbour's fence. It was a quiet street, a thoroughfare to nowhere. On Friday nights,

Dad unloaded his greeting card samples from his Cortina, box by box, and we carried them upstairs to store in the bedroom cupboards. On Saturdays and Sundays, he used the car for football. He would either be the linesman or the referee in some younger men's weekend game. My dad kept coloured flags and corner posts in the garage, and bashed hard mud off his boots on the steps. The studs on his boots left a honeycomb of holes in the dry turf he trod home from the pitch, and I remember sliding my fingers through the cavities with wonder. My brother and I fought to play with his crustaceous whistle and his bulbous stopwatch, the symbols of authority.

My brother was good at all sports except football. I was good at none, but slightly less bad at football than all the others. I thought I was all right, but one night I heard my dad on the phone to a friend saying, 'Mark plays football like a goalpost,' and when I grew up I was always second-to-last to be chosen for the team. The only thing that saved me from being last was that people liked me. I wonder how much that saved my dad. At his funeral, I asked my uncle why he did not press us harder, why he spent time training everybody else's children but us. He said my dad was no good at football either, and so didn't believe we could be. It was a bigger shock to me than my grandfather's revealed violence: that my dad could not play football.

My mum pulled my dad out of the tailoring factory, taught him to read, persuaded him to go for a job as a greeting-card salesman and, when his company went bust, talked him into going out on his own. Together, my parents rose rapidly in the world. Mum matriculated through the Workers Educational Association and went to university on a mature student's grant. Dad earned good money. My mum told me it was something to be a salesman, a 'rep', in the 1970s. For a year, they hired a deaf-mute woman to help in the house with cleaning. A man came around to do the garden. My brother went to a private kindergarten. I don't understand why we took in lodgers, but we hosted first a fourteen-year-old from France in his summer holidays, then a sixteen-year-old from Holland, then an eighteen-year-old university student from London, then another eighteen-year-old university student from the north-east of England—and my mum, at thirty-two, had an affair with him, left my father and took us with her.

When I was twelve, my mum, my brother, my stepfather and I all moved to the south of England, to a rented terrace house on the main road through a garrison town where there were no Jewish people. I was sad to leave my father, whom I still loved, but immeasurably relieved that I wouldn't have to sing my bar mitzvah because there was nobody in the area who could teach me my portion. Around my thirteenth birthday, I took a train and coach up to Leeds, and said a blessing in the downstairs room in the synagogue where men sat shivah for their dead relatives in the morning, and I became a man under Jewish law without singing.

In my book *Sex & Money*, I included a long chapter about growing up, touching on my grandfather—but not his violence—and, more painfully, on my dad. I wanted to write to apologise to him. I wanted to write about my dad, because I knew nobody else ever would. My words, and his obituaries in Jewish newspapers, are all he will leave behind. I tried to be generous, but I knew I was simply judging him again.

Long after our respective books had been published, I spoke to Gloria about my dad. She said she couldn't understand why my mum had married Gerry. 'I got a tape-recording of the wedding speech he made,' she said, 'and I was appalled (remember, I'd never met him). He sounded like a very uneducated, yobbish kind of person.

'Our house was full of books. She was a nurse—and nurses aren't stupid—and a secretary. And Gerry was living in a rented caravan in the slums.'

I felt so hurt for my dad. Who do we think we are, we clever people? Who do we think we are, we Benjamins? (Because I am a Benjamin in all but name, my surname an accident of patrilineality.) My dad never beat his kids, never spent the housekeeping on beer and whisky, never shouted a round for his mates and tipped the barmaid with money that should have gone towards clothes for his children. (He never lived in a caravan, either; my aunt was thinking of someone else.) I understood for the first time the significance of my dad's mantra, 'I don't drink, I don't smoke, I don't back horses.' I had heard it so often, it seemed like drinking, smoking and backing horses were the only things you could do in life to stop your world from disintegrating and your wife running off with the lodger and taking away your kids. I always thought he was being sanctimonious, defining himself by the things he did not do. Now I know he was saying, 'I'm not just some uneducated yob who lives in a rented caravan in the slums.'

A year after my father's funeral was the ceremony to lay the headstone. I cannot wrench much about it from my memory. I was staying with a friend in Hull, talking over the phone from a pub. People told me there was no need to go, but I thought my family would hate me even more if I did not. My uncle, so kind at the funeral, made a point of not talking to me one year later, except to acknowledge me as 'the rebel without a cause'.

I can't separate my dad's tombstone-unveiling day from my grandfather's. Although he was buried in 1988, my grandad's final headstone was raised many years later, because the first one contained a spelling mistake in its Hebrew inscription. There is an international shortage of Jewish monumental masons. Few stones are hand-carved any more, and the people who operate the Hebrew masonry typesetting programs cannot necessarily read the words. I happened to be back in the UK, so I must have travelled to Leeds, because I saw my grandfather's friends at the cemetery and one of them said, 'I remember you from the drinking days,' and I wanted to have a drink with him again, to talk about grandfather, but the way he said 'the drinking days' meant they were over.

My stepmother asked me to visit her. I'd been married and divorced since we last met. She had heard I looked like my dad, so she wanted to see me. She wanted to have him in the room again. In my family, we believed that she pressured him to marry her, that he only took her because he needed somebody to wash his clothes and cook his meals, but that day I realised he was the love of her life and now he had gone.

My brother, who has his own real and tender grudges, would not come into her flat, but she and I sat for a couple of hours and talked about my dad. She sorted out some photographs for me, and gave me his military service record, in which he was commended for his 'sober habits'. I asked why he had enjoyed the army, why he thought it was a good thing to have somebody telling him what to do.

'Your father didn't know what to do,' she said.

It occurs to me that, as with my grandfather, no-one will bother to write about my dad, the semi-literate orphan in the army who did not know what to do. If I was going to write about him, this is what I'd say.

He loved Liverpool. He enjoyed the Beatles. He sang 'She Loves You' as he bounced me on his knee. He owned few records, they were all by Shirley Bassey and they were all presents. When he was young, he went to see Bill Haley and his Comets play 'Rock Around the Clock'. He used to wear a kind of quiff. He laughed easily and boomingly. He watched a lot of television. Westerns and war films were his favourites. When I was little, when he tucked me in bed, he told me stories about his time in the army, at drill and on the firing range, and sang me marching songs such as 'Bless 'em All' and another in which the troops vow to murder the bugler who wakes them up every morning. From the army, he still called knives and forks 'eating irons'. He played poker in the back room one night a week. He liked books about the army, in particular about national servicemen. He was a big man who reminded people of Fred Flintstone or Yogi Bear. His bristles scratched like my grandfather's. He drove badly, crunching his gears, because he had learned to drive as a truck driver in the army. He told jokes. He loved the aunt who had brought him up. He lied about not eating bacon. He wore a proud signet ring with a Star of David. He always called my uncle 'our kid'. My uncle always called him by his Jewish name, 'Yankel'. He loved football. When we were children, he came home every evening in his Cortina and my brother and I would rush to meet him and grab the legs of his pressed trousers, laughing. He didn't smoke, he didn't drink and he didn't back the horses.

# BIRTHDAY PARTY EVER

oprah blew up on tv not literally
obviously i was avoiding carbs then, so no cake
or lollies chips or rice big deal.

heres a highway to the sky,
incredible present, do you realise,
barry gibb. the star of the
show exhaled noisily. have you noticed that
the dams froggy; & the rivers greasy.

with every second language you 'reconcile'
it gets easier, but harder for everyone around you.
your fairy godmother appeared at your fiftieth,
restoring your foreskin & teething mug.
you were younger than madonna, stammered more
cutely than ian thorpe.
out on the street were
the echoes of the yard.

to go 'backwards' is to
approach the vegie garden or slagheap,
romantic places once but depressing now,
or are they rather neutral, a late therapeutic effect,

our shirts merging with the sunset.
i accept my nickname gracefully, remove the tacks
from the effigy. my accent was enough to
prove me an idiot i just needed the apparatus
of recipes, a boxful of lamingtons is a
windfall to anyone & so is autumn:
everywhere seems like the ground when youre up.
homecomers prefer to have a window seat:
to see the pinata identifying with mistletoe,
if i was oprah,
& you were a rake.

MICHAEL FARRELL

# HOW TO KILL A CANE TOAD

ROBERT DREWE

AFTER the gunshots, and the bats' screeching and flapping, they'd lie in bed at night wondering what they'd got themselves into. The blasts, then Janine's agitated fingers tapping on his thigh in an increasingly accusatory way while the bats panicked and stray lead shot pattered on the roof and tinkled down into the gutter: this wasn't how they had imagined country living.

Those lifestyle magazines of hers celebrating a 'tree change' from the city to a simpler existence where they'd grow organic produce, breathe blossom-scented air and perform rewarding physical tasks in rural clothing while a grazing horse or two added interest to the scenery somehow never referred to the human element. *Getting back to basics* never mentioned the local inhabitants. Those first weeks, random shotgun explosions had punctuated their daylight hours of vegetable planting, fence mending and house renovation. Now, as a windy spring edged into a humid summer, the shotgun woke them at night as well.

Gunfire is more chilling at night. It came from nearby, but the squally winds and the enveloping orchards and plantations—a dense maze of trees curving and stretching up the echoing hills all the way to the western horizon—made it hard to pin down the source. Down at the general store for the morning milk, bread and newspaper, gritty-eyed from broken sleep, Dan finally asked Cliff Porteous, the proprietor, 'Who shoots guns at night around here?'

Just as Dan's daily presence and purchases—the city broadsheet, the high-fibre bread, the low-fat milk—appeared to amuse Cliff, the question seemed to entertain him. 'Oh, old Mango Ken gets shitty with the birds in his trees. Then the fruit bats at night. After a few scotches he decides to scare them away.' Cliff looked on the verge of laughter. 'Don't know when he sleeps.'

He was referring to their nearest neighbour, an orchardist named Ken Riddell. But despite this logical explanation, the day-and-night gunshots, the pellets peppering the tin roof, the shrieking fruit bats and interrupted sleep still unnerved them and soured everything. They woke tired and rattled in the morning and they went to bed tired and rattled at night.

This wasn't like a noisy-party problem in the city, where a phone call to the local cops sorted it out, where a constable knocked on the door and told the neighbours to turn it down. An old farmer's livelihood was involved. And *neighbour* meant something different in the bush. At this early stage they didn't want to come across as arrogant city blow-ins, the sort who moved to the country and then immediately complained about cows and roosters disturbing the peace, and the smell of fertiliser and pesticides.

So their shotgun annoyance not only continued but also swelled to include other irritations: Dan's snoring and Janine's increasing abstraction, as well as the area's voracious mosquitoes, speeding motorists, vanishing tradesmen (whenever a good surf was running) and, as the nights warmed and electrical storms blazed and crackled over the Pacific, the sudden appearance and clamour of cane toads.

One mid-December afternoon Ken Riddell stopped his tractor by the dividing fence, introduced himself and welcomed them to the district. So characteristically rustic did he seem in his overalls and his tattered straw hat draw-stringed under his chin, he could have been a storybook Farmer Giles or Old MacDonald. This was their chance to bring up the night-time blasts. But how could they start whinging to him right off the bat when the sociable old gunman was inviting them over that night for drinks?

It would have seemed uncivil. And they were grateful to be asked. Apart from smirking Cliff Porteous at the store, Greg Roylance, the estate agent who'd sold them the property, and various elusive, surf-preferring electricians and plumbers, they hadn't met any locals. As they watched the sun sink behind the dark corridors of nut plantations and orchards (row upon row of suddenly forbidding trees), sipping oddly unsatisfying gin and tonics, their optimism steadily ebbing with the daylight and the application of mosquito repellent, they'd begun to question, as with so much else, the myth of country hospitality.

But now, with another neighbouring couple, the Eastaughs, also guests this Saturday evening on the verandah of Ken and Elaine Riddells' Federation farmhouse, at least some sort of social life was unfolding. Eagerly anticipating a beer, Dan heard himself break the ice: 'So how do you deal with all these cane toads?' That croaking cacophony, like a hundred different telephone dial-tones, was beginning to grate as much as the shotgun pellets on the roof.

'Cane toads?' Mango Ken responded, in the loud interrogative manner someone might say 'hyenas?' or 'manatees?'

'Aren't they disgusting?' said Janine, a little too earnestly. 'The way they destroy the wildlife! I hate the way they'll eat anything they can fit into their mouths.'

'Toads?' boomed Mango Ken again. As he passed the drinks around, his hands managed four glasses at once. His brown fingers, cracked and swollen enough to burst, looked like pork sausages in the pan. He was eighty-plus, his face the dry yellow of chamois leather, with deep crotchety lines criss-crossing his cheeks and an old-fashioned pink hearing aid like a lump of bubblegum stuck in each ear.

'I googled them,' Janine went on, raising her voice. (She'd just noticed the hearing aids, too.) 'They're feral, a scientific import gone wrong. They're venomous and the females produce thirty-five thousand eggs every mating.' Her voice seemed surprisingly shrill. 'How do we fight those numbers?'

*A twelve-gauge?* Dan almost suggested.

'The old three wood!' Mango Ken yelled abruptly. His eyes lit up and he stood and teed off, miming a vigorous golf swing. His broad, bony shoulders looked as if they still had a bit of toad-belting left in them. He took a swig of his scotch, coughed and cleared his throat. 'If you could be bothered.' He thumped his chest. 'I've got enough on my plate.'

His verandah overlooked twenty hectares of mangoes, guavas and avocados and, on the higher slopes, five more hectares of Cavendish and ladyfinger bananas. Right now the Riddells were harvesting about half a hectare of cane toads as well. Attracted by the swarms of Christmas beetles battering against the louvres, a lumpy carpet of toads was inching towards the house lights.

'No, no, no.' His wife, Elaine, spoke up. 'Toads don't mind a wallop. It's a waste of time to whack them. By next morning they've recovered and hopped away.'

[69]

The old woman put down her scotch and grabbed a plastic shopping bag from somewhere. 'I like to avoid poison spurts!' she shouted, thrusting her hand in the bag. The nearest toad was squatting proprietorially on the back step calmly licking up Christmas beetles. Elaine stooped down and snatched it up. She must have been hitting eighty herself, but in three deft movements she grabbed the toad in the bag, flipped the bag inside out and tied a knot in it. Like a mouldy windfall mango, lemon-coloured, ovoid and spotty, the toad glared out through the plastic.

'*Voila!*' she said. 'The toad is in the bag.'

'The same way you Paddington people pick up your poodle's poop,' the other male guest, Macca Ken Eastaugh, offered, slyly. He was younger than the other Ken by about forty years, but two farmer Kens in the neighbourhood apparently made nicknames necessary. Macca Ken had thirty hectares of macadamia trees stretching up the hill behind the Riddells' orchard.

Dan almost pointed out that they'd come from Thornleigh, a far less trendy Sydney suburb than Paddington, and one better suited to a high school teacher's and a librarian's salaries. They had retired early, taken their superannuation, bought an old farmhouse on some land, and started—they fervently hoped—a serene country life. But he let it go. Country people were forever teasing newcomers. He sipped his beer and said, 'So now you have a cane toad in a bag.'

'Just pop him in the freezer!' roared Elaine, and she opened the fridge and did so. 'And Mr Toad goes quietly bye-byes.'

Dan imagined opening the freezer next day. In their new life he did the cooking. First thing in the morning he took out the meat to thaw. He thought out loud. 'All those warty frozen toads goggling out from the steak and ice-cream.'

'You reckon toads are bad?' said Macca Ken. He was thickset, with an ex-footballer's drum-like torso and a couple of basal-cell carcinomas glistening on his nose like half-pearls. 'Try fingers in the fridge.'

'Fish fingers?' said Janine.

'Human,' said Geraldine Eastaugh. 'Human fingers, for God's sake.'

'God's what?' yelled Mango Ken.

Macca Ken rolled his eyes. 'Fingers in the fridge!' He leaned back in his chair. 'You tell it, Geraldine.'

'Ken was in the force back in the eighties. Out in the far west even the young coppers had to do a bit of forensics.'

Macca Ken broke in. '*Big* distances to cover in the boondocks. Bodies to be identified. Shotgun homicides. Highway accidents. Imaginative rural suicides. No DNA testing to make it easy back then.' Now that he had everyone's attention he paused to take a long sip of beer. 'Hot weather to take into account. If I wanted to finish before dawn, get any sleep at all, I'd snip off the victim's fingers for later ID. Take 'em with me and pop 'em in the freezer at home.'

'I'll say this,' said Geraldine. 'Toad iceblocks are no big deal compared to a freezer full of fingers. Cop them first thing in the morning, they'll wake you up in a hurry. Bitten fingernails, wedding rings, nail polish, the lot.'

For a moment the others fell silent, drinking and gazing out at the patch of toad-filled light on the lawn.

'And I was first trimester at the time with Jade and not keeping anything down.'

'It was easy enough to handle,' said Macca Ken. 'I managed pretty well. Best years of my life in some ways.'

The older Ken had been lost in reverie, his nose in his scotch glass, but now he'd had an idea worth mentioning. 'There's always the Dettol method.'

'Dettol?' wondered Dan.

'Dettol antiseptic. Give the toads a squirt. Instant death.'

'He dabs it behind his ears too, before he goes anywhere,' confided his wife. 'Like perfume.'

As if guiltily caught out, Mango Ken turned on her, reddening. 'And I haven't died of paralysis ticks, have I? You get a paralysis tick burrowed in behind your ear and even if you cut the bastard out, your nerves go. You want a face sagging like melted wax, go right ahead.'

'The old bloke's full of good advice,' Macca Ken said, grinning. He raised his voice. 'Tell 'em your hangover cure.'

'Hangovers?' roared the old man. 'Well, you've got your best cure in the world running right round your property. The bloody fence.'

Dan thought of the electrified fence keeping the Riddells' cows out of his new lettuces and tomatoes. He laughed. 'Really.'

'There's enough voltage to really clear the head if you grab the fence with both hands.'

Taking a rise out of the city folks again. 'Oh, sure,' Dan said.

'He's not kidding,' shouted Elaine. 'With a bad hangover, he even wets his hands first.'

'I don't know about you people,' said Janine, 'but I can't stop looking at the fridge and wondering if your toad's frozen yet.'

Although the blasts no longer seemed mysterious or frightening, the nightly hubbub had had its effect. Janine now wore earplugs to bed. They helped block

ROBERT DREWE

out the gunshots, bats and toads, and also Dan's snoring. The humid summer on
top of the noise had pushed him into bad sleep patterns, which developed into a
sleep apnoea that made him doze off at inconvenient times in the day and
abruptly jerk awake in the middle of the night. When he did pass out, as if to
catch up on weeks of lost sleep, he snored loudly enough to drown out even the
loudest toads.

In his insomniac hours his mind strayed from one anxiety to the next, most
of them revolving around their precipitous move to the country. His worries
centred on Janine, the way her personality and moods were changing. Not only
was she blocking herself off from him at night, in the daytime she'd started disap-
pearing for long solitary drives into the hinterland.

He felt increasingly cut off. The tree-change adventure had begun with a
mutual wish to spend more time together in their middle years. Instead she was
drawing away. She seemed to be seeking a baffling sort of independence. Even her
speech patterns, her choice of vocabulary, had become isolating: first-person
singular. She rarely said *we* or *our* any more; everything was I and me and mine.
When he asked her, 'What happened to *us* and *our*?' she gave him her recently
acquired Mona Lisa smile.

'We're all on our individual journeys, Daniel,' she said, smug as a guru.

*Daniel*? What happened to *Dan*? What bloody journey was this?

*Just communing with nature,* or *absorbing the environment,* or *exploring the
country lanes,* or *getting to know the region,* she'd say enigmatically when she
returned home, and briefly mention scenic mountain ridges or pretty waterfalls
that she must share with him sometime.

Those ridges and cascades and ferny lanes must have been exceptionally
picturesque, Dan thought, to distract her for hours afterwards, right up to and
including her inserting her earplugs and going to bed.

She was heading to bed increasingly early. Immediately after dinner—no tele-
vision, no reading, no nightcap, no conversation about the day—she'd yawn and
turn in. Earplugged and nightdressed, she'd pass him outside the bathroom, peck
his cheek and disappear by 8.30 or nine, her heavy sigh coinciding with a similar
exhalation from the mattress as she flopped into bed and wound the bedclothes
protectively around her.

Of course he asked her if there was another man.

'Oh, please!' she said.

What could he do but make a hurt, defiant stand? Faced with her departure
from his presence, the brush-off, the shrouded lump on the far side of the bed

(not even tropical temperatures dissuaded her from a sheet and blanket), Dan moved into the spare bedroom. Then, rather than face the room's monkish austerity, he began staying up late. He'd finish the bottle of wine he had opened for dinner as well as the untouched glass he'd poured for her. And as the evening cacophony intruded on his melancholy like a flotilla of approaching motorboats, he'd lurch up from the table, grab the Dettol dispenser and a torch, and step outside to kill cane toads.

Dan felt squeamish at first, but he remembered the harm they were doing to the environment. Picking them off with the spray-gun to the sound of intermittent gunshots next door gave toad hunting a mock-military feel. Mango Ken was right. It was a startlingly effective method of execution. One squirt and the enemy instantly imploded, mustering just enough strength to drag itself into the shrubbery, considerately dig its own grave and inter itself.

Pacing around the dew-drenched lawn, half-full of wine, juggling the spray-gun and torch, strafing the grass, the driveway, the near paddocks, he'd shoot forty, fifty, sixty of the knobbly bastards a night. Like fish in a barrel really. And why not? The greedy feral trespassers were on the march—south, north and west across the country, gobbling up or poisoning everything—lizards, snakes, rare frogs, birds, insects, fish. The nice, normal Australian wildlife.

No matter how tired, downhearted and confused, no matter how drunk, before facing the spare bedroom each night he had a duty to patrol his territory and kill as many of the invaders as possible.

It was an overcast March morning with sputtering showers greasing the highway when Dan went for the bread and papers and saw four police cars, three state rescue service vehicles and a fire truck pulled up outside Cliff Porteous's store. Radios crackled and officers were hunched by one of the patrol cars, writing on clipboards, comparing information and sipping takeaway coffee.

Inside the store the mood was sombre. Local people gathered in small, murmuring groups by the magazine racks, eyes glittering with news. Porteous, unsmiling for once, filled Dan in. 'He was on his way here two hours ago as usual,' he said. 'Old Ken Riddell I'm talking about.' Making a right turn off the Pacific Highway, Mango Ken's car had been broadsided by a tanker carrying milk up to Brisbane. 'Drove right over him. Killed him instantly.'

There was some head-shaking about Mango Ken's bad hearing, questions about his eyesight, too; even suggestions that he was too old to be driving. A danger to himself and others. Then again, that section of the highway was a known deathtrap, and it was raining. What had intrigued the police at the crash scene, however, was all the busted shotgun cartridges and loose shot in Mango Ken's car.

That night Dan stayed up even later than usual, killing toads. The earlier rain had softened the soil and moistened the undergrowth and brought toads out in big numbers. When he was prowling about on execution patrol the toads always fell quiet at the approach of his torch, but their sudden stillness tonight didn't explain the wider, deeper silence across the damp lawn and weedy paddocks and surrounding orchards.

As midnight approached, the property was more than merely quiet, there was an eerie absence of noise. A sound vacuum. Of course, he realised, for the first night since they'd moved here there were no shotgun blasts. And hence no screeching bats, or lead shot clattering on the roof. Without the distraction of noise, the night seemed darker, too, the stars more distant.

He quickly despatched twenty-four toads (he always kept a tally). But his pants were drenched and muddy and the night felt uncomfortably humid. Standing alone on the dewy lawn with his spray-gun, the thin beam of his torch seeking the tell-tale lumps that were distant toads, he had a sudden sharp picture of himself as country-dwelling, toad-hunting man. This was the way this dismal man spent his evenings. Toad Man. The image struck him as too pathetic for words.

And then the air was shattered by a shotgun blast. And another. A salvo. Pellets tinkled on the roof and pattered on the leaves of the trees and onto his water tank, and fell around him like hail. Another blast sounded, and another. All the fruit bats of the tropics appeared to be whirling and flapping and shrieking over his head. He ran for the shelter of the verandah, deafened and dazed by noise.

Even with earplugs Janine must have been woken by the din because she came out on the verandah too, and stood on the steps in her nightdress, her arms folded across her breasts, staring into the dark. She was counting the blasts, and continued counting them off aloud. Finally they stopped. 'Twenty-one,' she said.

Self-consciously, he put down the torch and spray-gun. 'What was that all about?' he said. Bats still flapped by them, wheeling and screeching into the sky.

'Looks like Elaine got his guns and gave Ken a 21-gun salute,' she said. 'Commemorating him.'

A few stragglers were returning indignantly to the mango orchard. After some territorial squabbling and rustling they settled back in the trees. There was a last protesting squeal and then the bats were silent.

'She probably had a few scotches, and who'd blame her?' he said.

Following the fusillade, the night seemed quieter than ever. Moonlight streaked across the lawn and paddocks. Not quite strangers, more like hesitant recent acquaintances, they stood awkwardly on the verandah, unsure of their next movements. Soon, as if at a given signal, the toads started croaking again, their dissonance quickly swelling to fill the void. Inappropriately, as wrong as a field of outboard motors, an ocean of tractors, they took over the night.

# HE REMEMBERS THE MOUNTAINS

Now Wollemi is only memory
few things are clear, but what I retain is sharper
in retrospect than in the event. No bitter
wind blows any more; there's no urgency
to camp, nor weariness. I conjure here
the ragged jaw of the Yodeller's Range—its peak
is capped by canines and molars, each one cleft
with awkward gaps—and every detail's clear.

Over the lip of that horizon ridge,
which is curling higher night by night, is nothing,
nothing I've known. Beneath its sensuousness,
I feel the suck of that massed wave; it rips
around my legs and grabs my shoulders, lofting
me over its crest into the wilderness.

PETER COGHILL

# THE QUESTION
# OF DECADENCE

As **FIONA MCGREGOR** TRAVELS THROUGH POLAND FOR PERFORMANCES WITH SENVOODOO, SHE REFLECTS ON PERCEPTIONS OF DECADENCE IN RELIGION, POLITICS AND THE ARTS

POPE Benedict XVI has arrived in Poland. We watch him on TV. I have always found his face ghoulish, but there is something cheerful, excited, even humble about the way he walks through the crowd. Arms stretch towards him like Balinese dancers'. People surge to touch him, kiss his hand, kneel before him. Cripples are pushed forward, babies offered. The Pope is on television every night on every channel. We have resurfaced from work amazed at this mania. We channel surf for a proper news bulletin but it is all *Papiez Papiez Papiez.* We were considering a trip to Kraków this weekend to see a friend's video installation. How grateful we are to have stayed in Łódź. More than a million people have descended on Kraków to see *Papiez.* He addresses them in Polish from the Archbishop's residence in the old town, a medieval maze of tiny narrow streets, now utterly choked. Kraków's population of one million has more than doubled for the Pope's visit. Up to 600,000 youths have attended a special service in the rain, on Błonie common just outside the city.

A subtitle runs across the bottom of the screen: Three dead in an earthquake in Java. There won't be a full report on this disaster for days.

The Pope is going to Auschwitz-Birkenau. There is great anticipation about his address. Will it be in German? Surely not. A hundred and fifty survivors will be there, as well as thousands of descendants of internees. Mandelbaum, a Polish Jew, shows his tattoo. He says he carried the bodies to the ovens. He worries he is viewed critically for this but, he says, If I hadn't carried the bodies I would have been one of them. I wouldn't have survived to bear witness.

The Ministry of Education wants to make religion (Catholicism) a matriculation subject. Students have begun protesting. Benedict XVI is not ecumenical like his predecessor, who reached out to Muslims and apologised to Jews for the Church's anti-Semitism. These weeping wounds. The Kaczyński brothers' vitriol towards Germany and Russia rampages on. Aren't they digging another grave for their country with this Catholic supremacy? All down Piotrkówska Street are life-size bronze statues of famous Łódźiania—many Jewish, some Protestant—from the past. Arthur Rubinstein playing his grand piano. Writer Julian Tuwim relaxing on a bench. Poznański, Scheibler and Grohmann conferring around a table. Władisław Reymont (a Catholic but, according to my friend Jola, secretly gay). Many Poles are nostalgic for their multicultural past. They point excitedly to the growing Jewish population in Warsaw, the sprinkling of Asians, Africans and South Americans who came from poor Socialist countries to get an education during Communism, and stayed. But how welcome really are non-Catholics in contemporary Poland? The young folk have camped all night on Błonie in the rain again. Mass is being said. The priest tells them not to take drugs. He rails against decadence. The audience claps and sings and cheers.

AñA was here during Jan Paweł II's landmark visit to Poland in 1979. She describes the atmosphere as electric. She was in Gdańsk fresh from Solidarity strikes and took the bus to Częstochowa to see the Pope's address. And when the Gdańsk bus pulled in, the crowd went crazy.

To be devoutly Catholic in Communist Poland was to be anti-Establishment. Television coverage of a pope's visit was therefore minimal. Fully punishing and closing down the Church was always deemed too risky in Poland, unlike the rest of Eastern Europe. Religion was tolerated but not encouraged.

Jan Paweł II represented freedom to a country struggling to regain its independence for the first time in sixty years. He spoke that day in solidarity with the workers: his support for democracy was a defiant gesture against a very powerful status quo. He was passionate and charismatic, his humanism evident. It was just before the AIDS pandemic began to obliterate large chunks of the population in Africa and move into Asia to do the same. It was before Jan Paweł II's damnation of homosexuality reached fever pitch. Before his proscription of condoms became staunch and criminally irresponsible. It was before he became a slick journeyman and international pop star.

Several days later, medical help has been brought to 2500 of Pope Benedict's fans in Kraków. They sing in the rain as his plane takes off. *We love you, we love you!* He isn't Jan Paweł, says one man, he isn't Polish, but he is the Pope and so we love him. He is good but he is not *my* pope, says Isabel Niedzielska, aged forty-five. Weeping, she adds, I'm sorry, I am crying but when I see him I think it is my papa. A subtitle bulletin tells us there are now 4285 dead in Java and 10,000 wounded. The only words in German that the Pope says at Auschwitz-Birkenau mean 'Life without value', to draw attention to the inhumanity of the phrase. The words he says in Polish are anodyne, cursory. He is revered for walking into the camp, as opposed to being driven in like the SS were. Before a phalanx of cameras he closes his eyes and puts his hands together for a moment of 'quiet' prayer. He makes no mention of the German Catholic Church during the war, of how the priests in Bavaria sat on their pews while cattle trucks full of Jews rattled past. The media interview Polish Jews who are dissatisified. The Kaczyńskis rave about what good Catholics the Poles are. Are Jews the only ones who are dissatisfied? Is everyone else really fooled by this orgy of pious self-congratulation? This hero worship and empty ceremony?

THE nightclub is covered in photographs of naked women. Big-breasted babes playing pool in ironic high heels. Five of them lounge in deckchairs, legs spread, faces thick with beards. In another photo that was also on the front page of the local paper today, three women recline on shelves in a grocery store, the grocer seated beside them, facing the camera. It's a witty, slickly produced series. Łódź Kaliska is the name of this art collective, as well as this nightclub (and the transit train station in Łódź).

We have come here to have a drink after our live performance of *Arterial*, a piece about loss and mourning. Tonight was our third performance in a month: we previously performed *Arterial* at a venue in the Gdańsk shipyards, as well as at Interakcje Action Art festival in the town of Piotrkow Trybunalski. Adam and his crew were waiting for us in the Manhattan cafeteria. Adam runs the gallery where we will present the video installation of *Arterial* in ten days time. Now, in Łódź Kaliska, truculent Adam sits at a table clutching a bloody mary. He is squat, florid, with a pointy nose and glasses; he emanates a bitter world-weariness. He has been running a gallery in his apartment since the days of Solidarity and Martial Law.

Łódź Kaliska nightclub is considered the city's grooviest underground venue. It is a modern addition to an old building, nicely worn in and packed with regulars. There is food on tables—sausages, strawberries, bread. Next door, lights flash over a dance floor. It is the club's tenth birthday party. There isn't the faintest whiff of drugs in the air.

An elegant girl on my right tells me she's going to live in Manchester for a year, on an exchange with an advertising agency. She is unaware of Łódź's historical tag as 'the Manchester of the east'. Her boyfriend lives in Fremantle. She tells me in careful English that she thinks Polish women are just as beautiful as French, English, or anyone. Her dark hair is pulled back, she has a swan neck, perfect skin, wide silver eyes. She is probably the most beautiful woman I have seen in Poland. On my left I'm aware of AñA and Adam getting into a heated discussion. The elegant girl asks me about Australia. I want to tell her how much we have in common, that Australia is also crippled by cultural cringe, that the Christian right is increasingly powerful. But in Australia it's a troika of the Catholic, Anglican and Pentecostal Churches such as Hillsong, while in Poland the Catholic Church rules as the one imperial deity.

I say, simply, You should go.

The girl has read in our publicity notes that I'm a writer.

What do you write? she giggles. Feminist tracts?

On the other side of the table Adam is raising his voice.

*Nie nie nie!* AñA is waving her hand.

My favourite Łódź Kaliska photograph is the one of the women in deckchairs, cigars between their moustachioed lips.

Later I learn that the visionaries of this series are men, and it loses much of its satirical power. The collective, begun in 1979, is one of Poland's most renowned avant-garde groups. Concentrating on photography intially, Łódź Kaliska became increasingly anti-art and Dada. In 2000 they adopted 'New Pop', which embraces advertising and new media, in 'an attempt to obscure the border between life and art'. Some of the work is explicitly anti-religious and iconoclastic, such as their *The Nation is Still Going Strong* series, which features naked women in Hitler moustaches delivering speeches, attending board meetings, and so on. The women, as emphasised in one of Łódź Kaliska's manifestos, must be fleshy, with huge breasts.

STANISŁAW Ignacy Witkiewicz, commonly known as Witkacy, has a reputation as a decadent. Born in 1885 and brought up to be an artist, his life has all the markers of the romantic outcast. He was suicidal, sexually anxious, sometimes drugged, and found little success in his lifetime. Scratch the surface and you find a rapacious intellect, an acute political sensibility and a life concerned more than anything else with the artistic quest.

Witkacy worked in many genres of writing and was also a painter. His theory has become part of the bedrock of avant-garde alongside the better known Westerners Brecht and Artaud. Theatre was central, Witkacy's most prolific period occurring in the 1920s with limited success in mounting productions. In the 1950s Kantor revived him. Indeed, Kantor's dark absurdism could not have existed without Witkacy. In *Janulka*, a four-act tragedy of singular weirdness, people die as casually as cigarettes are lit. Nobody blinks when they come back to life. The main characters include feathered monsters. *Janulka* is a grand hallucination with, as seems mandatory in Polish art, serious political intent.

Witkacy's 1932 novel *Insatiability*, set in the near future, contains his favourite themes of artistic degradation and political threat. It depicts a decaying Western civilisation threatened by a Sino-Mongolian army that rules all territory from the Pacific to the Baltic. Hawkers peddle 'Murti-Bing' pills, named after a Mongolian philosopher who produced an edible version of the 'philosophy of life'. If you took a Murti-Bing pill you ceased being vexed by ontological concerns, your spiritual hunger was sated. The novel ends with the Western army surrendering to the Eastern. The disgruntled, perverted artists stop their carousing and metaphysical agonising and begin to write marches and socially useful odes. They also become schizophrenics. It's a vision as prescient as that of George Orwell, one of the few Western writers that twentieth-century Easterners embraced as someone who understood the regimes they lived under.

Like Orwell, Witkacy was as critical of capitalism as he was of communism, describing the former as a 'gigantic tumour which for quite some time has grown luxuriantly on the diseased body of mankind, pretending to represent it in its entirety, and yet, like every tumour, it has laid waste to the body, from which it has siphoned off the juices indispensable for life ...' But while Orwell seems to have arrived at his vision through lucid and fearless reasoning, Witkacy arrived at his through a cauldron of paranoid, apocalyptic obsessions. In 1939 he fled the Nazi invasion to the Ukraine with his lover Czesława Korzeniowska. Soon enough they found themselves in the frontline of the Soviets, and in a forest clearing one night Witkacy drank poison, Korzeniowska waking to find him dead.

While recovering from a nervous breakdown in the 1910s, Witkacy came to the Southern Hemisphere on an anthropological expedition with his best friend

Bronisław Malinowski, for whom his romantic feelings were never resolved. By 1914 Malinowski was an anthropologist of repute, having already published his first book, *The Family Among the Australian Aborigines*. Australia made little impression on Witkacy, but he loved the tropics.

It seems glib to dismiss Witkacy as a decadent—though Oscar Wilde may contend that the decadent cuts the deepest subversion—his main concerns being for form, which required constant technical experimentation, and the ideal of individual freedom within social equality. His drug-taking, like Aldous Huxley's, was part experiment, part pleasure-seeking, and pre-dated the Englishman's by some years although it was never to gain the same recognition. In a witty critique called *The Nitwit's Smirk* Witkacy scoffs at 'Huxley's literary caricatures … That's the way it is with everything: harass homegrown originality but welcome the same thing several years later when it comes from abroad.'

Witkacy marked codes for each drug in the corner of canvases done under the influence. His paintings are in just about every modern art museum in Poland. They leap out from the walls, dominating their neighbours. The portraits remind me a little of Van Gogh, in the psychotic vigour of the brushwork and the lurid colours. These and the fantasy landscapes are not peyote or cocaine, but Witkacy's beloved tropics.

In Łódź Muzeum Sztuki we stand before *Flight*. In its melting distortions we make out devilish faces, claw-like hands, weapons, threatening gestures. It's a vision of hell and a vision of life at its most primal and energetic, a sort of fecund jungle. We want to see more of Witkacy's work, but only a fraction of the collection is on display. Łódź Muzeum Sztuki was begun in the 1920s by an artists' collective. Currently housed in Maurycy Poznański's run-down villa, it is the most extensive collection of avant-garde art in the country, and one of the best in the world. As usual, we seem to be the only visitors. The *babcia* security guards follow us around as we examine the art beneath the flicker and hum of malfunctioning neon.

There are Jonasz Stern's collages of bones and prayer shawls, some of the most eloquent laments I've seen on the Holocaust—Stern survived the camps as a teenager. There are Magdalena Abakanowicz's giant fabric sculptures. A textile artist, Abakanowicz worked with the human body as element, creating woven skins of people. There are Kantor's emballages, costumes from his Cricot 2 Theatre and a desk from *Dead Class*. There is a beautiful installation of tombstones in sand, inscripted with Hebrew; there are videos by Zbigniew Warpechowski. Joseph Beuys, Fernand Léger, Max Ernst, Bridget Riley, Mirosław Bałka: all the twentieth-century luminaries are here. I don't remember the name of the Polish artist who made the boat installation on the top floor. Shown first in a larger space, the piece was then donated to the museum. It is so big it fills the room, and when you enter, you enter the installation itself immediately, the ribbed chamber of the hull giving the impression of the inside of a whale.

In his essay 'The Pill of Murti-Bing', which opens *The Captive Mind*, Czesław Miłosz examines capitulation. The swallowing of the pill is a metaphor for the desire of the alienated intellectual to *belong*. Supposedly egalitarian dialectical materialism has replaced (supposedly egalitarian) religion. The intellectual relishes the downfall of the bourgeoisie—wasn't life absurd before with its endless grotesque cycle of self-gratification?—he is on a mission to save humankind. There is his ineluctable need to be part of the human stream, to speak from it, there is his subjective impotence in the communist context and the inevitable damnation of his work should it speak from outside the stream. Humanity has been organised into one homogenous mass, and to speak of humanity as all artists must, is to speak in one homogenous voice. But to be denied one's own voice is to be denied one's humanity.

Having lost a large number of works during the war, Łódź Muzeum Sztuki accumulated most of its collection during the most oppressive years of Polish Communism. It is remarkable how much brilliant art there is here, not concerned with obedient themes. The Polish proclivity for abstraction becomes trenchant criticism. Abakanowicz's work in particular exudes menace and constriction.

*The Captive Mind* is written out of a despairing conviction that Soviet Communism will take over all of Europe, if not the world, and dominate for centuries. It posits religion as a benign force from the past (did *anybody* foresee the current rise of religion?). Yet Miłosz's insight is dazzling. 'The Pill of Murti-Bing' is more than anything about self-censorship and the apathy inside us all. Miłosz isn't talking about police banging down doors at 3 a.m. to arrest dissidents at gunpoint. He is talking about the quiet decision individuals make to swallow the dictates of the status quo and regurgitate them in their work. He writes: 'The objective conditions necessary to the realisation of a work of art are, as we know, a highly complex phenomenon, involving one's public, the possibility of contact with it, the general atmosphere, and above all freedom from involuntary subjective control.'

I find these words chilling in their relevance to our times. In Australia and similar economies, opportunities decrease as quickly as wealth accumulates; artists and writers are struggling to find their public. The atmosphere is too comfortable to merit comparisons to totalitarian regimes, but there is a palpable sense of tyranny in the air, caused precisely by the very comfort supposed to protect us. As we become more corporatised, personal wealth and personal space are favoured over communal. Laws tightened to protect the individual (from broken footpaths, fire, illness, unkind words) also cut the individual off. Public space is strictly regulated and under surveillance; freedom of speech is declining. Everything from the water-regulating authority through universities to arts organisations is run on a profit-based system. The buck is passed to the shareholder: individualism eats itself. The market narrows, and the market rules: artists are increasingly restricted. They must change their ways, or elicit favours, or get very lucky. In running this obstacle course, one never knows how far down the slippery slope one is.

As Australia slips to number 35 (31 in 2005) on the Reporters Without Borders Press Freedom Index, journalists are also blistering from the dance of obedience. (Finland is ranked no. 1; the United States 56, down from 44). Public servants and educationalists are following suit. At Interakcje, Zbigniew Warpechowski gave a lecture that addressed these concerns in Poland (ranked no. 60, down from 55). It was striking to hear a man born in the 1930s, who experienced life under Nazism then Stalinism, declare the new conservatism as restrictive as anything he had previously lived through.

In his 1940 essay 'Inside the Whale' Orwell writes of liberalism under threat, largely through an examination of Henry Miller's writing, dismissed by most critics at the time as a relic of the decadent 1920s. One of the most brilliant political minds of the twentieth century, whose allegorical novels still resonate, writing in the midst of the twentieth century's totalitarian madness, Orwell doesn't advocate a literature of literal signage. He goes deeper to the pulse of the individual within the collective, championing Miller's acceptance of a world process outside his control. 'Good novels are not written by orthodoxy-sniffers, nor by people who are conscience-stricken about their own unorthodoxy. Good novels are written by people who are *not frightened*.'

I wonder if the artist who constructed the boat installation in Łódź Muzeum Sztuki had read 'Inside the Whale'. He made the piece decades after Orwell's essay and *The Captive Mind* were written. Standing inside it is to feel at once protected and suffocated, and squeezing it into an undersized room only exaggerates this effect. The whale inside which Orwell puts Miller is transparent. Through slats of the installation we can see walls, a window, buildings. This is not the Poland of Witkacy or Miłosz, nor the Europe of Orwell and Miller. But the ideal of individual freedom within social equality still eludes us, and liberalism is again subjugated by a strict hierarchical order, full of terror, dogmatism and piety. 'Get inside the whale', says Orwell, '—or rather, admit that you are inside the whale (for you *are*, of course). Give yourself over to the world process, stop fighting against it or pretending that you control it; simply accept it, endure it, record it.'

ADAM lets us into his apartment with barely a grunt as a greeting. He says he has a hangover. The argument between him and AñA at Łódź Kaliska turns out to have been about how to install Version II of *Arterial*. We filmed it in residency at the Performance Space in Sydney six months before coming to Poland, so the video installation was made before Version I, the live performance, and has already been shown in Sydney and Beijing.

In Version II, the bloodpath wraps through the space, leading the audience to three screens. It is a 16-minute-long triptych, the right and left screens concentrating on a single figure until about halfway through when they converge, creating temporal distortions. While the audience surrounds the live performance, the video installation surrounds the audience. Removed from the sound and smell of bleeding in real time, the experience is more ethereal, and painterly, the bloodpath alone able to be viewed intimately. The medium is well suited to the sense of infinity suggested by the live performance, but there is an element crucial and particular to the video installation: the final image in the loop of the empty, stained shrouds draped in the centre of the bloodpath, marking the disappearance of the body, and the trace of the sacrifice undergone. The shrouds for us have a predominantly Catholic symbolism, although we are not at all hostile to cross-cultural interpretations, and aware that the shrouded woman today evokes Islam for many. Later, I will come across the work of Cuban artist AñA Mendieta, who worked extensively with blood and shrouds, and feel enormous kinship. But while Mendieta used blood as an external medium for its powerful totemic meaning, central to senVoodoo's *Arterial* is the act of bleeding itself. The work, whether live or in video installation, would be meaningless if the blood spilt were not our own. Mendieta was influenced by Octavio Paz's ideas of sacrifice as present in the Mexican combination of Catholic and Aztec cultures; Paz in turn was influenced by Georges Bataille and Roger Caillois's concept of excess and *fiesta*—or the carnivalesque—and the communal renewal these rituals offer.

We can see *Arterial* wrapping beautifully into these rooms. Adam's apartment consists of a kitchen, most of which is filled by a long wooden table; a large room used as an office and bedroom; and a bathroom. On the other side of the corridor the conjoined exhibition rooms look onto the street. Wschodnia Street, which means 'east', is parallel to Piotrówska Street. One block from the phone spruikers and trendy shops, we are back in rough-as-guts Poland. Below, men congregate in a doorway drinking beer from cans; beyond them kids are playing in a courtyard. Adam has a preconception about our installation; he wants it mounted like this, not like that. I don't think you've taken my space into account, he grumbles. The paper is heavy and it isn't possible to hang it the way Adam envisages. It takes almost an hour to persuade him, and I am glad for the distraction of Malutka, Adam's mischievous black cat, which reminds me of my much missed one at home. We have thirty metres of bloodpath now. From Piotrków Trybunalski through Gdańsk to Łódź, our songline is ready for its next incarnation.

Adam can't imagine where he can fit the third screen. He is argumentative and irritable, to the extent that we wonder why he invited us to show here. But he realises gradually that our idea is valid, and slowly begins to relax. He clears a space on the cluttered table and serves us barley soup. He lights up when he hears of our adventures in the strange museums of Łódź. Have you been to the Museum of Artistic Books? Have you been to Atlas Sztuki? Yes, you must go to the Jewish Cemetery, the old Jewish quarter began just up there. A Jewish family lived here before the war, he tells us. Their son came back to visit a few years ago. He was pleased to see it was a gallery because his father had been a very cultured man.

We tell Adam we are interested in the historical museum housed in the Poznański Palace, but it is closed every time we go, in spite of the fact that the building is one of the most sumptuously restored in the city. Adam shrugs: he doesn't think much of this particular museum. He says: An Israeli performance artist who came here last year said to me, When I see this building I understand anti-Semitism.

I don't know whether or not Izrael Poznański was Łódź's richest industrialist, but he was certainly its most ostentatious. Looked at in this way he is the epitome of the decadent Jew, archetype of the supposed moral degeneracy of the urban space. I wonder what the Israeli performance artist thought of Łódź's many German Protestant industrialists. I wonder whether it is ostentation that is offensive, or wealth per se. If material excess is the problem here, I wonder if a miser is morally superior to a profligate. Is the sin in the earning or in the spending?

In his *Diary Volume One*, written in Argentina in 1953–56, iconoclastic Polish writer Witold Gombrowicz says:

Why doesn't the world like Jews? Because, of course, they are more capable, they have money, and they create competition … There is simply no more brilliant people … The Jewish genius is most intimately connected with illness, defeat, degradation. Brilliant because it is ill. Higher because it is degraded. Creative because it is abnormal … This people [sic], like Michelangelo, Chopin, or Beethoven, is decadence that transforms itself into creativity and progress.

This reminds me a little of the straight person's praise for the creative *élan* of gay men; the gay man's praise for the political savvy of lesbians; the white man's praise for the black man's rhythm; the rich man's praise for the poor man's humility; the praise of men in general for the generosity and compassion of women. It is axiomatic that adversity can increase strength—it's the physics of survival—muscles are built from the scars of resistance. But reinforcements of otherness only help maintain distance from our fellow humans. Attributing qualities and talents to biological circumstance enables us equally to blame our failings on impersonal causes. Thus we are all fated to be; there's no point in trying to change. Such strategies also enable the conventional classes to justify hostility to any sort of non-conformist.

Gombrowicz's logic is uncomfortably close to that of the Nazis he so despised, except that for them decadence was an unambiguous pejorative. Hitler's list of deviants was a roll call of twentieth-century brilliance: Mann, Proust, Picasso, Freud. His Degenerate Art (*Entartete Kunst*) exhibition mounted in Munich in 1937 included works by luminaries such as Nolde, Otto Dix and Max Beckman. If not *other* to the Nazis by virtue of race or politics, these artists and writers transgressed with their style. The Degenerate Art exhibition was immensely more popular than its politically correct counterpart, the *Grosse Deutsche Kunstausstellung* (Great German Art Exhibition). Not all the punters would have railed in condemnation of paintings with such scandalous titles as *The negro becomes the racial ideal of degenerate art.*

For Witkacy, artists were even worse off under socialism than leading the decadent lives fostered by interwar liberalism. But Witkacy belied his convictions by his own example—he predicted time and again the end of art, yet he could not live without it and his own toil produced work that would forever change his region's culture. Still, both his and Gombrowicz's logic can feed the persistent myth that Weimar decadence, in particular sexual deviance, both caused and characterised Nazism.

As I travel through Poland, one of the most acclaimed novels in Australia is Christos Tsiolkas's *Dead Europe*, which deals with anti-Semitism in a Europe where global capitalism is shot through with ancient peasant culture. Tsiolkas spoke of Western decadence in several interviews, as well as in the publicity notes for the novel. He defines the West as Australia, America and Europe. It's unclear what place Eastern Europe has in Tsiolkas's definition, if any—but it is clear that decadence is excess, and morally reprehensible. Tsiolkas says:

> There is a danger in excess and the danger is a spiritual and moral emptiness … The outpouring of grief over the (death of the last) Pope, the revival of fundamentalism, all of this cannot hide the clear truth that we are unprepared to give ourselves over to the rejection of materialism and ego demanded of us by the Gospels. And not only Christians, I think long-term Muslims and Jews are also decadent in the West. So we create spiritualities that require no discipline or sacrifice. Call it the New Age, it too stinks of decadence.

In Tsiolkas's novel it is carnal excess that is used most explicitly to represent decadence. Sex and drugs are abominations. *Dead Europe*'s codes of sin are familiarly Judeo-Christian; they chime with those of all religions that place the body at the bottom of the pyramid of human identity, and the conventional family at the top of the social one. They are the same codes preached by Benedict XVI, Sheikh Al-Hilaly and George Bush.

What the West and the East, the right and the left and all organised religions agree upon is the condemnation of pleasure. But could it be that puritanism is one of contemporary society's greatest dangers, with its soul-destroying work ethic, which denies subversion, reflection and any sort of cultural activity not explicitly utilitarian? Let alone its hatred of sexuality.

There is a danger in blanket proscriptions of carnal excess, for it is fundamental to the carnivalesque, which is one of the most powerful tools we have for dissent. And who are the moral arbiters of this excess? Relying on the Holy Books plays into the hands of their often corrupt and unreliable priests. Without sexual deviance we wouldn't have sexual liberation—intrinsic to civil rights—as biblical codes favour men and procreation. The Gospels may be a good guide for basic ethics, but if St Paul condemns homosexuality and Leviticus the wearing of garments woven from two kinds of fabric, and the Old Testament no matter how beautifully written is so relentlessly misogynistic, then we need common sense more than anything to determine how to live today.

Witkacy, Tsiolkas and Benedict XVI all speak of a collapsing moral order, but none can point to a time and place where the ideal existed. Haven't humans in the East and the West overindulged for millennia? And where does religious excess fall in all of this? Must it end in murder before it is resisted, let alone criticised?

*Decadence*—degeneration, decay. The attrition of the outmoded that new growth may begin. An organic process, as potentially frightening as death itself.

In this sense decadence can be shrinkage, the taboo trajectory of capitalism, for no politician wants to go on television and talk about the inevitability of economic decay.

Benedict XVI has arrived in Warsaw and is railing against secularism. Scores more people have died in suicide bomb attacks in Baghdad. Secularism might be exactly what we need.

# FULL

# IMMERSION

**VANESSA RUSSELL** RECOUNTS THE CIRCUMSTANCES SURROUNDING
HER BAPTISM INTO THE CHURCH OF THE CHRISTADELPHIANS

'ACTUALLY, Vanessa,' the Examining Brother said, creaking forwards in the best
cane chair, 'we aren't told that the fruit Adam and Eve partook of in the Garden
of Eden was an apple.' I nodded, bowing my head, and picked at the scarlet hair
dye that stained my cuticles. Brother Barry Hepworth looked around the audience
of sixty Brethren and Sisters with barely contained triumph. He had wanted to
set me straight for years. This was my punishment for reading Malcolm X when
I was fifteen and declaring Jesus' soul-man blackness in Sunday school.

My family were terrified. We were all crammed into a cousin's home in
Rowville for my baptism into the faith. Solemn but happy Brethren and Sisters
spilled from the lounge room into the salmon-coloured kitchen, lining the halls
with fold-up camp chairs and balancing note-filled King James Version Bibles on
their knees. If you read the Bible correctly, they preached, baptism is the only way
to salvation.

I nearly hadn't made it through Brother Barry's preliminary examination. This
was unheard of. Nobody had ever, not in the whole five generations of my family's
belief, been close to rejection before. The preliminary examination is a longer
version of the baptismal examination and is held a few days before the baptism.

In a process long perfected through fourteen years of attendance at Sunday school, the examiner recites questions from the Baptismal Examiner and the applicant responds.

'Is there a devil?' the examiner asks.

'No,' answers the applicant.

'What does the term "devil" mean?'

'Sin in the flesh.'

'Where does it say that?'

'Romans 7:17, 18.'

'Read it out, please.'

' "Now then it is no more I that do it, but sin that dwelleth in me. For I know that in me (that is, in my flesh) dwelleth no good thing." '

'Very good.'


I RAN into trouble with Brother Barry when he tried to make me pledge that I would never go to the theatre, movies, football matches and 'the like'—worldly pursuits, in other words.

The generally accepted sidestep for this line of enquiry is to say, 'I will try to avoid such places.' This is to allow leeway for the slightly more liberal members of the faith, such as my family, who regularly watched TV. For Brother Barry the faith was becoming lax and standards were falling. It was his duty to bring me back from the brink of apostasy.

'Do we attend worldly pursuits?' he asked in my preliminary examination.

'It's best to avoid them,' I said.

Brother Barry's eyebrows went into spasm.

'Avoid?' he said. 'I think you mean it's best if we never go.'

'No,' I said, 'it's best to avoid them.'

For an hour he pushed. For an hour I didn't buckle. Our sticking point was football matches. I don't know how Brother Barry and I got stuck on football. It must have been the principle.

Football. I am so ignorant about the game that when I was younger and working Saturdays in the local newsagency I noticed everyone buying black and white streamers. I assumed everyone was having black and white parties. When I returned home Mum laughed and said, 'The Magpies were in the Grand Final today.'

When I refused to tell Brother Barry that I would never, not under any circumstances, attend a football match, he panicked and fled. He drove one minute around the corner to my grandparents' place and ten minutes later Grandad rang and told me that he'd sorted it out.

'It's best to avoid those places, hey, kiddo?' Grandad said.

'Yep.'

'Yeah, don't worry about old Barry boy, he gets into a bit of a flap every now and then. I've sorted him out. See you on Sat'day, kid.'

I SHOULD have foreseen it. I'd been born into the faith and had gone with my parents every Sunday to a hired hall in Wantirna, a hired hall because they didn't believe in owning 'pagan' churches. Every Sunday I had sprawled at my parents' feet on a rug on the hall's polished wooden floor and had coloured in with the riches of my Crayola Caddy amid interruptions of hymns and prayers that we had to stand up for.

Brother Barry made his children sit and read on the green vinyl concertina chairs after his youngest daughter, Georgie, was banned from drawing after she coloured in too loudly with a texta. He would have liked the rest of the children to follow, but he couldn't drum up the support. We children barely noticed the adults' rituals.

During my baptismal examination Brother Barry threw in a question that he might have prepared me for had we not become entangled with the issue of football.

'What's the highlight of our week?' he asked.

I floundered. *Frontline*? Friday night fish 'n' chips? Wednesday night's block of chocolate? Brother Barry's eyebrows danced.

'The breaking of bread,' he said, eventually.

'Oh,' I said.

Every Sunday the Brethren and Sisters break bread, drink wine and ask forgiveness for their sins. A loaf of bread is divided into eight chunks, placed on eight heavy glass plates, then passed from baptised hand to baptised hand where a pinch is torn and eaten. It is like eating death. The wine is poured into eight glass jugs where the Brethren and Sisters fill their own tiny wine glasses then throw back their heads to take a swallow of wine. It is vile: bargain basement because some were worried that people might get a taste for it.

One week an unknown visitor to the rented hall broke into the locked cupboard where the wine was kept and poured some into a glass. It was so revolting that after a taste the intruder poured the rest back.

I was eighteen when I decided I wanted to eat the bread and wine. The first Gulf War was starting and Armageddon was close. I had no smart responses left to the perennial Sunday school question: 'What will you do when Jesus returns?'

The question meant: what will become of you after you have been judged unworthy because you are not baptised? I thought: I will be alone; everyone I know will be saved.

Protocol meant that first I had to write a letter to the Head Brother. This was Robert Winterton, my first cousin once removed and one of my favourite members of the faith. For years he'd entertained me with impressions of the knights who say 'Ni'. No-one else found him funny. Silly man, Grandma hissed whenever he bobbed past to deliver the announcements after the breaking of bread.

At the conclusion of that week's announcements, which consisted of the news that Brother and Sister Charlie Sorrel sent greetings from Woy Woy, Robert said with an almost sinful degree of enthusiasm, 'We're very pleased to announce that we have received a letter requesting baptism.'

'Dear Rob …' he read.

I hunkered down in my seat and pulled the borrowed hat over my eyes.

'… I have been attending Sunday school since I was four and have realised that I will only be saved through baptism. Please make the necessary arrangements. Yours faithfully …'

Everyone, even the lounging teenagers playing Game Boys behind the back of Brother Barry held their breath wondering who it was going to be this time. With the forthcoming war the barely twenty-somethings had been converting in chronological age order. I was way out of line—ahead of me should have been Sam and Georgie, Kirsten and Nick, and maybe even that wayward pal of mine, Bronwyn.

'… Vanessa.'

A collective sharp intake of breath sucked the oxygen out of the room. I started to cry. As soon as the concluding hymn ended, streams of Brethren and Sisters congratulated me. Brother Barry's mother-in-law held me in her cotton wool arms and told me that the next week would be frightening, but I had the love of my Brothers and Sisters. Several joked and said they weren't expecting my name. Sam, Georgie, Kirsten, Nick and Bronwyn shuffled away.

While I was having my hat knocked off with enthusiastic hugs, the Arranging Brethren were gathering in a circle in the antechamber. The Arranging Brethren were an elected group of seven men who administrated the faith. One of them would examine me. I was desperately hoping for Brother Arthur Quinn, a gentle and patient man, but he'd examined the last applicant and there was a strict rota system. Oh, please, no.

Brother Barry broke through the chain of congratulating Brethren and Sisters and took me to the antechamber.

'I will be your Examining Brother,' he said.

'Fantastic,' I said, my tone of voice betraying my first sinful wish towards a Brother not five minutes after I'd applied to join.

'First of all,' he said, 'we'll need you to change this letter.'

'What's wrong with it?' I said, my first act of defiance against a Brother five minutes and ten seconds after I'd decided to live in eternity with him.

'It's not right,' he said. 'In the future, nobody will know who "Rob" and "Vanessa" were.'

We're not supposed to have a future, I thought, Jesus is coming back at any second. Remember?

I added my last name to my Christian name and crossed out 'Rob' (rather messily and impatiently) and wrote 'Mr Winterton', as if I were writing to a stranger for life insurance. Brother Barry arranged a time to come over during the week and put me through the preliminary examination. It was right in the middle of *Frontline*.

Baptism day. I was dressed in a not-very-demure hot-pink dress and desperately trying to tuck my disastrously dyed red hair up into my new Sunday hat. Five minutes to go and Brother Barry hadn't arrived. A hymn rattled out of an asthmatic organ. Late-arriving Brethren and Sisters pushed through the throng to get to the kitchen with cream-filled party cakes while early arrivals shifted in their already uncomfortable camp chairs. I hadn't heard from Brother Barry since the preliminary examination. One minute to go.

'Still on?' Brother Barry whispered in my ear. He creaked into the cane chair and addressed the audience. The organ music faded to a stop, camp chairs were hastily snapped open and King James Version Bibles fell open to Genesis 1:1.

'Let's start with Adam and Eve,' he said.

The crowd shuffled. It was going to be a long night.

'What caused the fall of Adam and Eve?' he asked.

'They took an apple from the tree …' I began.

'Actually, Vanessa,' he said, 'we aren't told that …'

I looked at Grandad. He raised his eyebrows and gave a rueful smile. The Brethren and Sisters squirmed for me. I fought down a glare at Brother Barry. So this was how it would be.

After two further hours of questioning Brother Barry came to the subject of 'worldly pursuits'. Despite his earlier Edenic produce lesson I felt confident that because of our stand-off at the preliminary examination he would allow me to use the sidestep.

'Do we attend worldly pursuits?' he asked.

'It's best to avoid them,' I said.

Brother Barry looked at me evenly then addressed the audience.

'Avoid?' he said. 'I think you mean it's best if we never go.'

I held my breath. I thought about my options. There weren't any. I could sit and argue. I could shame my family. I glanced at Grandad. He rolled his eyes.

'Yes,' I said.

Brother Barry stretched, and the cane chair cracked. He asked if any Brothers had more questions. After a silent minute I went to prepare in the laundry.

I wore the baptismal gown, a white cotton top-to-toe shroud underneath which my hot-pink bathers were clearly visible. I walked barefoot into the aluminium garage, holding up the gown's hem. In the middle of the garage the baptismal bath was assembled. It was homemade, about thirty years old; a plastic pool-liner had been cut to fit a coffin-shaped frame. I stepped into the bath at the direction of the Bath Brother who had stayed outside tending it. The water was warm. The Bath Brother told me to sit down and I waited, mind blank, for everyone to troop out to witness.

Brother Barry marched over. I thought I might cry. He placed his hand on my head and I shuddered.

'Do you agree to abide by the laws of God as laid out in the Holy Bible?' he intoned.

'I do,' I said.

'Then I baptise you, and may your sins be washed away.' He mumbled into my ear, 'Hold your nose,' and pushed back my head. Underwater I was held down by Brother Barry and two Brothers who pushed down on my legs and arms. Full immersion, or the baptism is invalid. After ten seconds, satisfied that I was fully immersed, they let me up. Brethren and Sisters were already walking back into the house.

I was sin-free. Everything looked brighter, in focus. I wondered what my first sin would be. I wouldn't, I thought, I'll never sin again.

I dressed back in my hot-pink dress that was too bright and tried to position my hat over my wet blazing red hair. I squelched up to the front to silence and Brother Barry welcomed the new Sister Vanessa. Sister Vanessa who hasn't sinned.

Afterwards my cousin Robert congratulated me. 'You're the first Sister to have Ronald McDonald hair,' he said. I laughed loudly, and my new Brothers and Sisters turned to glare. Brother Barry's eyebrows twitched and I wondered how long I would last.

HARMONIC
*For Dean Frenkel*

The ribbon
        of sound in which
a man becomes
a bird—
his throat
        alive
and
tremulous
with    pitch of
soil and leaf and
swirl
of rising heat—
sings,
as Ovid knew,
the strange and siren language of the clouds:

The breadth of this man's
body,    bone and
muscle, the
        burr of bass
grounds
(for now)
        the spilling
liquid notes that
strain and dive like gannets
in the shimmer of the summer day.

When will we, too,
        listeners, singers,
slip
into that feathered form
and find the breaking,
        lifting language of that simple
voice?
When will we be that bird,
        entire
and soar—
soar
into the endless breathing of the fluted air?


ROSE LUCAS

## I FOUND THE SIX OF SPADES
## IN CAT BA TOWN

I found a six of spades in Cat Ba Town
near the Bia Hoi warehouse
      kegs here thrown or humped off
a hydrofoil both by mouths
bumps and arms in suckle

    Not just any six
of spades, *the* six of spades. Mine. Somebody
millennia ago ensured I'd find it. Here
      these smoggy waves from Haiphong
      ship a fragrant peekaboo to my nose
      and a bin of prawns with bum hands

      Here where sampans bonk at flotsam
      in the bay
      as if clapping
    at me. My luck, miasmic
wasn't positive, until now, I'd not had much of a run
here, but there
it was. Vietnamese blackjack. That card—kaboom!

Manna maybe
though aged, bent and reeking
of rather dead smelt. It was
the perfect card to eureka, this
      fan of cartography

already fishing out this here five
of hearts in some dive bar hole aboard an Old
Muddy queen in Dubuque
then my club queen in a blue swim
grotto, Vanuatu
Now this? How
did they know
I was to win today
as if today was my own trophy catch?

KENT MACCARTER

# WAITING FOR MR MOWBRAY

PAUL MORGAN

WHEN someone dies, the way we hear of it forever colours how we remember them. A newspaper obituary, with its elegiac tone, makes the death seem inevitable and somehow right: the climax of a fast-moving short story. Familiar phrases help to lubricate the shock: 'distinguished career … much loved by those who knew him … sadly missed by family and friends'. Finding out by telephone gives the death an extra urgency, as though hearing an eyewitness report. You will always remember that moment, standing with the phone to your ear and staring through the window at the garden, listening to the details: the when, the where, who found the body, and the cause of death. Sometimes, less often these days, we find out in a letter. 'I thought you ought to know … what a character … great loss to the trade.' The news decrees the opening of a wine bottle and suitable, saddened words around the kitchen table. 'Poor old bugger, at least it was quick.' And later, after a second bottle has been started, it seems all right to make less kindly remarks. 'He wasn't a saint, of course. I remember the time …'

When I returned from holiday and heard that Anthony Mowbray had died, however, I received the news from all directions. It was hard to believe he had actually gone. We weren't close by any means. It was just that somehow he had always been there, like a familiar monument you walk past every day (that general of bronze gazing bravely at the railway station). I had bumped into Anthony (never 'Tony') just before I left on my long-awaited holiday in North Africa, and he excitedly told me—in confidence, of course—that he was about to pull off the biggest deal of his life. We must have lunch when I got back and he'd tell me all about. I genially agreed, knowing neither of us would make the effort. Then when I did return, there were urgent messages from friends on my answering machine telling me of his sudden death, the news in several letters (one with a paper-clipped obituary from the *Age* attached), and another from a solicitor I did not know. After expressing sincere condolences and so on, she wrote that Mr Mowbray had appointed me executor of his will, and that she looked forward to hearing from me soon.

I groaned. I was sorry to hear the news, of course, but this wasn't what I needed after a long flight from Dubai and with all the threads of my own business to pick up. Anthony was not someone I would have called a friend exactly. I doubted whether anyone did. When I had opened my first gallery (specialising in early twentieth-century Australian art) it happened to be near Anthony's premises in North Fitzroy and we soon began passing business each other's way. Asked to value the paintings in a deceased estate, I'd make sure I bought any pictures of interest, but also tipped him a wink if there was any furniture worth looking at before it went on public sale. Later he would return the favour. I guess it would have been on one of those occasions that he asked me to be executor of his will. I must have agreed and promptly forgotten. It was probably after cele-brating a satisfactory auction where we and a few other dealers had managed to 'ring in' everything of value with deliberately low bids, to divide up between ourselves afterwards. Well, that was how things were done in those days.

Anthony Mowbray was never quite as respectable, then, as his later public image suggested. Twice chairman of the Australian Antique Trade Association, he became recognisable everywhere at sale rooms and trade fairs. Tall, with a mop of curly white hair and dressed in a rumpled linen suit with a vaguely regimen-tal tie, he always seemed to be surrounded by a group of eager listeners, explaining some elaborate point about eighteenth-century joinery, or the influence of British and Indian styles on each other during the Raj. Every piece of furniture he showed you had a story, it seemed. And every story he told led to a piece that had just arrived in a new consignment that day, if you'd be interested to see before it went on display …?

One Saturday afternoon I saw him charm a couple in his cavernous treasure-cave of a shop, telling them the story of an Indian bureau he had noticed them admiring. Made of scented cedar and inlaid with decorated panels, it had been bought by a French adventurer in the seventeenth century. He had taken it back to his chateau at Lalinde in the Dordogne, where it was used by him, his son and his grandson after him, before the whirlwind of the French Revolution. Somehow the bureau turned up in an English manor house, and was later shipped to Australia, where it survived a shipwreck and was bought by a squatter in the Western District of Victoria. And now here the bureau was before them, as beautiful as the day it was made 300 years ago in Pondicherry, he said while running his hand over its delicate carving. His accent became more English and precise at times like this, as though he were a visiting academic generously sharing his knowledge rather than a dealer spinning a yarn. (I knew for a fact he had knocked it together from three other broken pieces and had no idea of their provenance.) The couple were entranced, and the man was already reaching for his credit card when Anthony said that, regrettably, the piece was not for sale and nothing that was said could change his mind. After they had left—almost pushed out the door—Anthony whistled to himself with a sly smile as he locked up. The following Monday, as he knew they would, the couple rang and offered twice the original price—an offer he felt obliged to accept.

That little desk was part of a fashion for Indian and oriental antiques that Anthony had helped to start in the 1970s. Before that time, 'antique' to most people had meant western European—anything from an exquisite Biedermeier couch to a grinning, red-faced Toby Jug. But then, with all things Eastern becoming fashionable again—from fabrics to philosophies—and the cost of shipping, and the trade connections he had begun to build up in India, Anthony was confident he was onto a good thing. Any businessman is lucky to have one really winning idea in a lifetime, and this was his: the realisation that people who could afford it were willing to fill their houses with beautiful objects from all around the world, not just France, England or, at a pinch, Germany.

Soon, every few months a new consignment would arrive from Madras, and later from Candy, Cochin or other Indian ports. For a dealer in antiques, the excitement of a container arriving never fades. The enormous truck pulled up outside Anthony's shop and the doors swung open for the first time since being sealed up on a faraway Indian afternoon. I swear you could smell the dust of that day and the spicy sweat of the stevedores who had carried the furniture in. Rubbing his hands together, Anthony walked up the bouncing metal drawbridge at the back of the truck and entered the long metallic cavern. He inhaled deeply and ran a fingertip over the surfaces of velvet and sweet, ornate timbers that he had last seen months earlier on the other side of the world. Then he turned, clapped, and said, 'Right, let's get this little lot inside!'

On occasions like this, his face was a mask of glee, grinning with self-satisfaction, as though he'd pulled off a particularly difficult conjuring trick. Indeed, seeing the marvellous, exotic contents of the container being unloaded, and Anthony himself fussing around and helping to carry the heavier items, he seemed like a time-traveller returning from a trip to the eighteenth century, where he had pulled on a frock-coat, bought an entire auction's worth of furniture and whisked it back to the present.

Though I liked Anthony and was grateful for his tip-offs, I still did not regard him as a friend, for the simple reason that I never really felt I knew him. He was like an actor doing a very good impersonation of an antique dealer, and I simply could not see him outside this role. What did he do in the evenings? Did he ever read? Listen to music? Have friends outside the trade? It was impossible to imagine. This conviction increased in the weeks after my return as I caught up with people, and the subject of Anthony's sudden death inevitably came up.

'There was more to him than that "charming rogue" front, of course,' I said, 'but what that "more" was, I've never really understood.'

'You do know he liked a bit of rough on the quiet, don't you?' said one acquaintance over coffee. 'I called round one weekend and he was quite seriously bashed, but pretended he'd fallen on the stairs. His face was like a bowl of fruit, all black and blue and red and yellow with bruises.'

'That English background was all a fake,' someone else told me over dinner in a restaurant. 'All that stuff about being the son of an English MP and being brought up in a country house. I happen to know he was born in Wagga. His parents ran the Provincial Hotel, a real dive in those days.'

'I can't tell you where he came from,' a woman said as we walked along the beach throwing sticks into the surf for her dog, 'but I know for a fact that he could speak Hindi like a native, not like someone who went to India to buy antiques a few times a year. Draw what conclusions you like from that ...'

There were no surprises in the will of Anthony Mowbray. When the time came for me to examine it at his solicitor's, I saw the bulk of the estate had been left to a niece in Perth. There was a bequest to the RSPCA (beneficiary of so many misanthropes' wills), and for all my work as executor, a muddy painting of *Box Hill at Dusk* by Jane Price, one of the more dreary painters of the Heidelberg School. I felt like Shakespeare's wife, whose only inheritance was her husband's second-best bed.

I had no doubt that, in Anthony's mind, his business affairs were in perfect order. Trying to reconstruct them from the chaos of his office was another matter, especially as—this being the antique trade—he did a fair bit of business on the basis of cash and a handshake. Receipts were generally works of fiction to keep tax and customs officials happy. If I had asked for the details relating to a particular nineteenth-century birdcage he had sold last year, I am sure he could have laid his hand on them within minutes. Whenever I needed to find something as his executor, though, I could only look around in despair at the overflowing shelves spilling papers onto the floor, the filing cabinets packed tightly with bulging manila folders, and the tin boxes stacked under tables and on top of a wardrobe he kept there. One of these tins contained a mouldering egg sandwich, which made me gag. I snapped the little coffin shut and took it straight out to the bin. Some were locked. Some only contained keys to other boxes tied together with greasy string but with no indication of which ones they would fit. One of them made a curious shuffling sound when I shook it. None of the keys fitted the lock, so after a few minutes work with a chisel I got it open, to find only the ashes of a burnt photograph.

Slowly, with the help of Anthony's solicitor and accountant, I began to make sense of it all. For every consignment of antiques bought, there were curt inventories (devoid of sales patter), bills of lading, customs declarations and certificates of payment. Sales were recorded by hand in a series of ledgers bound in red fabric stained with ink spots. His profits were mostly invested in fixed-interest bonds, but regular amounts were also transferred to an account in Chennai, so that he was able to pay for the next consignment in local currency. And so the process began again. Letters from India showed how much his business was valued there, as he returned season after season, year after year, extending his networks across the country. Looking back, I guess a lot of people came to rely on him and trusted his word. One winter, long after I had lost touch with Anthony, he contracted pneumonia. Then there were complications. He ended up in hospital and had to recuperate for over a month. When you run your own business, getting ill is no joke, as I knew myself. Thousands of dollars worth of furniture he had bought at auction was left unpaid for and awaiting instructions at a port on the Bengal coast. When he finally had the strength to make enquiries, it turned out everything had been kept safely for him. 'You are a gentleman,' the letter said. 'We knew there must be a reason, and you would send instructions and pay when you could.' How quaint. Was this the Mowbray we knew?

If I was not getting to know Anthony any better, my respect for his business skills increased on those wintry Sunday afternoons at his premises, huddled by a little two-bar electric heater and poring over the paperwork of his life. I found myself almost enjoying the process of sorting out his affairs. It reminded me of when I was a child, filling in an outlined scene with crayons until it was bright with primary colours. The yellow sun in a blue sky shone down on a red bus driving between green fields where a brown cow peacefully grazed. After the weeks of colouring in Anthony's business dealings, however, it became clear there was one area that stayed curiously blank: his final consignment, the one he had told me about the last time I had seen him.

The inventory for this ran to fifty pages, and I could sense Anthony's excitement in the tone of the correspondence. It was his biggest deal ever in India: the purchase of the entire contents of a maharajah's palace that was being sold for conversion to a hotel. The purchase had gone through; the money had been paid (an amount that looked astonishingly big in rupees); there was confirmation from his agent that everything had been packed up, and then … nothing. I wasn't too concerned at first. The businesses he dealt with were ones he had known and trusted for years. Had he really been conned? Surely he was too smart for that, and anyway—I figured—if Anthony Mowbray was involved in any swindle, he was far more likely to be the agent, not the victim. No, I felt confident that there wasn't any funny business here. It was just that the consignment—the entire contents and furnishings of the Maharajah of Jawahlpore's palace—had simply disappeared.

I tried to reconstruct how the deal was done, kneeling on the floor and fanning out all the documents in date order around me. It became obvious that the consignment was being held in storage somewhere in India, waiting for final instructions to collect and ship to the Port of Melbourne. But what if the heart attack had happened before he had a chance to do this? And what if, as it seemed, he had never written down the location of the warehouse? I spent the best part of a week trying to follow this paper trail. By Friday I was exhausted from repeated explanations of why I was phoning banks, lawyers and shipping agents. No, they did not know where Mr Murthu had moved after arranging the sale. The firm of Srinavasan & Srinavasan had closed down last month, had I not been notified? Mr Bhadra Sujit? Did I mean perhaps Mr Sujit Bhadra? But when I spoke to Sujit, he too had never heard of Anthony Mowbray.

'I'm sorry to hear of your loss. He sounds a most interesting person, and perhaps my late father was acquainted. I regret I never had the chance to meet your friend …' Sujit Bhadra obviously had time to chat, but I cut him off abruptly. I was on a mission.

After all my work, I had just one new piece of information in my palm. The warehouse where everything had been delivered was somewhere in the state of Tamil Nadu, and was probably owned by someone called Rashid (first name possibly Vijay). It wasn't much to go on, but it was something. That evening, after a quick meal, I settled down with a bottle of wine at the computer in my St Kilda apartment and hunted down an online telephone directory for Tamil Nadu. Searching for 'Rashid' brought up almost a hundred names. I decided to start from the end of the list, took a deep breath, and called the first number.

It was after midnight when I finished the last call. My ear was aching from the pressure of holding the phone there for so long. I poured the last of the wine into my glass and took it out onto the balcony to finish before going to bed. That was that, then. Not one of the Rashids I had spoken to even recognised the name 'Mowbray'. The trail had gone cold. I would write to the solicitor the next day saying I had done all I reasonably could as executor. The last consignment was lost.

Sitting with my feet up on the balustrade, I stared out into the darkness of the bay. Here and there the lights of distant container ships twinkled as they made their way into port from the sea lanes and the ocean beyond. Somewhere out there, in faraway India, deep in a warren of laneways, there would be a great wooden door secured by iron bars and large, rusting padlocks. People walked by every day on their way to work, hardly noticing it. But behind those doors lay an enormous warehouse filled with the contents of a maharajah's palace. I flipped through the thick wad of the inventory typed on flimsy, pale blue paper, and imagined walking through the shadowy silence of that warehouse, like being in a luxurious cathedral. There were seventy-five tables (various). Four hundred and fifty chairs (ditto). One throne (chipped). A thousand silver knives, forks and spoons, plus sundry other cutlery. Ceremonial swords (with scabbards). Fifty chandeliers, embroidered velvet sofas, and carven beds and wardrobes. A fresco on a plaster wall, the whole removed intact, showing a princess and her attendants in a silk pavilion, preparing for a swim. Bolts of fabric, spangled cushions, and ten palanquins covered in gold leaf. A hundred ceremonial saddles of red leather were piled into a pyramid, and towering over all of this, a great canopied howdah, the shape of a castle, for riding on an elephant.

I could picture the scene: already one monsoon's rain had leaked through the roof, setting some of the rich fabrics to rot. The wind had blown in shiny blue-winged beetles, which had started a colony, laying eggs in the painted woodwork that would turn into larvae and bore their way out the following spring. From a broken sewer, rats too had entered the warehouse and started to nest deep in mattresses and the carcasses of sofas, suckling new generations that would soon spread throughout the warehouse and all its exotic contents stacked neatly in long, silent rows.

'Why don't you just sell it all, before it turns to dust?' I could hear Mr Rashid's son plead. 'It's been over a year now. No-one would blame you. No-one would even know …'

'I am waiting to hear from the owner,' says his father in a slow, patient voice that shows they have had this conversation many times before. 'He will come. Mr Mowbray will keep his word. He will come, just you see.'

# VOYAGING

History books tell us they were the first form
of transport, and it makes sense
considering how much water there is in the world.
Here, it is all they ever had, sufficient
for the rough crossings to islands,
the hauling in of the sea's bounty
and those who collected it. In the museum,
there are replicas of these canoes, tightly bound
and woven. The ones we make
are a hazy imitation using long strips of bark
and small stones as ballast.
Ever hopeful, you always add a mast
And sometimes sails, selecting leaves
Or feathery ferns to catch the breeze, reminding me
Of feluccas on the Nile.

Launching them is always difficult, involving
the wetting of boots, drenched sleeves, sinking ships.
It's lucky there is such a store of bark in the undergrowth
so we don't have to watch our fortunes
and all our hopes disappearing before the first rapid.

I remember trying to step ashore at Elephant Island,
falling knee-deep into the lukewarm river,
a baptism of sorts, like walking into the Ganges,
claimed by holy water.

In the end, one of the boats always makes it through
the roughest patches, precarious, fragile as a moth,
but tough, too, in its nonchalant navigation
of submerged rocks, whirlpools, cataracts.
Think of Zarafa, the giraffe that travelled
thousands of miles from the Sahara to Paris,
her luminous eyes and knobbled knees
carted down the Nile, First Cataract,
Second Cataract, all the way to Alexandria.
Her captors expected her to die, the arduous
journey likely to drown her spirit,
but she negotiated water crossings, rivers
the way she approached men's hearts:
fearless and full of love.

ADRIENNE EBERHARD

# YOU DID NOT READ FAULKNER!

SOPHIE CUNNINGHAM TALKS TO LUKE DAVIES ABOUT HIS SHIFTING
BETWEEN FORMS—AND FINDS HIS HEART STILL LIES WITH POETRY

LUKE Davies was born in Sydney in 1962 and published his first poetry collection, *Four Plots for Magnets*, in 1982. It was twelve years before his second poetry collection, *Absolute Event Horizon*, was published. His novels *Candy* (1997), *Isabelle the Navigator* (2000) and *God of Speed* (2008) were all published by Allen & Unwin, as were the poetry collections *Running With Light* (1999) and *Totem* (2004). Both these collections won awards. Davies co-wrote the screenplay of *Candy* with Neil Armfield, and that film was released in 2006. He has been writing film reviews for the *Monthly* since early 2007.

Luke and I first met when I was a publisher at Allen & Unwin and he signed a contract for the novel *Candy*. At the time he was a long-time resident of Bondi Beach, but he has recently moved to Los Angeles. I interviewed him at Hotel Lindrum in Melbourne, when he was here to promote the extraordinary *God of Speed*.

**Sophie Cunningham: What was your first published work? Poetry?**
Luke Davies: *Four Plots for Magnets*, a slim little collector's item now. Four-hundred-copy print run, twenty years old, 1982.

**SC: So it was before a lot of the experiences you write about in** *Candy*.

LD: I always wrote during those bad times, which is actually what's different from the narrator in *Candy*, you don't really have a sense that he has that life, but we brought that back into the film.

In fact, at the *God of Speed* launch [the launcher] Jane [Gleeson-White] said, 'I want to read you a poem from this book of his. This is a poem called "The Death Fires Danced at Night".' I was sitting there shocked. Anyway, she read this poem from *Four Plots for Magnets*, which is clearly influenced by *The Rime of the Ancient Mariner*. It's a four-line poem that goes:

O to be in the Arctic,
with an albatross in the air,
I'd load my blazing crossbow
and tie it to my hair.

I was like, oh God, even back then … that's kind of really 'Luke'.

**SC: And the next publication was also poetry.**

LD: Yes, that was after the nightmare—Angus & Robertson, HarperCollins, 1994, *Absolute Event Horizon*. It was out the other side of all that stuff and rehab.

**SC: When you were growing up, did you have a sense of yourself as being a poet, or did you think of yourself more broadly: as a writer?**

LD: It was a mixture of both. It was both poetry and prose that I became completely immersed in and obsessed with at the age of thirteen.

**SC: Were there particular writers who inspired you, who got you thinking about yourself in this way?**

LD: Yes, there was a moment where the whole universe changed. The initial moment was the discovery of *Cannery Row* in the school bookshelves, and that was the moment where my life changed completely and forever. The memory of that is incredibly vivid. It's like the first adult memory of the me now, here, sitting here with adult consciousness—the sense of continuum from that moment is incredibly satisfying, that this thing happened there that gave me the meaning and direction in my life. What happened after that was very rapid—this moment of reading *Cannery Row*—discovering this world that existed …

**SC: Do you mean the world that the novel created, or the world of writing?**

LD: No, it was really the world of the experience of feeling like a full human being, like an adult as opposed to a child, like somebody who had autonomy as opposed to someone who was told what to do. And practically rather than symbolically that was a turning point from twelve years old [when I was] given these class sets of books, with groovy seventies English teachers and a moral message—they would be American books and there was drugs and stuff in them. They were lame, and at twelve years old I knew they were lame. And at thirteen I discovered Steinbeck with that beautiful lilting sense of humour and the way in which I wasn't being condescended to, and it was like 'oh my God'.

Within three months of that experience I had discovered Faulkner, and it was like Steinbeck was the door that opened, but [with] Faulkner I stepped into this infinite palace and I've been roaming around it ever since. I didn't really get what was going on in Faulkner when I was thirteen, but I knew that I was in an incredible place.

**SC: Was it the language that evoked these feelings in you, even if you didn't get exactly what the words were about?**

LD: Yes, with Faulkner it became language more than with Steinbeck. There was a whole lot of stuff going on there. I don't put Steinbeck in the same category as Faulkner, but my emotional fondness for Steinbeck is unbreakable ... I can always go back to Steinbeck and recognise that his body of work is erratic but some of it is really great, but I love it. I love it. Whereas Faulkner is, by any definition, important and incredible. *As I Lay Dying* was the first one, probably one of the easiest Faulkners to read, over the Christmas holidays at the end of 1975. Anyway, I had a confrontation with an English teacher who asked, 'What did you read [over the holidays]?' and when I said Faulkner he said, 'You did not read Faulkner!'

**SC: As I listen to you talk about these writers I wonder if my asking about your writing of poetry versus your writing of prose is a false distinction. Do you just see all language as poetry?**

LD: I don't think I've yet worked out the answer to that question. As the fantasy continued, as I became fourteen, fifteen, sixteen, I very much saw myself as a poet. I was obsessed with searching for poetry. I loved anything in the English classes that was to do with poetry, which most of the other kids hated.

I was this spacey kid, completely happy spending weekends wandering the State Library of New South Wales and going through the poetry shelves and finding people who were no doubt obscure then and are still obscure now. Lost, forgotten books of Welsh poets or whoever. It was infinite—the possibility for discovery of this stuff excited me constantly. So I thought I was a poet. But as that fantasy continued, in a sense the concept of being able to be a writer was too grand, because as a fourteen-year-old kid you try and start writing what you think is a novel or a short story and you pretty quickly find out how fucking difficult it is to get that first foolscap page written.

SC: Because I've worked with you in the past I've seen early drafts of your work and it seems to me that you write in short pieces that you then pull together. Say, with *Candy*, you wrote it almost as short stories.

LD: Well, it began its life as two or three things, yes.

SC: And with *God of Speed* you wrote quite intense sequences that were quite short and then had a bit of editorial struggle really to get the order right, all that kind of stuff.

LD: And *Isabelle* was, to some extent, episodic too.

SC: Is that a poet thing to do?

LD: I think that's a good point, and I think instinctively that I would tend to agree with it. I'd probably need to think about it a bit. It's probably a bit more complex than that.

SC: It seems to me that in both your prose and your poems, there's a central image that you write out from.

LD: Yes, absolutely. I do find that something that comes to me very clearly—a rock-solid overall image of what this poem is or even of what this chapter is or what this novel is.

SC: *With God of Speed* you seemed from the beginning to have a very strong sense of what you wanted the novel to do.

LD: I knew from day one what it was going to feel like. I didn't know the details and I didn't know what the struggle was going to be like to get there, but I never really wavered. The overall sense of what the book was going to be—what the tonal and emotional texture and temperature were going to be. That's the thing, it's almost like a visionary sort of thing: I know that, so now I've got to get there. You've got to put in the work and build the thing brick by brick.

SC: If you had to pick, is there any form you like writing in most?

LD: If I could get the recognition I felt I deserved for the thing I do that is most important, it's the poetry. Poetry feels like the spine. But I'm also really wary about that thing of precious poetic novels. That can be a barb: oh, he writes novels like a poet.

SC: Talk to me about writing screenplays. Is it a different part of the brain you use when you write them?

LD: It absolutely is. What I find strange is that if you were having a discussion just about poetry and prose, if they were the [only] two things I did—well, there are certain things of me as a poet that make it into my prose, but there aren't really things about me as a prose writer that make it into my poetry. You can't go backwards and stuff something bigger than that into the neck of the bottle. But you would say that these two things are far apart, and yes, maybe they come from different parts of the brain. In fact, I would say poetry comes from the limbic stem in some ways, and prose is these additional layers of thousands of years of civilisation and Western consciousness.

Then you look at screenplay writing and suddenly these two things [poetry and prose] seem unbelievably similar because that's so different.

**SC: Is the difference painful and difficult, or exhilarating and liberating?**

LD: It's exhilarating and liberating. One of the interesting things is that with the poetry and prose—even though you're at your best when you've stepped out of the way of yourself and your ego—the poem or the novel is the end product itself, it is the art object and you are effectively autonomous in creating it … but it's absolutely different with a screenplay. The document that you write is not in any way the art object.

Information matters in the screenplay, clarity of communication matters in a screenplay. Pretty language gets in the way of good screenplays. So screenplay is much more about good story, and in the journey towards creating a screenplay there's less ego involved, and it is for two reasons. One is that it's a bullet point blueprint for a visual medium that's going to belong to someone else, it's going to be someone else's vision ultimately, unless you're a writer-director. The second is that there are so many people involved along the way. You're not in control of every decision, and not just for reasons of the director. Sometimes even budgetry constraints will force you to change a scene. It's practical. You don't have to be so practical in a novel. Blow up a building: sure. Set a scene in Iceland: sure.

**SC: How did you cope with that kind of collaboration?**

LD: The *Candy* experience was a dream in so many ways, partly because Neil Armfield is such an incredibly talented and generous person, with whom a friendship developed parallel to the collaborative professional experience, which went on for five or more years because it was so hard to get a film like that funded. It's also connected to recovering from drug addiction, because I had to learn ways of stepping out of the way of myself, as I said, discarding the ego, which is such a problematic part of ourselves.

**SC: Was Neil your script editor or did you have another script editor?**

LD: No, that was a different sort of situation. Neil was the co-writer and he was the boss, he was the director of the film. We had a script editor, John Collee. He was the guy who wrote *Master and Commander*. John is an incredibly sweet, incredibly smart guy and really commercial, admittedly commercial, not speaking out of school to say that, and he has no ego, it's the most delightful thing. He's got a great understanding of structure, and from the perspective of *Candy* being a dark, difficult, indie film with drugs as its subject matter, the relationship with John was really interesting because he just throws ideas at you, and nine out of ten would be just, like, oh my God, what the fuck is he thinking? And I'd say, 'John, yeah, that doesn't quite work, that's not kind of the direction we're heading.' And he'd say, 'No problems. How about this? How about this?' And one out of ten would be just like, God, this is brilliant, this is so insightful, he has understood what we need to do to get ourselves out of this hole or this hole.

SC: **Do you think that emphasis on narrative is going to be useful to your prose in the future?**

LD: Absolutely. I had a vivid sensation of how incredible it was, this learning curve, this opportunity. This guy [Armfield] has been doing beautiful theatre for thirty years. He understands character and economy like I never have. My own screenplay, left to my own devices, would not have been as good.

SC: **What screenplays are you working on at the moment?**

LD: I got accepted into this AFC program called IndiVision—as writer-director. I love what I do as a poet, novelist and hopefully screenwriter, but another thing since the age of fourteen, fifteen, that I've fantasised about, is I've always wanted to make movies.

SC: **As in direct movies or produce them?**

LD: No, direct. Two or three years after the Steinbeck moment I had the Werner Herzog moment with *Aguirre, the Wrath of God*. So I applied for this program and I got it, and if all works out I'm going to be making this low-budget Australian thriller that I wrote about an eleven-year-old boy and his seven-year-old sister being chased through the bush by the man who has just killed their father. I have written this really deliberately kind of L-plates film. [And] I've also written this … supposedly sci-fi film, [though] really it's just a film about male friendship, which I've wanted to explore in a particular way. It's about all sorts of things: it's about robots and cops and what makes us human.

SC: **Is the desire to direct related to actually having a bit more control over what you called the art object, which as a screenplay writer you don't have?**

LD: Yes, and as a novelist you kind of have, and certainly as a poet you have. Everyone leaves you alone as a poet! It's absolutely connected to that. I loved the experience of *Candy* and I loved the end result but it's not my end result, and having certain kinds of controlling tendencies within, I want to have the experience of sinking or swimming on my own overarching vision: this music, or that camera angle or that way of expressing that emotional moment. It's all about the same thing, though, it's all about the desire to create the same spine-tingling moment for the audience member or reader who is receptive, in the way that I have been, to those experiences—those experiences that make life worth living. That experience of being fully alive is … sometimes it's [caused by] other moments—sex, affection, family, companionship—but so often it's that moment of artistic arrest: this extraordinary moment of deep gratitude. And I feel that really strongly still, eighteen years down the track from drugs, this very conscious striving to live in the present more fully. Those years of addiction were so horrendously not *that*.

SC: Was the drug addiction about avoiding the present? Is that too simple?
LD: Yes, it is probably too simple but it's a good summary; [though] in some ways the chase for the drug moment was an attempt to eternalise the present. But it was a Faustian bargain. They never work, if you read the literature.

SC: Another shift in your work is that since *Candy* you've more clearly stepped into other people's stories. Was that a relief? That shift away from semi-autobiograhical writing? Or was it difficult to move out of your own experience?
LD: It was neither a relief nor … well, 'difficult' is too harsh a word, but I've a conscious sense that it's a struggle to move into that territory [but] it is absolutely necessary … the gaze has to turn outwards. Things can be investigated in much more exciting ways if you can begin to turn the gaze outwards.

SC: You told me earlier that you've begun a meditation practice. What kind of monasteries have you been going to?
LD: In the last twelve months I've been to two Benedictine ones, one outside Sydney, one in the desert outside Los Angeles.

SC: You're going back to your Catholic roots?
LD: Sort of. Not really. I'm exploring solitude and ritual [but] whatever monastery is available, I'll go happily. One Camoldoni, it's pretty obscure, sort of Benedictine; and one Buddhist in the boondocks of Canada, it's called the Birken Forest Monastery, and the nearest town is a town called Kamloops in British Columbia, it's about six hours by car north-east of Vancouver. It is seriously in the middle of nowhere, and very ascetic—it was the most ascetic of my four experiences in terms of the vow of silence being close to complete and no solid foods after the 11 a.m. meal and it was really intense.

After all these years, [it was] time to enter into the utter insanity of the mind in cascading freefall—how fucking difficult that is. [I feel like] a baby at the beginning of this mountain …

SC: At least you can see the mountain.
LD: Yes.

SC: **To get back to your interest in direction and your desire for more control—can one ever control a film?**

LD: Yes, there's a lot of fear surrounding that: what do I think I'm doing, I've never worked with actors and what will that be like? I don't know, I'm sure that's a journey in itself.

SC: **Are you working on poetry or prose at the moment? Do you have a novel project?**

LD: I am going through the experience of poetry pouring out obsessively. I know that a lot of people say poetry is a young man's thing … [but] I don't want to feel my strength waning. I fret about that because it's the most important thing within me, and suddenly in my mid forties I've got this feeling of 'Oh, this is good, it is [still] happening.'

Anyway, I've almost finished my next book and that's a really exciting feeling. It's a very clear body of work that began when the *Totem* drawbridge shut. It's coherent, it's been four years, and I've just begun to write a few poems that don't belong to that any more, so [maybe] there's a future book.

SC: **When you say you think the last three or four poems might sit somewhere else, is that because a poetry book or a cycle tends to come out of a particular set of experiences or a particular exploration, or is it about getting to a different technical place?**

LD: It's all of those things. It's a really lovely sense of strength. It definitely comes out of a particular set of experiences. *Totem* was clearly and consciously a paean to love in many, many forms; it was a sort of exploration of exuberance and gratitude and sexuality. There was a whole lot of stuff going on in *Totem* that was coherently controlled. This new book comes out of a darker place. You could say that it's an exploration of unease. It's like you create the ocean and you know you've got to get to the other shore, so there's some technical stuff going on there too. It's like it has a coherent form that's completely different from *Totem* because I wanted and needed to do something completely different from *Totem*. They're psalms, basically, it's psalmodic, and it's not as tightly controlled as *Totem*. It's like they're almost prose paragraphs some of them, it's like they follow the breath and it's left-justified … there's the beginning of your line, it might be one line, it might take up four lines, but I'm not trying to rhyme and scan and stuff like that.

SC: **Is following the breath related to meditation?**

LD: Oh yes, and yoga as well. It's just the most important realisation, and it's a return to some pretty primal roots because I've been thinking a lot about the origins of prehistory and breath and storytelling and ways of remembering poetry when it was oral. But that's another story.

**SC: So what are you doing with prose at the moment?**

LD: For the first time since Allen & Unwin said yes to the book of Howard Hughes [now *God of Speed*], which then got superseded by *Isabelle*, for the first time, in other words, in twelve or thirteen years, I have no obligations and it's a great feeling. I haven't yet started writing the new thing, but there are two different things. Some time in the next month or two that first day is going to come where I open a blank page and it's going to be, okay, I'm just going to write something here and see where this thing goes.

One [idea] is new, pristine, and it's an opportunity to go to different places than I have before. It got really ugly with Howard Hughes in the middle … when I got into serious research, I hit a point where it was like, what the fuck are you doing here, Luke? This man is horrible in so many ways. And it was difficult.

**SC: Were you having to commit to projects because you were trying to make a living as a writer?**

LD: No. There was a naiveté then for which I have a great nostalgia now.

**SC: You thought you could knock off Howard in a year or so and be done with him?**

LD: All that stuff, yes. Really it was all such extraordinary icing in a kind of … what if I could write a novel? What if I could make a living?

**SC: So how long did Howard take?**

LD: The light bulb moment where I thought: I'm going to write this, I can't quite pin it down. It was either late '93 or sometime in '94 that I wrote the first two chapters of Howard Hughes. One of them was the transcendental moment with connectedness with the god figure [while] masturbating in the cockpit when hurtling towards the ocean at breakneck speed. The other one was a strange mixture of three things which are now spread through the novel in different ways: the bad plane crash, Beverly Hills 1946; the day of the flight that occurs the night before the moment in which the book is now set, in 1973; and the round-the-world record, 1938. These things were all mixed in together and the masturbation scene was connected to that but I didn't [have the] facts. The actual fact was that there were three other guys in that plane and it didn't make sense to set that [scene] there. But that's thirteen years or possibly fourteen years since the first chapter—with many breaks and interruptions, which I think were all absolutely necessary.

In the middle years with Howard Hughes I was experiencing not only the ugliness but the practical difficulty of having written myself into a mess where it might have been sensible to think about giving up [but] I clung to his voice. I just had this determination to get it right. And so I finally [began] the journey with [my editor] Alice Truax where the book found its necessary form and leanness.

[Alice said to me:] 'I've identified this, these are the types of writing you do, these are the pulses running through the book, this is when you've got ecstatic, you're king of the world, you're a god, flight. Here's this dysfunctional, ugly, sexual blackness. Here's some drug addiction stuff. There's this. There's that.' She'd divided it all into codes to [show me] the structure. [Then she said,] 'This clashes with this, this shouldn't butt up against this.' Unbelievably practical American stuff. It was really great.

SC: **What's it like living in LA? It's strange that you should live there after you have finished Howard Hughes, because in some ways he is such an American character. How does it impact on your sense of yourself as a writer?**

LD: I love it, it's a gentle city as well and there are great people there, and there are also lunatics there—it's a city of such contrast. [After a recent relationship break-up] it was like, okay, fuck it, I can be wherever I want. Life in Sydney is packed in boxes and I think I'm going to leave it that way at the moment. Definitely part of it was getting an agent. Practical reasons. I want to sell scripts, I want to make some money. I want some breathing-space money.

But beyond those practical things this other thing has arisen—I'm still writing my poetry and my prose and [being in LA] is really affecting it. Being in overwhelming and always foreign circumstances is definitely affecting my poetry. It's been a surge. I went over [to LA] with all these very methodical, practical plans, but then, beyond the plans [the move] sparked off all this other creative activity, which is very pleasing. This kind of exile, it's an appropriate state to be in because it's time for a change and it's appropriate to be experiencing great difficulty in moving out of the comfort zone into the discomfort zone.

# TWO CIRCLES OF LOVE

## Circle 1

She longs to go back to the trapeze
of legs and arms—the visits in his
voice—how he configured her body
to the embrace of his words. Go back

to first love, when she was next to him
moving in time with his shadow
through the alleys of his sight
to all the lost countries inside him.

She still sleeps next to his name
knuckled against her thigh.
His room still locked in her life.

When her voice kneeled near his bed
he was fine exotic silk
and the curtains crossed out the light.

She cries—no tears on her face—
she is crying inside her body;
his name, the first page of her life.

## Circle 2
*Pas de Deux*

The weightlifter night holds them together.
Mario, streetwise, lithe as a golfer; Shani,
eighteen—her name smudged on his pillow.
She tries to empty her eyes but his body
is so beautiful its shape spills on her hands.

They touch a pleasure older than Africa
and she is a glove enclosing his whole life—
the jewels of his semen white as ferns in the frost,
then after sex, lost countries of sleep.

For so many nights they watched the moon's spinnaker
turn on the night's hinge. She became pregnant
and names grow inside her, Angello, Lucretia, Giovanni.
When they strolled together a cloud's glide covered them
and the walked-under moon traced their shapes
on the sidewalk—'Mario! Your shadow next to me
moves on a carpet your voice makes and the night sings.'

Summer sleeps on the harbour and just after dawn,
when the sun is a huge apricot, her fingers wake
to the drift of his skin. They are not married or partnered.
Leaving him she walks home past the wind's maul—
she is graceful as a yacht, its sails
curving their tongue round the wind—
her absence remains a warm shape under him.

Over time love fades until he becomes nameless,
his world no bigger than a finger. He moves to Italy,
draws a circle round that part of his life.
She remembers how the wind opened his door
and walked in, how daylight blew across
the carpet—and his shadow would touch her—
his name asleep on her hands.

Now the room is locked and her life weeps.

JOHN MILLETT

# TRACES

the waves
    lick indentations scratched in sand—
        her burred letters

the waves
    leave ruins where sandcastles stood
        scour foundations

        the anemone hairs on his arms
          blow southerly
          to the north

        he scribes letters on her back,
          invisible tattoos
                a bluebottle's shadow
                smoke rings on carnival night
      *w  a  n  t   t o ...?*

        on her skin salty prisms fratch

    before dusk they pull shirts over swimmers
        the linen tough as history

        she whispers mirror writing into a bottle—
        oh moon, will you read her postcard?

                                        lightning flashes codes
                                        before thunder


she, perfumed
rises and goes to his garden—
        its beer
        its green neon moon

                        the closer she …
                        the faster he …

                                if she ebbed,
                                how high would the tide rise?

                                        underwater, invisible
                                        gut secures the hook
                                        to the line.


JULIE CHEVALIER

# WASTELANDS OF THE CROWN

NOVELIST AND FORMER PASTORALIST **JIM MORGAN** EXPLORES THE
PIONEERING LIVES OF TWO ANCESTORS

… the British nation may be an example to the whole world for their wisdom, care,
and justice in planting colonies; their caution in stocking the provinces with people
of sober lives and conversations from this mother kingdom …

— Jonathan Swift, *Gulliver's Travels*

I WAS born in Adelaide in 1932 and when I was four they removed my tonsils
and circumcised me for good measure, the latter without telling me. Arriving at
the age of twelve, hyperactive, redheaded, I was invited to join the managing
director of the Mutooroo Pastoral Company on his monthly inspection of the
runs, three properties covering 3000 square miles of the north-east of South
Australia, from Yunta to Broken Hill up on the NSW border and west to Lake
Frome—or thereabouts. I went up by train, changing at Terowie to the Silverton
narrow gauge, swaying and rattling through the night to arrive at Cockburn in

the early hours, having hung over the rails of the observation platform of the last carriage for an hour, counting kangaroos and observing stations and sidings: Paratoo, Yunta, Manna Hill, Mingary and at last Cockburn. W.S. Findlay was there to meet us in his large American car and take us to breakfast at the outstation Lake Dismal, with its overseer whose nerves were shredded by responsibility and a wife who kept back the tide of dust blowing in from moving stock. This was my introduction to the organisation of which I was to be managing director twenty-five years later.

Everyone has two grandfathers, no more no less, not necessarily alive and kicking, but somewhere in the background. What is unusual about mine is that they not only knew each other as children, but also lived next door to each other and, despite a difference in temperament like a ditch if not a chasm between them, were best mates. Grandfathers are one thing, great-grandfathers another—we each have four of them and must think hard to be able to name them all.

Two of my great-grandfathers come readily to mind: William Morgan and Peter Waite. The former was a wholesale grocer and for a while premier of South Australia, the latter was possibly Australia's outstanding sheep farmer of the nineteenth century. Both were immigrants from Britain. One came from Bedfordshire, one from Fife, and both young men grew up breathing in the fumes of industrial revolution and religious dissent and received enough education to hold their own in the public arena. Both came to have houses that were dignified by rooms described as libraries. According to my father, 'William Morgan throughout was an avid reader and a buyer of books', whereas 'Peter Waite seldom used the library, nor did anyone else', though these contrasting judgements may possess some bias by descent.

Aged twelve, for a week, I sat in the back of Mr Findlay's Pontiac, ready to leap out and open the gates, mainly so-called 'Waite' gates, a clever variation with an adjustable latch of the basic cockie's wire gate. In 1944 the runs were in the grip of drought and the bush looked black. The inspection took a week, two nights at each homestead: Mulyungarie, Mutooroo and Lilydale, each house more or less seventy miles from the next with many stops in between at boundary riders' huts. In those days the huts were all inhabited, even during the Second World War; sometimes by one man, usually past his prime or in the grip of alcoholism; sometimes by two, a younger and an older, whose days would be spent maintaining waters, inspecting stock and fencing, and fetching wood and water for their own survival. The buildings were spaced every hour or so of driving, and ranged from solid stone buildings with slate floors to one room of corrugated iron with an earth floor, tricked out with wooden shelves lined with pages pinked from the *Women's Weekly*. There would be johnnie cakes or jam tart baked in anticipation of the visit, the word of our arrival having gone out over the station telephone line, an improvement carried out in 1910 by the same W.S. Findlay soon after he joined the company, despite fears that ready communication would tempt employees to talk rather than do their job.

The sheep farmer had several daughters, two of whom were known to us children as 'the Aunts' though in fact they were great-aunts. Though both born in South Australia, they kept a Scottish way of speaking about 'gals' and the game of 'goff'. They ate 'cheecken' in the 'keetchen' and declared certain things 'eeveel': pies and pasties, tomato sauce, bananas, for instance. Both were well read and could dominate a meeting in which they were the only women, with a natural authority, not just bullying; neither married, though there were opportunities, so it is said. They had much to do with our family in my childhood, especially with my father whom they had given £500 a decade before my birth to go to England and marry my mother who was languishing there, her mother disapproving of penniless colonials.

Throughout my childhood, there was a daily telephone conversation with my father, who, on coming home from his chambers, would sit at the crouching black instrument of the time at the foot of the stairs beneath the rise of the upper flight, somewhat dark, but in a way private, although his resounding Morgan voice could be heard upwards and abroad from this point that was almost central to the large house's being. I can't quite remember who rang whom; I think it depended somewhat on which party had something to communicate, considered urgent. In these overheard conversations concerning the events of the day, large and small, there would be long silences at my father's end interspersed by his habitual uttering of a drawn-out 'Yersss' and bursts of laughter.

My grandfather, James Waite, the sheep farmer's elder son, worked all his life in England as a consulting engineer and only came back to South Australia on his wife's death, travelling by merchant ship in a convoy towards the close of the war, so that I knew him but never knew my other grandfather, Ranembe Morgan, or either of their fathers, the two great-grandfathers in question. Ranembe was a cheerful teller of tales to all and sundry, and much of what I know about William Morgan comes from him, including the story of how his father, the young immigrant, was saved from a certain death at the hands of the warlike Murray Bend mob, who were inclined to deal with overlanding colonials in a summary fashion, by another Aborigine named Ranembe who swam him across the Murray on his back. So that my grandfather, the first of five subsequent generations, was named after him and was always known as 'Ran'. A Tasmanian literary lady, Cassandra Pybus, to whom I told the story at a Freud conference in the seaside town of Lorne, said it was an unforgivable piece of appropriation.

The passage of time and the whims of family are strangely selective when it comes to deciding what shall be recorded and remembered from generation to generation. 'Both families appear to have been destroyers,' my father writes in the foreword to his family history, describing how my grandfather Ranembe Morgan, William Morgan's son, was 'assigned the task of sorting and disposing of his father's papers'. Thus portraits of the two men, friends and neighbours, depend almost entirely on formal accounts of their careers that give little flavour and lack the detail that can light up a life for posterity.

At first, all went well for William Morgan: a trip to the Victorian goldfields with some success, then purchase with the proceeds plus a small inheritance of the business of wholesale grocer in Hindley Street, which never ceased to thrive. He married and had children and became engaged with the community in a way that Peter Waite never was: Waite's engagement was with sheep and the saltbush plains. In contrast Morgan had the life of the city: family, business and public. He seemed to have all that was required to be not only the 'coming man', as his wife once described him, but also the man of the hour. In 1867 he was persuaded to stand for the Legislative Council and a committee of thirty-one supporters was formed to secure his return, including four members of the upper house, five of the lower, eight justices of the peace and one doctor. On 20 July 1867 the *Weekly Mail* published a formal request by a round dozen gentlemen that William Morgan Esq. JP would allow himself to be nominated 'feeling assured that, from your long experience and knowledge of what tends to our best interests, you would ably represent the Colony', pledging themselves to use their best exertions to secure his return, this modest backing compared with that of a hundred supporters listed for Emanuel Solomon in the very next column of the same newspaper. In his published acceptance, Morgan pleads that, given the lengthened period of ten-year terms in the Legislative Council, general character means more than expression of opinion on topics of the day, confining his remarks to support for borrowing reasonable amounts of English capital for 'reproductive' works and those calculated to open up the resources of the province, his regret for the temporary distress among the working classes, his support for unfettered trade with the Riverina district, and his opposition to 'any impost or restriction calculated to fetter or embarrass the development of the resources of our pastoral, mineral or agricultural interests'—in other words, free trade.

A couple of days later, a meeting was held at the new Town Hall for the purpose of considering who were the most fit and proper persons to represent the province in the Legislative Council. Question and answer was the order of the evening rather than formal speeches. It seems the meeting had been called by those in favour of increased protection, and candidates gave their views on that subject and that of the preferential treatment of squatters. By the time William Morgan spoke, the audience was inclined to uproar and the report in the *Weekly Mail* later referred to 'drunken behaviour of lawyers' clerks'.

Morgan opened his remarks using the classic mode of self-deprecation, saying that he was 'not much up to that kind of thing' and that he hoped they would hear him out patiently. He went on to say: that 'want of work' was the most important issue; that immigration should be discontinued for a year and Sutherland's Act repealed; that protection in its existing form was unfair and only supported by men who derived personal profit from it; that northern squatters in dry country should hold land at a peppercorn rent rather than leave it unoccupied (Peter Waite would have approved of this sentiment); that prospectors should have mining leases for nothing, providing they worked them—'that principle had been found to act well in Chili [*sic*]'.

Questions and answers followed in which candidate Skelton, a man with some antipathy towards Morgan, played a leading part. He asked whether someone establishing a 'manufactory' should be granted a bonus, to which Morgan replied that great care should be taken. Candidate Raphael then asked whether Morgan was a squatter. Morgan told Raphael he had no more right to ask this question than he had to ask Raphael if he lent money at 25 per cent. A Dr Spicer moved that Mr Morgan 'should not be heard until he answers the question whether or not he is a squatter'. Morgan refused to answer, saying it was his private business. A Mr Bean took the chair, asking Morgan to answer the question, but there came a chorus of 'He's gone, he's not here.' At this point the gaslights almost went out. The meeting ended with a farcical wrangle about the gas being turned down when the mayor had left the building, over whether this was deliberate or a coincidental fault.

It was not a promising start to a political career. But William Morgan's candidature must subsequently have been approved, for he stood and was elected second in the poll, well behind Crozier but ahead of Solomon, all three taking up their seats later that year in the Legislative Council.

At first all went well. In 1865 William Morgan was one of the eleven founders of the Bank of Adelaide, and in 1867, at the age of thirty-eight, he was elected to the Adelaide Club in his rise from Bedfordshire farm boy to colonial gentleman. He became a partner in wheat broking firm Morgan Connor & Glyde and was a local director of the AMP Society. But it was probably about this time that he met the man who was to be his nemesis, John Higginson, and became involved in the supply of flour to the French penal colony New Caledonia. New Caledonia looms large in his life from about 1870 onwards. On the one hand there was his continued prosperity as merchant, a calling that was never to fail him. Would that he had stuck to this business, which from 1870 became exclusively wholesale and operated from a building in Currie Street on a block of freehold land he had bought some time earlier, a site later occupied by the Adelaide Steamship Company.

Compared with South Australia, New Caledonia with its Melanesian population leavened with a dash of Polynesian, a French possession since 1853, must have seemed to the Bedfordshire man quite exotic and a suitable conduit for the entrepreneurial side of his character. Nevertheless, it is hard to reconcile a man in his prime, his mid forties, a member of the legislative council of a thriving new political entity, popular, successful in his local business of merchant and shipping agent, a family man with a fine house pullulating with business associates and distinguished visitors should go to another house in another community, even more fledgling and quite foreign. Having come to South Australia aged nineteen, his success there was not enough. He looked for another challenge, somewhere more exotic—South Australia, despite its natural and even man-made charms, was hardly that, unlike Grande Terre of New Caledonia with its contrasting mix of subtropical east coast and largely Kanak population and the bleaker west coast of gum trees and cattle country worked by Caldoches—settlers of European descent.

Once in New Caledonia William Morgan was treated as a person of some importance by the governor and allotted three *assignés*—convicts released on good behaviour to work outside the penitentiary—one was his valet, one his cook and the role of the third I have forgotten if I ever knew it. Their stories have been passed down by Ranembe, a vivid raconteur: the valet who shaved William each morning had cut the throat of a customer who displeased him back in France; the cook, worse still, had surprised his wife and her lover in the act, killed the man, cut out his heart, cooked it and made the wife eat it.

Morgan and John Higginson built a sugar refinery with a great castellated brick chimney that still stands lonely in a field, some distance from the town. There was another partner, a New Zealander whom Morgan did not like, but in the end relationships did not affect the outcome, as grasshoppers demolished the young shoots. There were other expeditions further afield to the north of Grande Terre, by ship along the Diahot River, deep and navigable, by whose side lay the Fern Hill gold mine and not so far away the diggings for copper at Balade.

To the end of his life William Morgan remained obsessed by copper, like some sickness of the mind that valued above all that which could be dug out of the ground. At home in Adelaide he continued to thrive in business and politics. He became premier and provided a period of stability when all the institutions as we know them on North Terrace—library, museum, art gallery, university—came into being. A town was named after him on the bend of the Murray. He retired from office on the grounds of pressure of business affairs, went back to England for the first time in an attempt to resuscitate his finances and died there of pernicious anaemia, leaving his widow and children unexpectedly penniless. The estate of Netherby, where the Morgans had lived next door to Urrbrae, the home of Peter Waite, my other South Australian great-grandfather, was sold up.

Meanwhile Waite prospered and continued to inspect and manage 11,500 square miles of northern South Australia with his entrepreneurial partner, Thomas Elder, in two separate ventures, but moved, after fifteen years, from the bush to town. The nature of this challenge, over an area almost half that of Scotland, perhaps needs some explanation.

Pastoralism takes place mainly in marginal areas where cultivation, usually through lack of rainfall, is not possible. Indigenous people live off the land in a direct manner, hunting and foraging. But colonists can only make the land work through the intermediary of a grazing domestic animal that produces either meat or wool for sale.

They enclosed land with walls or fences and introduced machinery and water reticulation, which enabled vast areas of wasteland to be stocked with little permanent labour. They worked out that cattle were bulky to transport, slow to breed up, expensive to fence in and liable to go bush. But above all, cattle's only product was meat, possessing a limited shelf life. Sheep, on the other hand, enabled those with capital and ingenuity to make huge areas of wasteland productive. Wool could be cut from the sheep's back, scoured and pressed in bales for transport to the markets of Europe, even years later.

What happened to the indigenous people on Thomas Elder and Peter Waite's outback runs? On Mutooroo it was said that there was no permanent surface water until the company put it there, so it was only in a good season that Aborigines came across from the Menindee Lakes. That may be true, as they do not play much part in the legends of the company. Not so in the Beltana Pastoral

Company in the lee of the Flinders Ranges, its watercourse country in the far north. The offical history of the Beltana Pastoral Company Limited tells how there was always a camp near the homestead from which the indigenous people went about their traditional activities, their maintenance subsidised to some extent by government rations; how Cordillo employed male and female Aborigines as shepherds and women worked on the famous wool scour with white stockmen until the chiacking got quite out of hand. There was a succession of legendary indigenous stockmen throughout the Beltana's history down to my day as a director in the late 1960s: Murtee Johnnie, Bunny Treloar and many more.

How was it that my great-grandfather, a young man in his mid twenties, could so rapidly and with such sure touch conceive and implement the infrastructure of extended sheep farming in the arid zone within the space of a few years with no previous experience? He had grown up on a farm in Fife of 320 acres. It was not the biggest in the district parish of Auchterderran, but a viable size. A mild climate allowed the cultivation of three-quarters of its acreage. Breeding herds or flocks were rare and in 1875 the number of sheep run in the whole of Fife was 70,000, compared with 260,000 on the Paratoo runs in the same year. Waite was the facilitator, the man who made the grandiose schemes viable. Elder was the visionary, importing camels from India complete with attendant 'Afghans' as early as 1862.

From the beginning Elder fostered his interests and those of his 'sheep farmers' by his election to the Legislative Council. But drought struck in the mid 1860s with huge losses, reputed to be 100,000, on his northern runs. That was when Waite made an impressive appearance before a parliamentary committee on the drought and in 1869, when Elder visited Europe, he made Waite 'Superintendent of his Northern Runs', which included Beltana, Umberatana and Lake Hope.

Waite was not the first man to build a fence but he was the first to do so to manage stock successfully on thousands of square miles. Until he arrived on the pastoral scene, flocks were shepherded and yarded overnight to prevent them wandering and falling prey to wild dogs. Waters were mainly small holes scooped out in creek beds or where a local catchment lent itself to their creation.

His much quoted dictum was 'big dams and small paddocks'. But there was a chasm between a phrase thrown off and its execution—to take a thousand square miles and cut it up with fences in a rational manner to produce more than a hundred paddocks, each paddock with water, either with access to a trough fed by a tank or by direct access to a dam, could not have happened overnight. At first, waters had to be developed where there was some possibility of supply, where there was a well or one could be dug. To some extent the government led the way, sinking a chain of such wells in the mid 1860s from Burra through the original north-eastern runs to provide a stock route for teamsters and drovers from the country on the Darling to Adelaide purveyors and markets until such time as the Adelaide–Broken Hill railway line was completed in 1887 under the aegis of Waite's next-door neighbour, Premier William Morgan. This chain of wells was known as the Peg Line; the wells were equipped with a steam pump or horse works to pump water into the great square tanks made of stone with lime mortar, walls feet thick, capacity perhaps 25,000 gallons. Four-inch cast-iron outlets ran water into giant troughs one hundred yards long for travelling stock. Those at the Gorge and Duffields still exist on the Mutooroo runs and are not to be forgotten by anyone who has cleaned them out.

All this needed great organisation where means of communication were sparse or non-existent—and men, capital and foresight. Fortunately workers had flooded into South Australia as the boom in copper boosted employment. From 1870 the overland telegraph established an instant connection between Adelaide and townships such as Burra and Beltana. From the outset Waite realised that tenure unsupported by capital was useless, that placement of stock depended on feed and water and that methods of control were dependent on labour.

Waite began developing the runs with careful planning and baffling speed. Early in the piece, not long after his appearance before the parliamentary inquiry following the drought, Waite purchased a shipload—265 tons—of wire from England, and fencing contractors were engaged to erect minimal but effective fences for sheep. There is some doubt whether the wire was black soft eight-gauge wire or the wire that still hangs about Mutooroo and Lilydale, sometimes known as Waite wire, a steely wire that being plaited cannot be tied with an ordinary fencing knot but must be spliced.

One of the first tasks would have been to build a fence enclosing an area about an existing water so that no part of the enclosed area was further than five miles from the watering point, as that was as far as lambing ewes could be expected to walk out and back to drink at least once a day. If it were a boundary fence, netting would have been used against dogs (and rabbits after 1880), a so-called vermin-proof fence, 3'8" high with netting, one plain wire and two barbs, according to Peter Waite—somewhat low by modern standards.

Waite lived on for twenty-five years after his partner, Thomas Elder, died, throughout that period remaining chairman of Elder Smith & Co Ltd, managing director of the Beltana Pastoral Company Ltd and a director of the Mutooroo Pastoral Company Ltd.

In 1913 his second son David, who had taken on the title of Inspector of Runs, disappeared at sea, perhaps mentally affected by a fall from a horse; the daughters having been consulted, Peter Waite wrote to the premier of South Australia, the Hon. A.H. Peake, regarding his intention to make over to the University of Adelaide his house, Urrbrae, and more than 200 acres to be used for agricultural and kindred studies. Later he bought and transferred another 163 acres to the university along with £60,000. On his death in 1922 the endowment became a reality and the Waite Institute instrumental in changing the face of huge areas of Australia through its research and development of trace elements and wheat varieties.

## LIFT

I check the drift
of a word to relieve
the weight of losing it

and, suddenly,
the worn dictionary
seems so heavy,
like a rock that turns
out to be ore—

the odd stratified word
making a comeback, cocky
among the dumped.

Nearby, contractors
bulldozing a lake of clay
call subterranean boulders
'floaters' as they surface
and, definitively, stay.

# DANDELIONS

*The sun never sets on the empire of the dandelion*
—Alfred Crosby

Sunbursts on a late
afternoon lawn, where gin might be served;
or they're back between cracks
like natural borders in the concrete
and won't be extracted, the tap
roots fattening on a mixture
of blind persistence
and victory. Ever thus—
seeds airborne, arriving like parachutes
since the Cretaceous, light
of a hundred million
of the Earth's solar revolutions
inspiring them, filament
bright. High time
—now children blow off seeds—
their advance was arrested,
the gardener thinks, annually
defeated, his new shed, the armoury,
his insult, to call them a weed.

ANDREW SANT

# GIVE

And these nodes that start to gnarl my fingers?
—Vivian Smith, 'The Return'

My small child, smooth, himself
distinguished only by dimples,
likes to place his fingertip
in pouches crept up on me,
despite me,
at knuckles and elbows. *Buttons,*
he says, and giggles
at these points of slackness, balloons
gone airless, the perished elastic
of a hand-me-down he never dreams
he'll wear, though once, it's true,
I encompassed him
snug as a bug before he shucked me off.
Now I let him try each joint, obedient
as a puppet, back and forth—when bent,
as sleek as anyone's,
but only straighten, and stiffen,
and there's the accommodation, ring upon ring,
the looser, lesser fit
between inside and out.

## LAMB

Seems to leap at some unseen will
surprising herself, ad libitum,
a sneeze, a seizure in motion, a tic
ecstatic, mini-mystic, pure impulse, hauled up
and dropped by magic, now limp as a hanky,
now all spring and muscle. Three weeks
and the ground, great fontanelle, still hasn't set
under her feet, too sweet to call cloven,
they are dolls' feet, tottering, abridged.
Sniffing us out by the toes, how we do this
upright and hard thing, she's nibbling
grass, leaf and plastic, everything grist
to a new soul-mill, runs rings around
small boy on trampoline, three years, who notes
twin marks on her neck where the eagle grabbed
and lost her to life, on her head twin buds
that will one day be all the horns
she has.

TRACY RYAN

# THE CHINESE SUBMARINE

TIM RICHARDS

NOTHING was fixed. Making that discovery drew the fifteen-year-old Carl to history. If you believed the British had prior knowledge of the assault on Pearl Harbour, were they right to allow the attack that would drag America into the war? Depending on how you chose to look at it, a fine line separated Winston the Hero from Churchill the Monster. And no matter how thoroughly you interrogated the facts, or how persuasively you argued a case, the truths you arrived at would always be provisional and subject to the discovery of new evidence and ways of seeing that would cast events in a different light.

Two decades on, historian Carl sees most of his youthful attitudes as symptomatic of clinical depression. Euphoria was to be feared as a state of mind that invited subversion.

The first rug-pull came when the eleven-year-old made his debut for Koorook Under Sixteens. Unable to produce a birth certificate, he'd worn the number 34 jersey belonging to the player officially registered as Neil Stevens. Carl was told to answer only to that name.

As Neil Stevens, he took the opposition apart, ghosting through packs, riding bumps, and always getting to where the ball fell. Early in the last quarter, with the game still in the balance, he stood under a high ball, and caught it a half-second before a fist smacked his ear. Instead of waiting for the penalty, he took off into the open, and weighed his options before making a dash for goal. As his third bounce took him within thirty meters, Carl heard his father on the boundary screaming, 'Kick it!' and, after slotting his fourth major, he turned to see Jack shouting, 'You little beauty!'

Carl Johanssen might have been wearing a borrowed jumper and boots, but he had something that couldn't be taken away: his dad's praise.

After the match, the coach shook his head. The young champ had drawn too much attention to himself. They'd better pray that Neil Stevens never came back from Bendigo.

Carl's head and feet were sore, but smiling team-mates recognised him with pats on the back, and it didn't matter that some called him Neil. He was dangerously happy. The boy tried to conceal this joy as he crossed the boundary to where his dad sat behind the wheel of the red ute.

Something had changed. The old man wanted to speak, but the words wouldn't come. Carl was embarrassed to see him so unsure of himself. Suddenly, big Jack's head jerked twice, and he clutched at his chest. Carl promised to get someone, but Jack grabbed his wrist and gasped, 'No time.'

In truth, Carl remembered little of what followed, certainly not how he moved Jack's huge frame across the seat to take the wheel. Fearing the ute would stall, he gunned two stop signs and nearly side-swiped a woman reversing from an angled park in Scott Street. At the clinic, the South African doctor did everything to resuscitate Jack, but getting him out of the vehicle ate up crucial time, and Carl's father was pronounced dead ten minutes before the ambulance arrived from Echuca.

Short of anything else to say, the doctor told him he'd been brave, and that his grandpa was a huge man. Corrected by the boy, the doctor asked how old his dad was. Carl said seventy, but he wasn't sure.

'I bet you loved him,' the doctor said.

All of 140 kilograms when his heart gave out, Jack Johanssen was huge in Carl's memory. Though he spoke little, his dad made words count, and Carl never saw two people so obsessed with each other as his parents were. Rarely leaving home, his mother channelled her energy into thinking of ways to please big Jack. Carl had always been conscious of his dad's age, and the likelihood that he could die any day. Whenever Jack left to oversee deliveries at the pub, or to visit mates in Bendigo or Echuca, the child ran to his room, buried his head under a pillow and imagined how impossible life would be if his dad didn't come back. His mum had never worked, and, having neither family nor friends, they'd be doomed. If she didn't find someone to remarry, Carl would be taken away, and how could she ever love someone the way she loved his dad?

It wasn't uncommon for Carl's parents to make love in the living room while he read a book or watched television nearby. This was so typical that he wouldn't have thought to mention it to friends at school. There, he was Barney, named after the ice-cream icon Barney Banana. This for having been born in Queensland, even though his Victorian parents returned when Carl was three.

He had just one strong memory of Queensland, where they'd lived in Kingaroy around the time local member Joh Bjelke-Petersen first became premier. They were standing in the street beside the truck Jack drove. His dad picked him up and held him high above his head, and Carl remembered thinking that if his dad could hold him there long enough, he'd see everything there was to see. But Nellie shouted to put the boy down, scared that Jack would damage himself.

Even if his teenage diaries had survived, they wouldn't tell him much that would be of interest now. Just football scores and goalkickers, and predictions about who would go on to become a champion. He was far too shy to write of the girls he fancied, and too self-absorbed to comment on the last days of the Fraser government. Anxieties would have prevented Carl from writing about his widowed mother.

It was now impossible to revisit that time without seeing it in the light of subsequent discoveries. With Jack gone, he and Nellie were everything to each other. His mum was pretty, nervous, always with a book in her hand once she'd cooked and cleaned, hopelessly fearful if required to venture outside.

The funeral was one of few times Carl saw Nellie abroad in Koorook, and she worked hard to bluff her way through. Barely a dozen mourners attended, the bulk of them people who knew Carl; a teacher, two friends, the principal from the local state school, the man who coached Carl's first and last game of football, his wife, two neighbours, big Jack's boss at the pub, and two drinking mates. The minister had never met Jack, and when he referred to him as John, Carl heard fingernails scraping a blackboard.

Afterwards, his mum cried for days, and told Carl not to answer when neighbours came to the door. She lay sprawled sideways across their big bed, clutching the sheets. Toast was all Carl could tempt her with. A week passed before Nellie collected herself to say that they didn't have much, but they'd get by. He hadn't believed her, sure there was no way they'd survive without Jack. But they did survive. It suited Nellie to clean the Grain Board's offices from four to seven each morning, that way she never had to speak to anyone. The pay was feeble, but with Carl's paper round there was enough for rent and food. Not a day went by without his mum saying how proud Jack would be to see them getting by without recourse to charity.

But their lives were ruled by unspoken fears. Carl hated the early morning, dreading the sound of the key turning in the lock when Nellie left for work. Twenty-five years later, he knew this fear wasn't that she'd come to harm, it was fear that she would find another man. Or a man would find her. Her reclusiveness only seemed to make her more vulnerable. If she was late home from work, and failed to beat his return from the paper round, Carl interrogated her, just as Jack used to. He'd insist that she'd been out, or answered the door, whenever he returned home from weekends away.

Nellie's fears for Carl were more obvious. With no money to spare, football was over, but she was suspicious of his friends, and asked paranoid questions if he was slow to return from the library.

'This isn't when you said you'd be back.'

'How can I know what's worth reading if I don't look at the books?'

'Why should I believe you?'

She asked that question thousands of times, her natural angst fuelled by the crime novels she asked him to borrow. His mother only spoke about current events or the world at large to say how things were sure to degenerate, that shocking bushfires or a new Depression were just around the corner.

But there was praise too. Nellie couldn't have been prouder of Carl's outstanding scholarship. She often reminded him how the second grade teacher, Miss Conrad, told Jack that Carl was slow, and might need to travel to Melbourne for an assessment. Jack answered that she might need to go to the city to get her jaw wired.

His mum read Carl's texts with more enthusiasm than he did. She'd wanted to stay on at school, but it wasn't possible. When he asked why, she said it just wasn't. He should thank his stars that he had the smarts to become a lawyer, or a doctor. Study was about making sure you got a job you could count on when things went bad.

If anything, the past—meaning the time before Jack saved her from certain doom—scared Nellie more than dark clouds on the horizon. The past taught her that sooner or later you were bound to lose everything.

At sixteen, tall enough to look stupid riding a paper round on an undersized bike, Carl came home to find Nellie sitting in front of an open drawer in his room, looking like she'd just found a stash of the porn his father read so voraciously. In her fingers, she cradled the medal Carl was awarded by the Humane Society for attempting to save his father's life. In the other hand, she held a pile of newspaper reports related to the incident.

He could keep the medal. She was proud of his efforts. But she was throwing out the cuttings. When you held on to things, they suffocated you.

*Suffocate* was a favourite word. Treat every day like a new beginning, or the Past would stand over your bed and mash your face with a pillow. All questions about Nellie's family—who they were, what they'd done—were met with the same response, *There was a fire*, as if her memories of them were indistinguishable from the treasures the flames consumed.

And that's how Carl knew that he and Nellie were different. He would have spent all his time remembering the lost people and things.

Andrew Vincent was twenty-five, and the owner of a Masters degree, when he arrived to teach senior English and history at Koorook High. Though he was young enough to play as a swooping half-forward for the football team, in truth he would have preferred to spend Saturdays reading or gardening at the house he rented just three doors from the Johanssens.

There was something calculating about Andrew Vincent that Carl still struggled to define twenty years later. He noted weaknesses of character in his students and held them over their heads like an extortionist. His was easily the finest mind in the staffroom, and since Carl was the school's star student it was natural that Vincent should take him under his wing.

Strolling to school, the fifth-former would find the teacher suddenly beside him, asking his thoughts on Machiavelli. Was there a difference between being a dispassionate observer of pragmatism in action and a heartless advocate of the same? If Carl's thoughts weren't equal to the teacher's challenge, he was given an essay to write. Vincent would not permit Carl's agile mind to drift towards law or economics.

The principal, Mrs Peng, shared Vincent's view that Carl should study history, philosophy and English at Melbourne University, but, much as Carl's mother valued the world of books, for her education was about securing prosperity. Fortunately, to argue that belief you had to look strangers in the eye, something Nellie couldn't do.

When Mrs Peng invited Carl to enter the history competition being run in conjunction with the Bicentenary, the boy expressed interest in writing about the period, exactly twenty years earlier, when the sudden death of Prime Minister Holt brought two 'locals'—John McEwen, the Country Party leader, and John Gorton, the senator from Kerang, to the forefront of Australian politics. Carl was fascinated by the tumult that follows the death of a leader.

Mr Vincent liked this idea so much so that he asked Carl to accompany him on a trip to Sydney. While the teacher attended the Test match against England, the boy could read the newspaper files in the Mitchell Library. But the pair would need to leave before daybreak, and wouldn't return to Koorook till two or three the following morning.

Save the journey from Kingaroy to Koorook when he was three, Carl had never been further than Bendigo. For all his reading and dreaminess, he'd no more imagined seeing Sydney than he would Atlantis. The idea that he might gain a place at Melbourne University was frightening, and Carl could see himself turning down such an offer to work in a newsagency in Kerang or Echuca. Get too big for yourself, and you'd be cut down.

'How do I know the man's not homosexual?' Nellie asked. Word was that Vincent had shown no interest in the women of the district.

Carl had never questioned anyone's sexuality, and was unaccustomed to considering ulterior motives. He thought Vincent was shy, and said that if his mother was worried, she should speak to the teacher, never for one moment believing she might act on this suggestion.

This meeting was a brief encounter at the Johanssens' front door. No chance that Nellie would invite the teacher in for coffee.

She told Vincent this trip was his idea, and would have to be carried out at his expense. What's more, it would be on his soul to ensure that no harm came to the boy in Sydney. Though smart, and man-like, her son was an innocent when it came to the city and its predators. Somewhat reluctantly, Nellie gave Carl permission to go.

The pair were two hours down the road, the sun massaging the horizon, when Vincent abruptly switched subject from Australian cultural life in the 1960s to offer his impressions of Carl's mother, a woman he'd glimpsed just twice in the two years he'd lived in Phipps Street.

'She's fierce, isn't she?'

'She finds it hard to talk to people.'

'Or trust them, I'd say.'

'She trusts you,' Carl said, wary of this talk.

'When she came to the door, I thought she must be your sister. It's tragic that an intelligent woman has to lock herself away like that.'

Nothing more was said for some time. Finally, Vincent suggested stopping at a service-station restaurant for breakfast. Never having considered the quality of his mother's mind, it shocked Carl to hear this praise. Vincent had noticed his mother, and Carl feared he would ask more questions, that Vincent might wish to gain some inkling of how best to court her. Until then, Carl had believed that he and his father were the only men who could respond to his mother's delicate beauty. Now there was another.

Between breakfast and the endless approach to Sydney through its southern suburbs, they spoke of Harold Holt, who was in the company of another man's wife the day he drowned at Portsea. This while Holt's 67-year-old deputy McEwen—a man who knew Australia better than anyone—fought a bushfire at Stanhope. Though Vincent admired both Gorton and the man known as Black Jack, he had little time for the blue-blooded, sycophantic Holt.

'Holt was copping some bad polls, and there was enough trouble in his personal life for people to suppose that his recklessness might have been deliberate.'

Though Carl knew the myth of the Chinese submarine that came to collect the Australian Prime Minister, he'd never read any suicide theories. Surely Holt could have the life of his choosing.

'That's what you'd think. But money doesn't always count for a lot. When he was a young bloke about your age, Holt had a girlfriend his dad said wasn't good enough for him. No sooner did Holt senior crush the affair than he raced off to marry the girl himself.'

The substance of this story impressed Carl less than the telling. There wasn't anything that Andrew Vincent hadn't thought about from another angle. Through his eyes, the happiest family could begin to look like the Mansons.

Nearly twenty years later, Carl Johanssen, senior lecturer in Australian Studies and author of three well-received books on Australian life in the sixties and seventies, recalled that he'd only ever won two things: the Humane Society's medal for attempting to save his father, and the Bicentennial Essay Prize. The latter was awarded for his mature analysis of the brief prime ministership of Jack McEwen.

Despite this maturity, Carl could see his youth only in terms of failing to save his mother.

Not that the Mitchell Library's resources seemed anything less than thrilling on the morning of 29 January 1988. Decades of contemporary reports were Carl's for the asking. The seven hours he had at his disposal would hardly be enough.

Since Holt drowned on the Mornington Peninsula, the scholar thought it best to start with the Melbourne *Age*'s accounts from December 1967 and January 1968. The 18 December issue would record that the nation's leader, 'normally a strong swimmer', had disappeared in treacherous waters off Cheviot Beach near Portsea. Everything about these newspapers interested Carl, from the job ads and television schedules to the brief page-two piece reporting that two young Australians, Alan McLean and Richard Ramsay, had been killed in an ambush at Nui Dat. Nothing could be read without feeling that you had an edge on those who read the paper on its day of publication.

For all the searching, Holt's body wouldn't be found, and the frontrunner for his job, Paul Hasluck, soon fell by the wayside. Within a day, the minor coalition partner, the Country Party, led by stand-in Prime Minister and arch-protectionist McEwen, declared that Billy McMahon was unacceptable to them as leader. Despite his lack of cabinet experience, Gorton began to be spoken of as the right sort of man to combat the ALP's charismatic leader, Gough Whitlam.

By Tuesday 21 December, with all hope of finding Holt gone, plans were made for a memorial service. Meanwhile, McEwen resisted pressure to hold a summit meeting on the situation in Vietnam, declaring that Australia would fight on. Noting this on his pad, Carl had just flicked the microfilm reader's forward switch when he caught sight of a photograph that forced him to halt and return.

There, next to a map detailing traffic plans for Holt's memorial service, was a black-and-white image of his mother. The more Carl thought this impossible, the more stark the resemblance became. A caption told him that this woman, Wendy Phillips, aged thirty-two, was pleading for information about her twelve-year-old daughter, Jenny. An adjacent article reported that the girl had been missing for thirty-six hours since last seen leaving Mooroolbark station after spending the morning shopping in the city.

Carl stared at the face of Nellie's doppelganger for some minutes before making a note to ask if her family, the Walshes, had near-relatives named Phillips.

With no follow-up in the next day's *Age*, Carl assumed the girl had been found. The Saturday edition would bring news of Emerson and Newcombe crushing Spain in the Davis Cup, along with an eight-page spread on the Holt memorial service. But on page nine, beside a report urging holiday drivers to relax, he found a small photo of the missing twelve-year-old Jenny Phillips. Police now held 'very grave fears' for the girl, after receiving a witness account that a child matching her description was dragged into a Volkswagen just seventy yards from the Phillips' home in Carron Vale Road.

Though this image, clipped from a class photograph, was of poor quality, Carl had no doubt who the girl was.

But, if the missing twelve-year-old Jenny Phillips now lived as Nellie Johanssen in Koorook, she would have been fourteen at his birth, and just thirty-two now. Had Jack stolen her? Impossible. No woman was more devoted to a man than his mother was to Jack.

Carl sped on to 1 January 1968. After stories detailing the birth of Australia's first quintuplets, much needed rain, and the five men lost in a plane crash near Bunyip, he found the same photo of young Jenny above a report that said Homicide detectives were treating the disappearance as a murder investigation.

Strangely, that was the last reference to the matter Carl found in the *Age*. Christian Barnard performed a heart transplant, the Beatles' *Magical Mystery Tour* premiered on British television, and the last-born of the Braham quins died. After McEwen successfully undermined the McMahon candidacy, war hero John Gorton was sworn in as Australian prime minister on 10 January 1968. But Jenny Phillips had ceased to be of interest to that paper's editors.

Reports in the *Sun* and the *Herald* followed the same pattern, with two exceptions. A photograph in the latter had 34-year-old Mark Phillips standing beside his wife and two of Jenny's three younger siblings, Cathy and Robert. The next morning's *Sun* published an identikit of the man seen driving the Volkswagen Beetle. With long dark hair and a thick beard, he might have been anyone, but he looked nothing like Jack as Carl remembered him. How old was Jack then? Fifty-five, fifty-six? This was someone much younger.

Seven hours passed in a blink. His arm aching from taking forty pages of notes, Carl hadn't stopped to eat or drink. He was due to meet Mr Vincent in front of the library at six-thirty, and he'd seen neither the Bridge nor the Opera House, just four images that would haunt the rest of his life.

Worn out from watching a laborious innings by the Englishman Broad, Mr Vincent spent most of the afternoon in the Sydney Cricket Ground bar, and now stank of beer and smoke. He told Carl this was the last time he'd attend a Test match. The five-day game was certain to be devoured by the thrill-packed abbreviated model.

If Carl was concerned about the teacher's fitness to drive, he was thankful that bitterness distracted Vincent from asking about his day in the library. Not until they were sharing a late hamburger near Goulburn did the older man question him.

'Black Jack and Holt were harder to nail than you thought?'

'I did something stupid. I looked up the fire that killed Mum's family.'

'Well,' Vincent said, struggling to find the proper response. 'You can't expect to make sense of tragedy. Count yourself lucky that your mum wasn't taken.'

Not yet the professional historian, eighteen-year-old Carl Johanssen extrapolated from a set of barely-knowns to question everything he believed. The rare love between his mother and her much older husband might now be considered perverse. Nellie's intense devotion, and her fear of dealing with people, could suggest something other than adoration and shyness.

Carl replayed scenes from the past. Big Jack returning drunk from three days away with mates to criticise Nellie's cooking and insinuate that some change out front meant that she'd been working in the garden. She never contradicted him. If Jack's anger threatened to spill over, it was Nellie who led him to the couch or the bedroom.

And Carl had wanted a love like that for himself. He'd wanted to find a girl who could love him with the same intensity that Nellie loved his dad.

Now everything was fucked up. Though he'd never had much, Carl entered that library as protagonist in his own story, only to become an incidental figure in a huge canvas, unsure if anything said to him had been sincere.

His mother saw the change in mood instantly, and her questions hinted that Vincent might have acted improperly during their long trip. Carl would only say that he couldn't do justice to his topic. Things were more complicated than he'd thought.

As it happened, Carl had little trouble drafting an essay that was deemed the best of those submitted from all parts of Australia. Holt's death brought divisions within the Liberal Party to the surface. Though McEwen didn't anoint Gorton so much as make clear a conviction that effective government would be impossible under McMahon, it was probably coincidence that McEwen retired about the same time Malcolm Fraser helped McMahon oust Gorton.

While some of his judgements now seemed naive, Carl was most taken by the young writer's interest in subversion. Since nothing was as it appeared on the surface, the invention of a Chinese sub to spirit Holt away was more or less inevitable. And half the things Carl wrote about the Holt case might have been written about his mother, whether she was born Helen 'Nellie' Walsh or Jennifer Phillips.

Carl watched her, but held his silence. Some mornings when she was out cleaning, he went through her things, but his mother held on to nothing that had outlived its utility. No diaries, no letters, no papers. The few images she had kept were of Carl as a child and Big Jack. Husband and wife never appeared together and, when photographed, his mother looked like she'd rather be anywhere than in front of a camera.

Knowing that family questions were instantly batted away with reference to the fire, Carl took a new tack. He asked Nellie to come with him to visit his dad's grave. As they stood beside an unmarked plot in a windswept cemetery, Carl pretended to have little memory of Jack other than his dying gasps and that time in Queensland when he was held high above Jack's head.

This amnesia infuriated his mother. If he didn't nurture the memory of his father, and all the sacrifices he'd made for them, what would he have to tell his children?

'But you and Dad haven't told me anything about your families, or where you came from. Only the fire.'

She said there was a pain so great that it didn't bear revisiting.

'Did you ever see your family's graves?'

Nellie took this as a chance to rehearse the story of herself as the nineteen-year-old with no-one in the world, and how Jack—sent by her dad's boss to ask if she needed help—stepped in to save her. But in this rehashing of an oft-told tale, there were two notable variations. Nellie didn't say, as she always had, that she'd fallen in love with him there and then. In this version, Jack was a coarse man, who used language she'd never heard at home. But he was sincere. He didn't ask her to love him. He just asked her to accept that the world she'd known was gone, and she'd be wise to make the best of things.

Carl might have asked if people said Jack was too old for her, or questioned the kind of love that a young woman—barely adult in her version—could expect from a rough-edged man three times her age. He did not. It wasn't just that she would have ruled these questions out of order. In reality, Carl's need to have the kidnap confirmed was matched by his fear of that confirmation. Truth was one thing when seen from a distance, quite another when it challenged the core of your being.

Things changed, subtly, in ways he still struggled to define. Though he'd expected Nellie to oppose his plan to study Arts at Melbourne University, she almost bundled him onto the bus at Echuca.

In the previous year, Nellie's attitude to many things had softened, the essay prize having made it inevitable that her son, the central focus of her life, would be lost to her. And Carl began to see her for what she was, a 32-year-old woman, still beautiful, still capable of starting a new life, or a new family, if she chose. Neither had a right to obstruct the other.

Not only did Nellie attend Speech Day to see Carl lauded as Dux of Humanities, but she wore a blue frock purchased for the occasion, and was by some distance the most striking woman at the gathering. Andrew Vincent couldn't wait to button-hole her.

'The skies are limitless for a boy with Carl's ability,' the teacher said.

Nellie said that the skies have a habit of being fickle.

The eighties boom was ready to bust when Carl arrived at Melbourne University in 1989. Needing money, he soon found a job proofreading for a suburban newspaper, and rented a room in a Brunswick share-house. There it took some resolve to avoid the chaos of his housemates' love affairs. Set up by rich parents, his co-tenants had no need for part-time work, and couldn't understand why Carl valued study more than partying.

He wrote to his mother twice a week, and her letters to him were more sentimental than their conversations had ever been. She asked Carl to list the books he'd been reading, and then attempted to borrow the same titles through the mobile library service.

Often, in his mind's eye, Carl saw himself looking up Mark and Wendy Phillips in the Melbourne telephone directory. Now in their early fifties, they might still reside in Mooroolbark.

Daydreams had Carl stalk these grandparents, following them to work, and insinuating himself into their lives. He'd be the quiet country boy who needed a safe place to board. And the Phillips would fail to grasp why they needed him, or why he reminded them of their lost daughter.

In none of these daydreams did he tell them the truth. Truth stalled all intent. How could it be true to say that the child the Phillips knew as their eldest daughter was still alive? Whoever Nellie might be, she was not the twelve-year-old Jenny.

Near the end of that first year, depressed by a failed romance with a spirited Dutch girl, Carl tried to compose a letter to his maternal grandmother. Even simple statements seemed impossible to craft. 'My name is Carl Johanssen, and I have reason to believe that I am your grandson.' He couldn't know that for sure. And would his mother forgive him for the impertinence? What if Jenny Phillips wasn't the girl dragged into the Volkswagen? Or what if Jenny had run from an abusive home? Everything he could claim to know was surmise.

Carl would spend the next seventeen years redrafting that letter in his head. There was a time, just after completing his dissertation, when he would walk through the streets of North Melbourne at night, imagining versions of the great family reunion. Often, for no obvious reason, he would enter a brothel, but choosing one woman from several always proved excruciatingly difficult. It wasn't until he'd spent a small fortune on these encounters that Carl realised the thing he wanted most was to be kissed passionately by a lover who thought him the finest man in the world, and that was something these women couldn't give him.

Every two weeks, he drove north to spend a weekend with his mother. Though Nellie had begun to connect with the world, first through distance education, then through qualifying to teach the third grade at Koorook Primary, her home life was unchanged. She gardened, prepared lessons and read crime stories. She rarely asked about Carl's personal life, and showed little interest in his accounts of the Victorian capital. Though many years had passed since Jack's death, he continued to grow in her estimation.

'There was something I remembered the other day,' Carl told her. 'I was six or seven, and Dad took me to the Swan Hill Pioneer Museum. Dad wanted a pie, and there were Japanese tourists waiting to be served. He must have said something offensive to them, because they moved away. But he followed one of the men, grabbed his collar, and punched him hard. Two or three times. We left then. That's all I remember.'

Nellie reacted as if Carl hadn't spoken. For the next few minutes, she seemed locked in a trance. Later, when they were eating chicken casserole, she said, apropos of nothing being discussed, that Jack had served with the occupational forces in Japan. He'd had some sort of trouble there, and carried a lot of ill-feeling for the Japanese.

When would Jack have told her that? If true, why never mention it until reminded of his temper? Trying to draw her out, Carl promised to research his father's military history.

'Your dad left you alone. Leave him in peace.'

Shortly after this, Carl wrote to the War Memorial, only to be advised that no Jack Johanssens served in Japan after the capitulation.

That was when the temptation to confront Nellie was strongest. Everything about their life was a lie. Was his father really Jack Johanssen? For all she knew, Jack could have spent the war in an Australian prison. By taking his lies and making them true, they'd become sustaining certainties. But much as he wanted to believe they'd be best served by the truth, Carl knew the truth had the power to obliterate them.

A student he'd tutored, Nancy, moved in for six months, his longest love affair, but their disagreements became increasingly heated. When Carl wasn't 'emotionally absent', he was a 'passive aggressive' in need of therapy. He might have agreed if Nancy hadn't been so concerned about his happiness. Disdain wasn't nearly so threatening as a woman with a powerful need to be kind. Therapy was for people who wouldn't be destroyed by the facts.

And it was always easier to be astute about other people's problems. The best reviews for Carl's book on the Whitlam government praised his sensitive reading of the Cairns–Morosi affair. Even Nellie admitted surprise at his levels of insight. But it suited Nellie to think him imperceptive, as the boy who would never issue the challenges that might bring her undone.

Having begun teaching with the belief that it was a necessary evil, something to be tolerated if you were a publicly funded researcher, Carl found that his students gave him more pleasure than anything else in life. If he could overcome his sense of being a hypocrite and a fraud, teaching might bring him the same happiness it brought his mother, who wallpapered her house with artworks produced by grade threes.

'You never let me draw.'

'I made you get jobs and learn to be independent. Otherwise, you would have spent your life day-dreaming.'

While conceding that, Carl defended the imaginative world. To what did Nellie respond when she looked at these paintings if not the wealth of a child's imagination?

Emily was by no means the most brilliant of Carl's students, but her sincerity touched him. It seemed odd that someone born in the Bicentennial year should have a special interest in early eighties pop music, but she'd grown up with her parents' videotapes of *Countdown* and *Rock Arena*. Her mother acted in television dramas, and, while filming one, she'd met Emily's father, a producer at the ABC.

'Do you know the Hoodoo Gurus?' Carl knew the name, but little more. There had been no music in his house. His father hated it.

According to Emily, the Hoodoo Gurus defined a peculiarly Australian brand of postmodernity, and she wanted to explore that in her 5000-word essay. She promised to supply some discs, so Carl would know what she was talking about.

'There must be music you like.'

'Music's a foreign language to me.'

When he asked if she wanted to be a musician, Emily thought the idea hilarious. She wanted to travel the world, but her great ambition was to teach art to young children.

Without thinking, Carl said she should meet his mother, who'd developed a late passion for the same thing, and it struck him that this was the first time he'd spoken of his mother's individuality.

Expecting his remark to be taken as something one utters automatically in the course of a friendly chat, he was surprised by Emily's eagerness to visit Nellie's classroom. 'She lives four hours drive away,' he cautioned, and thought no more of it.

The essay Emily submitted was clumsily expressed, and too heavily reliant on pre-digested cultural theory, but her analysis of the Hoodoo Gurus' borrowings and distillations merited a solid B. Only when officially recording this mark did Carl notice that the nineteen-year-old Emily Phillips had a home address in Croydon, a suburb just down the road from Mooroolbark. Little wonder she seemed so familiar. The recorded next of kin—*Robert Phillips, father*—was 90 per cent likely to be Jenny's younger brother.

Everything seemed pointed, as if destiny were using this girl to drag Carl back into the fold, an idea totally at odds with his trust in impersonal fate. In the days prior to handing back the essay, Carl's imagination ran amok. He saw himself asking Emily to come to his office. There, he told her bluntly that he believed himself to be her first cousin. In another scenario, he saw himself driving unannounced to Emily's home in Croydon, where he told all to Robert Phillips, an uncle ten years older than himself.

The most dramatic fantasy had Carl driving his young student to his mother's home in Koorook, fully aware that he hadn't taken anyone there since Andrew Vincent—now a headmaster in Perth—had come to enquire about the Sydney trip. At first, Nellie would be curious about this girl and Carl's interest in her, only for it to gradually dawn who Emily was, and what Carl must have known all along.

But would forcing that connection liberate his mother, or introduce her to a new form of captivity? Whoever she was now, or had been, she didn't need pity. Notoriety might kill her.

Whatever Carl chose, he couldn't pretend to be doing it for anyone but himself, be that the eleven-year-old failing to thump life back into Jack's chest, or the historian living in bad faith with the truth.

*Emily, this is a solid piece of work that evidences a superior understanding of the HG's music, the context of its production, and the sixties cultural influences that coloured their style. At times, it would benefit from less convoluted sentences, and a more critical appreciation of the theoretical frames you apply. However, your ideas merit consideration, and this is a thoughtful essay. B*

*PS. If you're still interested, we can make a time for you to come up to Koorook. Though she's an unusual woman, my mother's a committed teacher. And you could ask her about your own grandparents. I believe they all knew one another in the dim, dark past.*

# DINING WITH THE PURE MERINOS

Try as you might
you can't dislike them,
this dining room of pure merinos,

the linen and the silver,
the splendid glasses, quart-pot size.
Everything you hear's assumption:

the acreage a century old
or closing in on two,
the money likewise, old not new,

a good school somewhere, single sex,
and paid for with a fifties wool cheque—
or QC's weekly fee.

They have, of course, their self-possession …
and, sometimes too, the Will to Power
that Nietzsche so admired.

Everything they say's connected;
you listen to the talk and how
the branches of each family tree

are intertwined with others,
a possum's hop from bough to bough.
You see it in the cheekbones, too—

male or female makes no difference—
symmetrical and rather high,
handed down like silver.

A few, it's true, have flown the fold,
played treason with their breeding—
but that's not obvious tonight.

A few (like you) are not quite seen:
mere courtiers, a service rendered.
How *does* one hover in a seat?

Outside this candlelit consensus
nothing real can quite exist.
Poverty, ill-luck, bad manners,

a tolerance for cheaper wine
or just a quarrel with the bill
may lift an eyebrow slightly—

some minor insect crawling by,
not needing any name.
You've been invited—there's no doubt—

and everything's politeness.
Your wife's been summoned too.
Together, you're alone.

'The rich are different': Scott Fitzgerald.
But these are merely God's well-off,
their gossip thick with givens,

well-meaning as a stone.

# RUMI
1207–2007

I have had enough of Rumi
the deserts and the dancing
the parables of camels
the donkeys and the roadside inns
the figs and nightingales.
I have had enough of oceans

and metaphors to net the world.
I'm tired of similes as maxims
the eyes of needles full of stars.

The unseen Friend remains unseen,
the sun and moon, the sea and air
persist in being physics.

'To find yourself give up the self'
is what the mystics say
but that's too high a price

despite that wedding-night surrender.
I'm reading *The Essential Rumi*.
Spare me then the 'inessential'.

Saying the ineffable
requires some little talk, it seems.
Rumi, poet, shows his wares

like moons beside the road.
Rumi, teacher, then ensures
you ride the camel of their meaning.

I have had enough of Rumi …
but still I see him dancing.

GEOFF PAGE

# THE OTHER WAY

**WAYNE MACAULEY** OFFERS A PERSONAL REFLECTION ON AUSTRALIAN
FICTION PUBLISHING

'IT'S very hard to make a definite assessment of this book.' In the course of
rejecting novels they probably should have published, big publishers sometimes,
kindly, enclose with your rejection letter a copy of their reader's report, should
your particular manuscript have got that far in the assessment process. The day
after receiving this particular rejection, I took a copy of the reader's report down
to the local library where I used the photocopy machine to photocopy this phrase
then enlarge it to ten times its original size. I then took this enlarged phrase home
and glued it to the wall above my desk. It's still there now: 'It's very hard to make
a definite assessment of this book.'

So what did the reader mean by this, and in what way did this form part of
the argument for the book's rejection? Because no matter which way you hold it
up and look at it, the reader clearly intended it to be taken as a negative comment.
The reader, basically, was not easily able to sum up the book, identify its genre
and therefore its market—and if they, the reader doing the reader's report, were
unable to sum it up and package it succinctly, then how on earth would the
marketing department? The book was rejected, in part, because the book could
not easily be explained.

Why is this a negative? What is it about the state of our current literary culture that says a work must be easily explained? What's wrong with not being easily able to explain or assess something? Isn't that the way it should be?

After a few more such misunderstandings (seven in all), my book was published. My eventual publisher, the Melbourne independent Black Pepper, thank goodness, had no such concerns. They saw difficulty of assessment as a cause for celebration, allowed its oddity to stand, even advertised it as 'eccentric and original' on the cover. On release I got a rave review in the *Age* and was stamped their 'Pick of the Week'. More good reviews followed. The book was put on the VCE English recommended reading list (alongside Dickens, Greene and Camus) and quickly went to a second edition.

So I didn't fall through the cracks, as it turned out, but I easily could have. There, down at the bottom of the publishing pecking order, was Black Pepper, picking through the tailings, finding the gems. Black Pepper is a cottage publisher, literally, working out of an old house in North Fitzroy. Kevin Pearson and Gail Hannah made their reputations initially as poetry publishers but have now also built an impressive fiction list. They operate on a shoestring. Every March they submit a list of proposed new titles to the Literature Board of the Australia Council for the subsidy on offer of $4000 per work of Australian fiction ($2500 for poetry). This allows them to typeset and print the book, but little else. They do the cover design in-house, as well as all editing and proofreading. They have no marketing department or publicist, no budget for either. They send out copies to reviewers at all the major dailies and journals and do a general mail-out to bookshops, but promotion of the book is left pretty much to the author—or if they decline, to the lap of the gods.

So is it good to get your book up with an independent publisher, instead of with one of the big ones? It depends what your expectations are. It is sometimes frustrating not having a full-time editor with plenty of paid time to help prepare your book for publication—but it can also be a blessing in disguise. I'm quite sure my book wouldn't be so 'eccentric and original' if a tribe of mainstream publisher's editors had got hold of it—they would have knocked that sort of crap out of it quick smart. A small publisher's editor is much more likely to accommodate an author's intentions, no matter how commercially misguided those intentions are. An original voice is not just allowed but actively encouraged. Limited editorial intervention (as is blessedly the case with Black Pepper) also puts the onus back on the writer to think about their work beforehand, to self-edit, in other words; to not hand over a rag-bag of material and expect the publishing house to pull it together and 'make it work'.

As for the marketing side of things, with no publicity and marketing department, any book published by a small independent publisher is at an obvious disadvantage in terms of sales. But equally, for the writer who has not thought about 'marketability' when writing their book (me, for example) this is an advantage. The book is not accepted (or subsequently packaged) because of its perceived ability to cater to the whims of a fickle buying public but because the publisher actually thinks it's good.

I wrote my first novel when I was thirty-three and didn't see it published till I was forty-six: it takes a lot of faith and good humour to keep hanging in there for that long. But over that time, as articles about the state of the post-1980s Australian publishing industry started to proliferate, I couldn't help wondering if what I was doing—putting my manuscript in an envelope and sending it off to Penguin, Random House, HarperCollins—might not be a complete waste of time. Throughout those years my other life was as an independent theatre-maker, working in the alternative Melbourne theatre scene, writing grant applications, scratching together the money (public and private), developing the project, finding the venue, helping with publicity, getting the thing on. In theatre I was making art entirely outside the mainstream, but with my novel I was desperately seeking mainstream approval. It took me a long time to figure it out: approval from whom? Not Sylvia Beach and Adrienne Monnier, that's for sure. I was seeking approval from nerdy bean-counters and gadfly publicists, most of whom worked out of Sydney. I was waiting on the big Yes from editors who with all the best will in the world couldn't say Yes anyway—they were at the mercy of forces much greater than them, that is to say, marketing.

I work casual hours in a bookshop (that's what happens when you don't get published till you're forty-six), in Receivals and Despatch; I see them come and I see them go. One moment we are taking them freshly baked out of their boxes and putting their shiny new price stickers on them, the next we are taking those barely scuffed price stickers off and packing them up as 'Returns', the unsold and unwanteds, sending them back whence they came. The shelf life of a book these days is short, too short. When the relevant staff member checks the system and notes that this thing (it is a 'thing', unlikely to have been read by the person doing the checking) hasn't racked up the required sales to justify its shelf space, off it goes to the knacker's yard.

So is there another way of doing things, a better way of building a conduit between writer and reader, something that will give us both a more satisfying, longer lasting and ultimately more enriching experience? I've become convinced that there is.

VERY little art survives in this country without some kind of government funding. As unpalatable as it is, we all need to get our snouts in the trough at some stage, if not directly then indirectly through government support to organisations higher up the food chain from whose table we then collect the crumbs. Many if not most books of literary fiction will have received some government support at some stage. But you've got to wonder whether this money is being spent wisely.

The principal source of funding for the production of Australian literature is the Literature Board of the Australia Council—any freelance writer trying to scratch a living will be very familiar with their booklets, their application forms and their closing dates. So too the Theatre Board for a person working in the performing arts. Let's compare for a moment how these two bodies work—the comparison, I think, is instructive.

At the Theatre Board, as with the Literature Board, the main area of funding from which a freelance artist such as myself could benefit is the New Work category, funding grants to individuals and/or small performance companies. If I want to make a piece of theatre, for example, from the ground up—write it, develop it with a director and actors, put it on, promote it—this is where I go. *All these stages* (and my ability to justify the money for them) become the criteria against which my proposal is assessed. At the Literature Board, on the other hand, under their New Work category the story is quite different. What you are applying for there is 'time to write', not 'funds to produce'. That is, you can't apply to self-publish, nor demonstrate publisher support for your project from any other than one with 'effective national distribution'. There is a distinct difference between the two boards' definitions of new work: at the Literature Board the creation of new work is *the writing of it*, at the Theatre Board it is its *writing, development, production and presentation.* At the Theatre Board you can apply for money to write, workshop, develop, rehearse, present and publicise your new work—in literary terms, to write, edit, typeset, print, publish, market and distribute your book. That is, to do precisely what you *can't* do under the Literature Board's current rules. They'll give you money to write, and will give money to a reputable publisher to help publish what you've written, but they won't let you do it all yourself because—well, I don't really know why.

Let's say the Literature Board gives you an Emerging Writers grant of $15,000 (twelve months of toasted cheese sandwiches) to write a book that a major publisher—let's call them X—has said they are interested in publishing. When it comes time to publish (assuming they've been able to 'make it work'), X will then go back to the Literature Board for a publishing subsidy of $4000. The question has to be asked: why should a major commercial publisher get a $4000 subsidy to publish a new work of Australian literary fiction that the taxpayer has already paid to have written? *If* commercial publishers want to publish new literature (do they? really?), then why don't *they* put their own money into it? Why don't they pay for the writing of the book they are supposedly so enamoured of? Yes, that's right, they won't, it's new literary fiction, they'll run a mile. *And this is a good thing.* Let them run. Let them publish no more Australian fiction but the lowest-common-denominator guaranteed bestsellers. Instead of spending our precious arts-funding dollars helping out these massive global businesses, encouraging them to do something they couldn't give a rat's about anyway, let's invest the money in new Australian literary fiction.

There are two ways of doing this. The first, obviously, is to better fund the infrastructure of small independent publishers, to help them deal with the massive quantities of fiction manuscripts they are now receiving and to help them better promote, market and distribute the books they select. (We're not talking big dollars here: the weekly wine-and-canapés budget of your average big publisher will do.) The second, and more problematic, is to fund new publishing ventures, including self-publishing.

Self-publishing: the hyphenated horror word that makes most literati reach for their revolvers. Family histories, bad story collections, worse poetry. But why not something else besides? Brilliant poetry by front-line poets, innovative fiction by the best going round, new unclassifiable genres of writing that might reach a whole new readership. It happens every day in the film and music businesses: as these industries become more corporatised and money-driven there is a definite move on the part of artists and arts consumers towards more independent, self-promoted art. The world of independent publishing, of which innovative self-publishing is a legitimate part, could do pretty well everything everyone is whingeing about not being done, if it just had a little bit of money to do it.

The physical production of a book (with all due respect) is not rocket science. The big commercial publishers no longer hold copyright over the mysteries of book-making. With digital technology for the layout and money for the printing costs, anyone can 'make' a book—that is, wrap a couple of hundred printed pages into a sheet of thin cardboard with a picture on the front. The challenge is to make a *good book*. A bigger challenge is to find your readers. But let's imagine that Literature Board policy has been overhauled and that I'm going to ask for money to write and publish my own book, or write and publish it through a small independent publisher that doesn't (yet) have 'effective national distribution'. The checks and balances are already there in the system. In any Literature Board grant application you already have to jump through a lot of hoops to prove the worthiness of your project: the same deal applies here. If the supporting material is bad, the project won't get funded. If the marketing strategy outlined is poor, the project won't get funded. If real thought hasn't been put into distribution, the project won't get funded. If the thing hasn't been properly costed, the project won't get funded. It happens every funding round over at the Theatre Board: your project proposal has to show artistic merit, but just as importantly, if you can't show realistic box-office returns and how you will achieve them, the project won't get funded. If independently published and self-published literature is subjected to the same quality control as independent and self-produced theatre, then I don't see what the problem is. Sure you can't quality-control everything, sure there'll be some bad work produced (had a look at what the commercial publishers are putting out lately?)—but at least something is happening.

For about the same amount we taxpayers 'gave' X to get their book written and published ($15,000 for the writer to write it, $4000 for the publishing subsidy), a new, innovative work of Australian fiction will be independently written, published, marketed and distributed. It will not have passed through the commercially biased filter of a big commercial publisher but through a peer assessment process that is committed to risk and innovation. With the Literature Board's financial leg-up, the writer and/or small publisher (the ones who believe in it most) will get out there and promote it, get it into the bookshops (which are now far more receptive to it since the Literature Board will also have overhauled its promotion of Australian literature strategies and will no longer waste money on pointless Books Alive promotions to the tune of $2 million a year but instead will encourage promotion of new independent Australian fiction). On a self-published title at $24.95 RRP with a 60 per cent return after the 40 per cent bookshop discount on 100 per cent of sales on a print run of 1000, the writer pockets $15,000—which they will now use to write their next book …

I, LIKE everyone else, I suspect, am sick to death of stories and articles decrying the state of Australian fiction. The trouble is, too many people have a vested interest in maintaining the status quo—it is only by giving power back to those who don't, those whose interest is in subverting if not overturning the status quo, that any kind of change can be effected. This takes money, government money preferably, money with strings but not rope-and-tackle attached: a small investment for a massive return. Forget the big publishers, they don't care. If they did they would have done something about it by now. Put the money where it matters, where it will *actually make a difference.*

I didn't fall through the cracks. I'm a bit greyer around the temples, but I didn't fall through the cracks. My second novel is out, again through Black Pepper. I sometimes resent the time lost but there's no point whingeing about it now. And above my desk, edifyingly, are two bits of paper. One is an extract from my first review: 'If more Australian literature was of this calibre, we'd be laughing.' The other, the phrase from that reader's report: 'It's very hard to make a definite assessment of this book.' They sit very comfortably together.

# SEAWEED

Sometimes out of the wet hillocks
a ragged company heaves and settles
in a prickly flush and weave
of beads and beards and weird limbs.

Riddled by fish, the seaweed moves
within itself, a loitering detail
of shredded uniforms and snorkel stems
swishing towards, away from the beach.

It's only when the sea tips over
in falling walls of white and green
that dark gorillas raise up their arms,
standing up in surrender, or is it praise?

DAVID MUSGRAVE

# THEIR HOOKS FIND HOLD DEEP IN OUR FLESH

[AUTHOR] KATE FIELDING
[ARTIST] MANDY ORD

DURING the federal government's recent apology to the Indigenous peoples of Australia I was tickled pink by Prime Minister Rudd's assertion that the *Bringing Them Home* report shouldn't be left to 'languish with the historians'. It offered the cheering suggestion that, far from tweed and elbow patches, the general public think historians work reclining on a chaise lounge while drinking devastating cocktails under beaded lampshades, smelling salts close at hand.

Languishing aside, Rudd's statement reframed the national debate about how to understand our past, emphasising that a generous, critical and impassioned engagement with our shared histories is both the joy and responsibility of all people. It was a fitting end to a bleak decade of John Howard's insistence that we could inherit the glory of previous generations but not liability for the results of their actions.

To take up the challenges posed by the apology it is essential that we pursue an exploration of our histories that is generous yet rigorous. This continues the brave work of many Indigenous and non-Indigenous people who have been speaking up about these difficult issues for years—work that sadly wasn't acknowledged in Rudd's speech.

Creative, reflective and charismatic storytelling and story-listening is required for a rich account of our past. The past was not two-dimensional nor text-based: it was made up of salted herrings, sudden squalls, the abandon of dancing and pairs of socks. Likewise the process of writing history engages the physical and the sensory: ducking through rain to visit memorials, smelling old cloth, deciphering loopy handwriting and eating impeccable home-baked sponge cakes during interviews.

*Their hooks find hold deep in our flesh* takes to heart the notion that to tell the diverse stories that comprise our history it is not enough to simply turn the same tools to a different task. We need a multitude of histories to be sung, danced, played, written, spoken and drawn.

We are all implicated in these histories. It is not enough to learn dispassionately the details of the past, nor should we deny its complexity. Why, when our world is so complex, should we expect the past to be anything different? The true challenge and pleasure of history lies in how we link the past to our present and allow it to change the stories we tell about ourselves.

The extracts presented in this and following issues of *Meanjin* are taken from a longer work created by author Kate Fielding and artists Mandy Ord, Clint Curé, Elizabeth McDowell and Ben Fox. It was originally presented as an honours thesis in the History Department of the University of Melbourne, and has been subsequently reworked with support from the Australia Council for the Arts.

KATE FIELDING

Over millions of years volcanic eruptions formed the Plains of western Victoria

Indigenous Australians arrived here around 20,000 years ago

Less than 200 years ago the British arrived and established their first foothold here. In 1841, near present day Colac, the Chief Protector of Aborigines George Augustus Robinson wrote in his journal 'On the evening when I amused the natives at Murry's with fireworks they, the natives, tried to emulate me. They lighted the end of a crooked stick in a shape like a boomerang and threw it in the air. The lighted end revolving in an extended circle through the air had a pleasing effect especially as the ignited missile ascended to a considerable altitude.'

I came here in 1977 (born 4 am)

It is night time and we are on top of the volcano. My mum, my dad, my brothers and me

... and some firecrackers...

... before they were illegal.

We are on top of Mt Leura and I am holding sparklers, dancing around. Camperdown twinkles below us.

**Down there I am scared of . . .**

a house with a tower

a skeleton in a backroom

a man who eats snakes

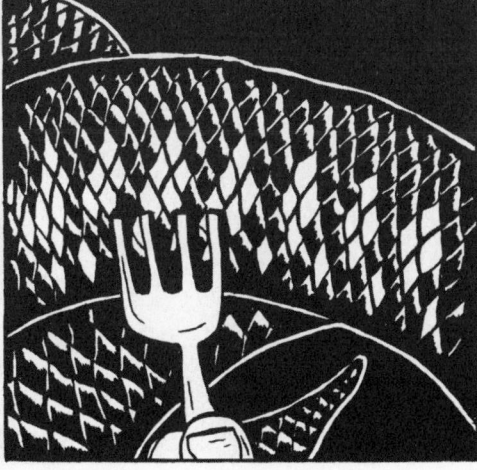

Up here we stand beneath the dome of night,
warm, black, the vertigo of space above us

spitting light,
in my hand.

Fear is buried
beneath my feet,
an imagined boil
of red lava and heat.

Dad says the volcano hasn't erupted for a very long time.
How long? A very very very long time. Dad knows about rocks.
He breaks scoria open to show me it's green olivine
heart, knows how to find thundereggs. But sometimes I
can't sleep. I imagine the paddocks of our farm melting
under the flow of lava. How fast can it move? Can I run
faster than it? Would we hear it coming? Do you burn
or drown? How do they **know** that it won't erupt?

Melbourne 2003

THE MAN FROM
CURDIE'S RIVER
AN AUTOBIOGRAPHY

DONALD MACLEAN

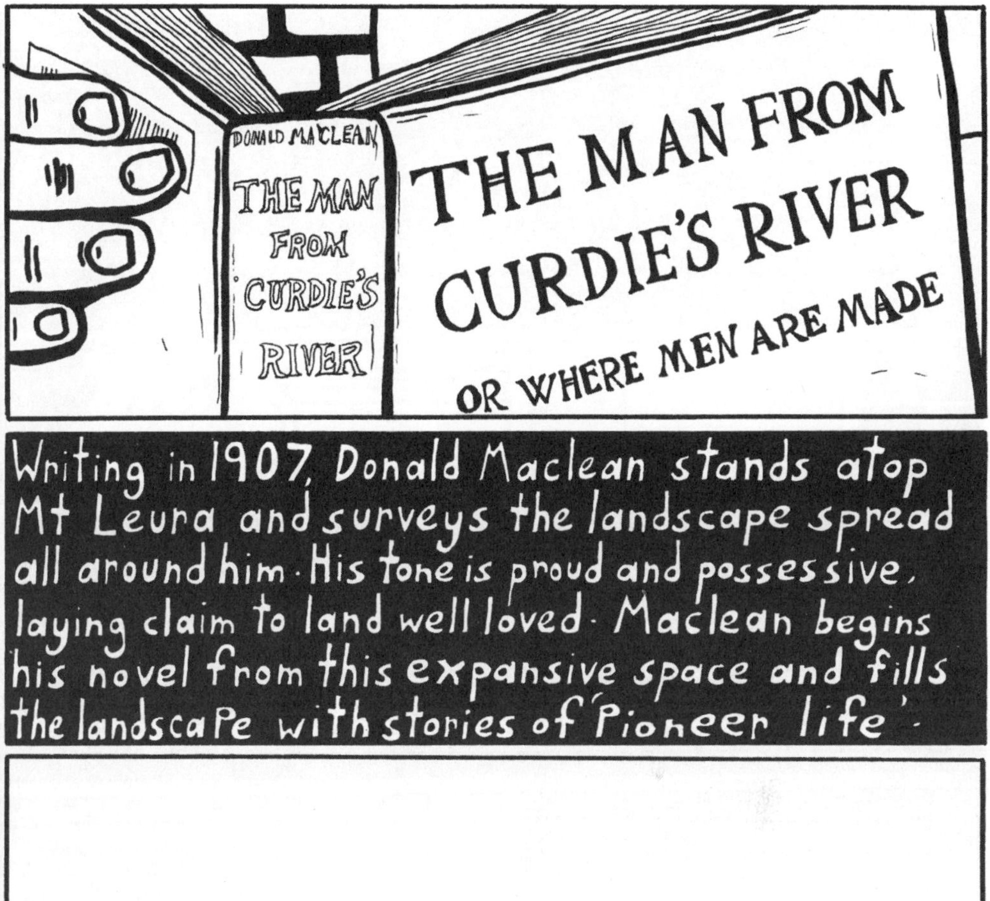

**THE MAN FROM CURDIE'S RIVER**

*OR WHERE MEN ARE MADE*

Writing in 1907, Donald Maclean stands atop Mt Leura and surveys the landscape spread all around him. His tone is proud and possessive, laying claim to land well loved. Maclean begins his novel from this expansive space and fills the landscape with stories of 'Pioneer life'.

"The train now standing on platform seven is the 6:18 to Warrnambool, stopping in Geelong, Winchelsea, Birregurra, Colac, Camperdown, Terang and terminating in Warrnambool with connections to Portland"

"All clear on platform seven please"

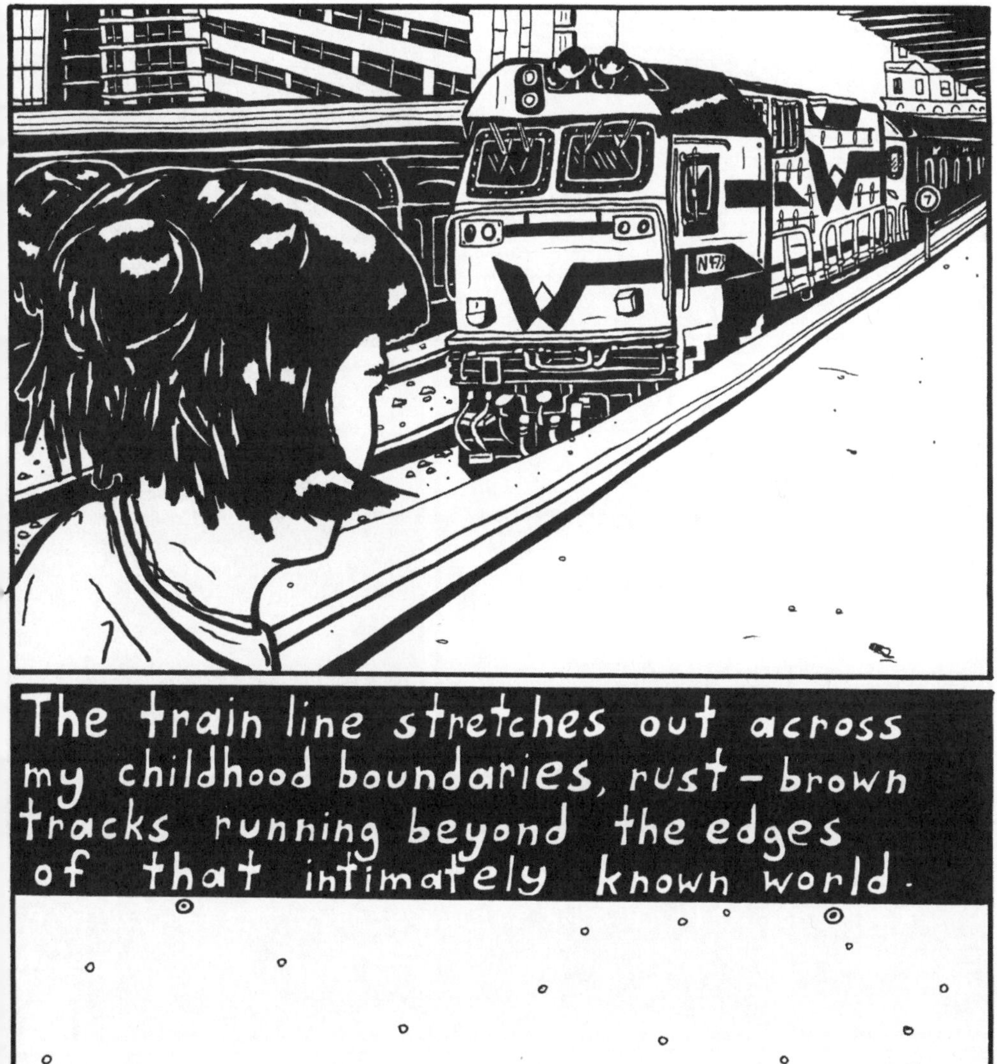

The train line stretches out across my childhood boundaries, rust-brown tracks running beyond the edges of that intimately known world.

Portland  Warrnambool  Terang  Camperdown  Colac  Geelong

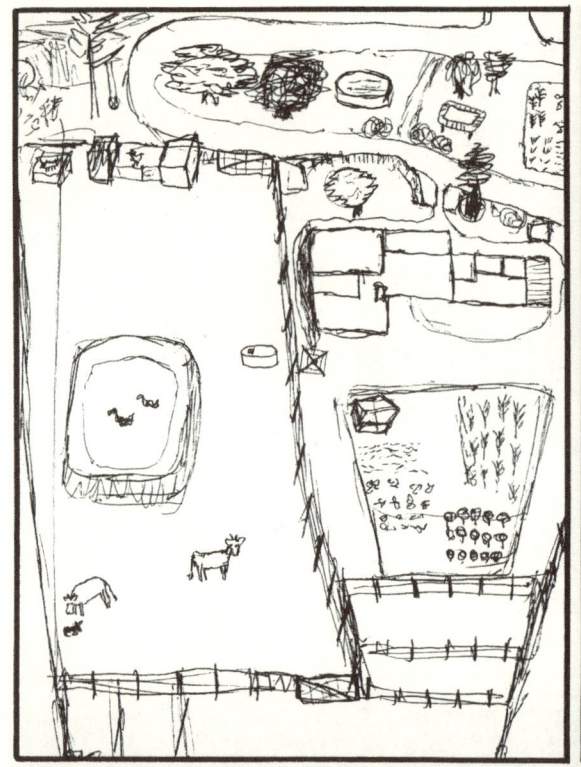

Drawing maps
of the house,
the farm, the
neighbours'
farm, I am
shocked by
sudden emotion,
the corporal
power of memory

The land of western Victoria is layered over with such maps, these of my siblings, these of the farmer before us, passages of experience and knowledge strung across the land. Other maps were made, maps which lay claim to land and described its shape scientifically, economically, geographically. Colonial maps.

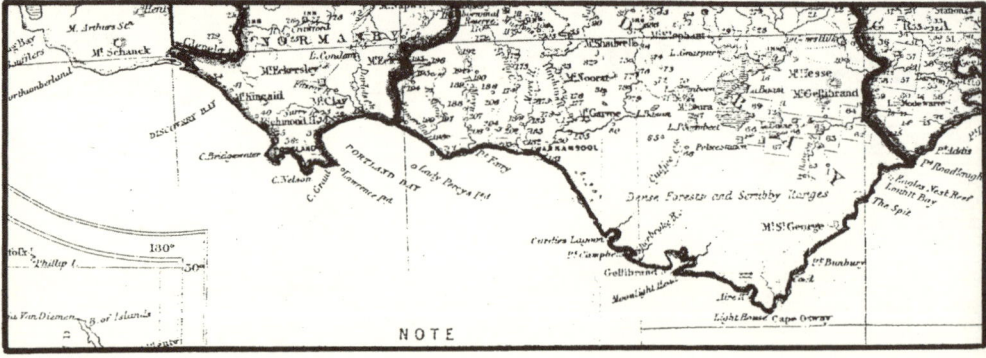

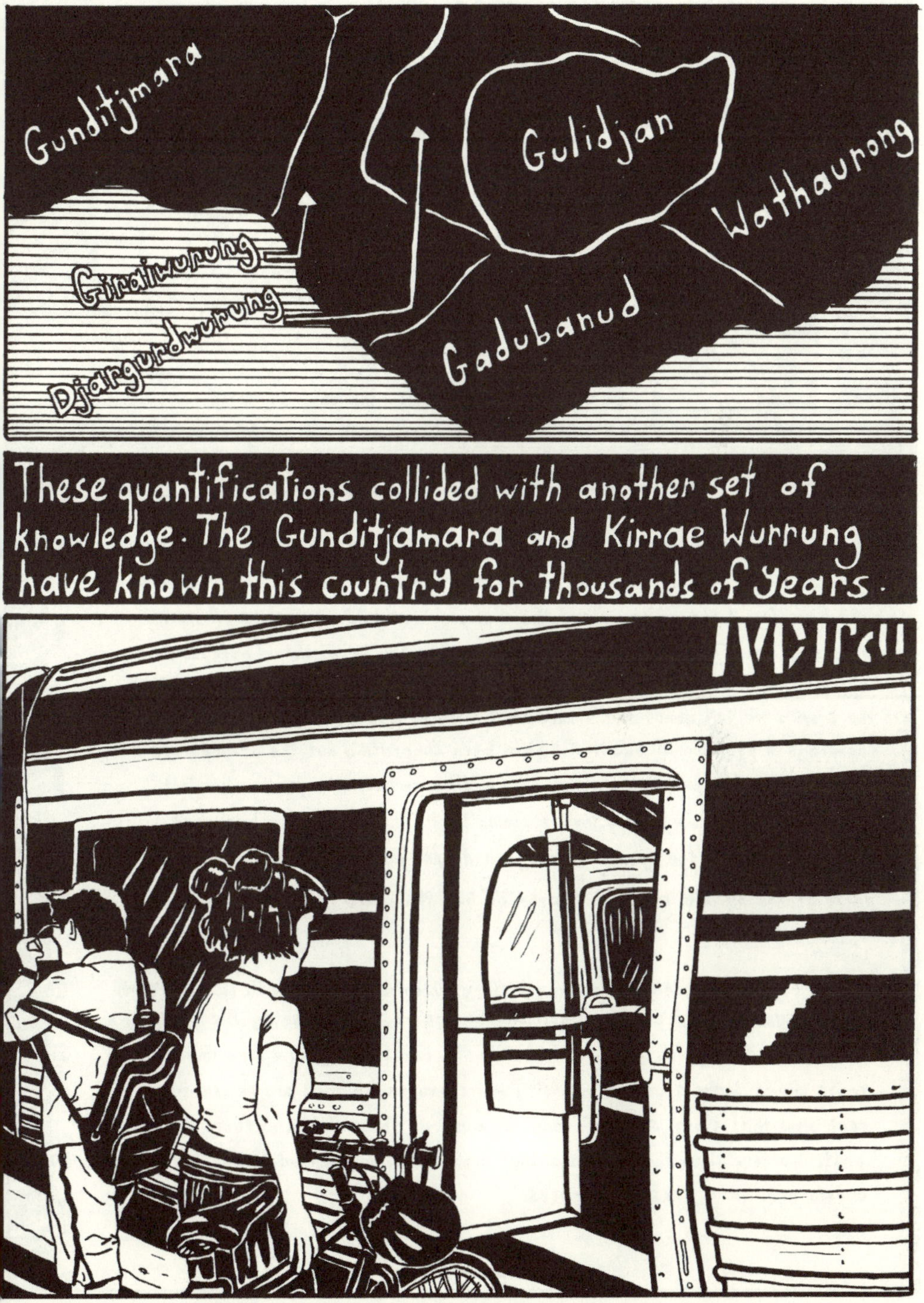

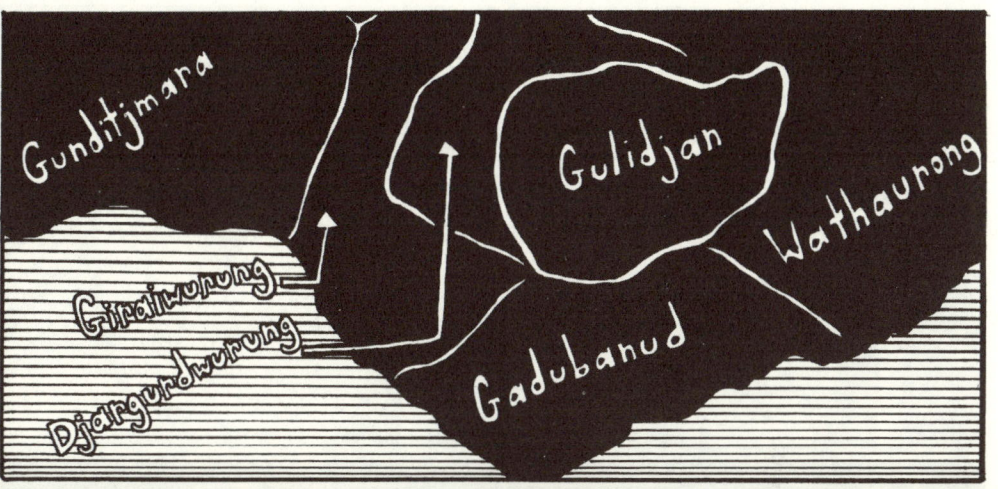

These quantifications collided with another set of knowledge. The Gunditjamara and Kirrae Wurrung have known this country for thousands of years.

It's five years since i first thought to question why a feature of my childhood coastline was called 'Massacre Point', and was shaken to find that it referred to the mass killing of Koori people. Perhaps it is impolite to interrogate an inheritance but I have found reason to pursue the stories I was told as a child of that community. Paul Fox gives shape to this pursuit when he writes 'The question is, do Australians inhabit a postcolonial world or a landscape of colonial memories?' Do the stories we tell about the places we live reinscribe a colonial mentality or encourage a postcolonial reality? I have been separating out the strands of inheritance and experience, setting my childhood memories against my adult knowledge that I occupy and love a stolen land. The stories I've been told empty of meaning, the spacious valleys and vast paddocks fill with missing parts of the puzzle, and I am scared of how the place I love so quickly becomes strange.

How to fearlessly unlearn a colonial history which is entwined with memory, myth and community? We are shaped not only by the past, but also by the stories we choose to tell about it. Stories leach into the landscape, give shape and meaning to its cliffs, leave spots of intensity in its geography that are reinscribed each time that story is told. These, as much as the material effects of the past, are crucial to the identities that communities forge, and to our own understandings of these landscapes.

On the weekends my three brothers
and I would light fires, make BMX
tracks and dress up. As the oldest child
I got to pick the costumes. This is my
brother Michael. I dressed him up as a
horse, a swagman, a ballerina and an
'Aborigine'. I knew all about 'Aborigines'.
They lived in the desert, wore grass to
cover their 'pee-nee'(penis) and carried
spears. Bouncing on the trampoline
at sunset I would
scare myself imagining
Tasmanian tigers
prowling up the paddock
to swallow me. I knew
that there had been
tigers here a long time
ago, and wasn't convinced
that they were all gone.
But I never thought about
'Aborigines' in these fields.

## H2

Home is, then the heart is.
Home is a poem halved.

Home is making peace
where the ocean
killed a man with a shark.

Peace is shadows listing
on a grassy path.

Paths are wet feet welding
home to heel at last.

Press kiss, home is
torn love, birthmarked.

TOBY DAVIDSON

Laura Carroll lives in Melbourne. She teaches English at La Trobe University, where she is also completing a PhD on film adaptation.

Julie Chevalier completed an MA in Writing (by research) at University of Technology Sydney. Her poems and short stories have been published in *Southerly*, *Island*, *Blue Dog*, *Overland*, *Poetrix* and *famous reporter*. Her poem 'Women of Antiquity 2002' was co-runner-up for the 2008 *Overland* Judith Wright Poetry Prize for New and Emerging Poets.

Peter Coghill is a physicist who lives in Sydney. His poems have appeared in *Blue Dog* and *Meanjin*.

Mark Dapin is a columnist and feature writer with 'Good Weekend' in *The Sydney Morning Herald* and *The Age*. He has written for most of the magazines in Australia, from *The Picture* to *The Australian Financial Review* Magazine, and for British newspapers such as *The Times* and *The Guardian*. His short stories have appeared in *Penthouse*, *Woman's Day*, *Ita* and a couple of anthologies.

Toby Davidson was born in Perth in 1977. He Later moved to Sydney where he co-founded the Citizens of Language readings. He now resides in Warrnambool and is completing a PhD in Australian poetry.

Brett Dionysius directed the Queensland Poetry Festival from 1997 to 2001 and is currently the editor of *papertiger: new world poetry*. He has published two collections of poetry. *Fatherlands* was short-listed in the 2002 Mary Gilmore Poetry Prize.

Robert Drewe is the author of seven novels, three collections of short stories and two books of nonfiction. His latest book of stories, *The Rip*, will be published by Hamish Hamilton/Penguin in October.

Ampersand Duck is a letterpress printer, bookbinder, book-arts teacher, designer and daydreamer. You will find her blog at www.ampersandduck.blogspot.com.

Adrienne Eberhard has an MA in twentieth-century travel writing. Her poems and short stories have been published in a wide range of Australian journals including *Southerly*, *Island*, *Westerly*, *Voices*, *Meanjin*, *Siglo* and *The Australian*. *Agamemnon's Poppies* (Black Pepper, 2003) was awarded equal second in the 2003–04 Anne Elder award.

Michael Farrell has published three books: *ode ode* (Salt, 2003); *Break Me Ouch*, a poetry comic book (3 Deep, 2006); and *a raiders guide* (Giramondo, 2008).

Kate Fielding develops innovative spaces for telling underrepresented histories in creative, playful and radical forms. She has filled research and public history roles with Museum Victoria, National Archives of Australia, National Museum of Australia, Heritage Victoria, Koorie Heritage Trust, History Council of Victoria and—currently—the Warburton Arts Project based in remote Western Australia.

Carol Jenkins is a Sydney writer whose work has appeared in *Island*, *Heat*, *Southerly*, *Cordite* and *Antipodes*. Her first book of poetry, *Fishing in the Devonian*, will be published early in 2009 by Puncher & Wattman. In 2007 she established River Road Press, which produces audio CDs of Australian poetry.

Martin Langford is the author of five books of poetry. His most recent publication is *Microtexts* (2005), a book of aphorisms and brief observations about poetics.

Caroline Lee is a writer and performer. Her play *The Three Interiors of Lola Strong* premiered at fortyfivedownstairs in 2003. She won the 2005 A.B. Natoli Prize for her short story 'the yo-yo' and has had stories published in *The Sleepers Almanac* and *Visible Ink*. The first draft of her novel *Stripped* was completed with the assistance of the 2005 Marion Eldridge Award for Emerging Woman Writers.

Rose Lucas is a Melbourne poet who teaches literature at Monash University. She is also a convenor of the July conference, Poetry and the Trace.

Wayne Macauley is a Melbourne writer whose short fiction has been widely published, most recently in *Meanjin* and *Island*. In 2005 and 2006 he was on the judging panel for the Unpublished Manuscript category of the Victorian Premier's Literary Awards. In 2007 he judged the Open Short Story category of the Boroondara Literary Awards. His second novel is *Caravan Story*.

Kent MacCarter is a writer and reviewer based in Melbourne. His poems focus on sound and texture of 'place'. Regarding sound specifically, his poems have been described as akin to reading jazz. This is his second appearance in *Meanjin*, adding to work also published in the United States, New Zealand and Singapore.

Andrew McDonald's books of poems are *Absence in Strange Countries* and *The One True History*; a third is gestating. After many years at SBS subtitling he moved to Canberra, where he works as an editor and counsellor.

Fiona McGregor has published three books of fiction. Her most recent novel, *Chemical Palace*, was short-listed for the NSW Premier's Awards. In 2008, *Strange Museums*, a book about Poland and performance art, will be published by UWAP. In 2009, Scribe will publish McGregor's next novel.

**John Millet** is the author of sixteen books of poetry that have been published in the USA, Ireland, New Zealand, France and Australia. He is the former editor of *Poetry Australia*. In 1996 he was awarded the Order of Australia for services to literature, and has won several national and international prizes for his poetry, including the Victorian Premier's Literary Award in 2002.

**Paul Mitchell** is a Melbourne fiction writer and poet. His latest books are a short-story collection, *Dodging the Bull* (Wakefield Press, 2007), and a poetry collection, *Awake Despite the Hour* (Five Islands Press, 2007). His novel-in-progress focuses on domestic violence in the Wimmera in the 1950s.

**Jim Morgan** grew up in Adelaide but lives in Melbourne and, despite appearances to the contrary, has no *animus revertandi* to South Australia, but for the purposes of this book, which may well be called 'Neighbours: Morgan & Waite, Modern Men', has just spent twelve months there—at least in his head.

**Paul Morgan** is the author of two widely praised novels, *The Pelagius Book* and *Turner's Paintbox*. Born in London, he studied philosophy and English at the University of Wales, and now lives in Melbourne.

**David Musgrave** lives in Sydney and is the founder of the publisher Puncher & Wattman. His poetry has been appearing in print since 1985 and he is the author of two books of poetry, *To Thalia* (2004) and *On Reflection* (2005).

**David Nichols** is a historian and a lecturer in Urban Planning in the School of Design, University of Melbourne. His interest in Pip Proud's work began in Red Eye Records, Sydney, 1991, on finding a battered copy of Proud's second album. He has facilitated some reissues and new recordings from Proud.

**Mandy Ord** is a Melbourne-based cartoonist and illustrator. She has self-published her comic stories; her work has also appeared in a broad cross-section of local and international anthologies. Her first graphic novel, *Rooftops*, was published by Finlay Lloyd in 2008.

**Geoff Page** is a Canberra-based poet. His most recent books are *Seriatim* (Salt, UK), *Lawrie & Shirley: the Final Cadenza: a Movie in Verse* (Pandanus Books), *80 Great Poems from Chaucer to Now* (UNSW Press) and *Agnostic Skies* (Five Islands Press).

**Pip Proud** was born in 1947 in Adelaide. He became renowned in underground circles as the composer and performer of some of the most uncompromising and extraordinary pop music of the 1960s, exemplified in the albums *Adreneline and Richard* (1968) and *A Bird in the Engine* (1969). After a long absence he returned to the music scene in 1995 when some of his material was re-released, and he has since recorded four new albums issued on the Emperor Jones label.

**Tim Richards** is the author of *Letters to Francesca*, *The Prince* and *Duckness*, and is currently writing with the assistance of an Established Writers' Grant from the Australia Council.

**Vanessa Russell** has written a novel called 'The Holy Bible', based on her experiences growing up within a small Christian sect. She has been published in Australia, New York, Nepal and Turkey. Currently living deep in the Irish-speaking Gaeltacht in Ireland, she can now say 'no worries' in two languages.

**Tracy Ryan** was born in Western Australia but has also lived in the United Kingdom and the United States. She has published several collections of poetry, the latest being *Scar Revision* (Fremantle Press, 2008). Her third novel, *Sweet*, is due out with Fremantle Press in late 2008.

**Andrew Sant's** latest book, *Speed & Other Liberties*, has recently been published by Salt. He is currently living in London.

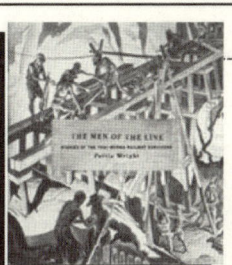

# 2009 Peter Blazey Fellowship - for life writing, biography and autobiography.

Applications are invited for the 2009 Peter Blazey Fellowship. This prestigious national award is presented annually to further a work in progress in the non-fiction fields of life writing, biography and autobiography.

The recipient will be supported in their work by a cash prize of $15,000, and a one-month residency at the Australian Centre at the University of Melbourne.

**Past winners include:**

**2008** Prize shared between Andrew Lindsay, for his work in progress *The God of Morphine*, and Dmetri Kakmi, for his work in progress *Motherland*.

**2007** Judith Pugh, for her work towards *Unstill Life: Art, Politics and Living with Clifton Pugh*, Allen & Unwin, 2008.

**2006** Robert Kenny, for his work towards *The Lamb Enters the Dreaming: Nathanael Pepper & the Ruptured World*, Scribe Publications, 2007.

**2005** Jennifer Compton, for her work towards *Who Doesn't Want Me to Dance?*.

**2004** Sara Hardy, for her work towards *The Unusual Life of Edna Walling*, Allen & Unwin, 2005.

For further information and application forms, please visit
**http://www.australian.unimelb.edu.au/public/awards/blazey.html**

Please direct enquiries to James Waghorne,
tel: +61 3 8344 4154; email jwag@unimelb.edu.au

Applications close: Monday 7 July 2008.

**dream large**

THE UNIVERSITY OF
MELBOURNE

# DOROTHY SARGENT ROSENBERG
# ANNUAL POETRY PRIZES, 2008

PRIZES ranging from $1000 to as much as $25,000 will be awarded for the finest lyric poems celebrating the human spirit. The contest is open to all writers, published or unpublished, who will be under the age of 40 on 6 November 2008. Entries must be postmarked on or before the third Saturday in October (18 October 2008). Only previously unpublished poems are eligible for prizes. Names of prize winners will be published on our website on 5 February 2009, together with a selection of the winning poems. Please visit our website www.DorothyPrizes.org for further information and to read poems by previous winners.

### Checklist of Contest Guidelines

- Entries must be postmarked on or before 18 October 2008.
- Past winners may re-enter until their prizes total in excess of $25,000.
- All entrants must be under the age of 40 on 6 November 2008.
- Submissions must be original, previously unpublished, and in English: no translations, please.
- Each entrant may submit up to three separate poems.
- Only one of the poems may be more than thirty lines in length.
- Each poem must be printed on a separate sheet.
- Submit two copies of each entry with your name, address, phone number and email address clearly marked on each page of one copy only.
- Include an index card with your name, address, phone number and email address and the titles of each of your submitted poems.
- Include a $10 entry fee payable to the Dorothy Sargent Rosenberg Memorial Fund. (This fee is not required for entries mailed from outside the USA.)
- Poems will not be returned. Include a stamped, self-addressed envelope if you wish us to acknowledge the receipt of your entry.

Mail entries to: **Dorothy Sargent Rosenberg Poetry Prizes, PO Box 2306, Orinda, California 9456**

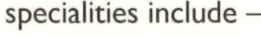